TRIPLE HOMICIDE

THRILLERS

JAMES PATTERSON

WITH MAXINE PAETRO AND JAMES O. BORN

GRAND CENTRAL
PUBLISHING

NEW YORK   BOSTON

Copyright © 2018 by JBP Business, LLC

Grand Central Publishing
Hachette Book Group
1290 Avenue of the Americas, New York, NY 10104
grandcentralpublishing.com
twitter.com/grandcentralpub

First Edition: July 2018
DETECTIVE CROSS originally published as trade paperback and ebook in May 2017
THE MEDICAL EXAMINER originally published as trade paperback and ebook in August 2017
MANHUNT originally published as trade paperback and ebook in November 2017

Grand Central Publishing is a division of Hachette Book Group, Inc. The Grand Central Publishing name and logo is a trademark of Hachette Book Group, Inc.

The publisher is not responsible for websites (or their content) that are not owned by the publisher.

The Hachette Speakers Bureau provides a wide range of authors for speaking events. To find out more, go to www.hachettespeakersbureau.com or call (866) 376-6591.

ISBNs: 978-1-5387-3058-4 (trade paperback), 978-1-5387-1471-3 (large print), 978-1-5387-3073-7 (ebook)

Printed in the United States of America

LSC-C

10 9 8 7 6 5 4 3 2

CONTENTS

DETECTIVE CROSS

AN ALEX CROSS STORY

JAMES PATTERSON

CHAPTER 1

BREE STONE WAS thirty minutes into her morning exercise and breathing hard as she ran east along a path by the Tidal Basin in Washington, DC. It was a gorgeous spring day in late March, warm with a fragrant breeze.

The Japanese cherry trees that lined the path were in full bloom, attracting early tourists. Bree had to dodge a few of them, but it was so pretty a setting and day that she didn't mind.

She was in her late thirties, but her legs felt stronger than they had when she was just out of college. So did her breathing, and that pleased her. The daily exercise was working.

Leaving the Tidal Basin, Bree cut past the statue of John Paul Jones and jogged in place, waiting to cross 17th Street SE beside a DC bus discharging and loading passengers. When the bus sighed and rolled away, Bree looped around the pedestrians to cross the street, toward the National Sylvan Theater and another grove of blooming cherry trees. The cherry blossoms only peaked once a year and she intended to enjoy them as much as possible. She'd just passed a knot of Japanese tourists when her cell phone rang.

She plucked the phone from the small fanny pack she wore, but did not stop or slow. Bree glanced at the unfamiliar phone number and let her voice mail take the call. She ran on and soon could see a team of National Park Police raising the fifty American flags surrounding the base of the Washington Monument. Her phone rang again, same number.

Irritated, she stopped and answered, "Bree Stone."

"Chief Bree Stone?"

The voice was male. Or was it? The tone wasn't deep.

"Who's calling, please?"

"Your worst nightmare, Chief. There's an IED on the National Mall. You should have answered my first call. Now you only have fifty-eight minutes to figure out where I left it."

The line died. Bree stared at the phone half a beat, then checked her watch. 7:28 a.m. Detonation: 8:26 a.m.? She hit a number on speed dial and surveyed the area, swallowing the impulse to get well off the Mall as fast as possible.

DC Metro Police Chief Jim Michaels answered on the second ring.

"Why is my chief of detectives calling me? I told her to take a few days off."

"I just got an anonymous call, Jim," Bree said. "An IED planted on the National Mall, set to go off at 8:26 a.m. We need to clear the area as fast as possible and bring in the dogs."

In the short silence that followed, Bree thought of something and started sprinting toward the men raising flags.

"Are you sure it wasn't a crank?" Chief Michaels said.

"Do you want to take the chance it isn't a crank?"

Michaels let out a sharp puff of breath and said, "I'll notify National Park and Capitol Hill Police. You sound like you're running. Where are you?"

"On the Mall. Going to high ground to spot the bomber on his way out of Dodge."

CHAPTER 2

IT WAS 7:36 A.M. when the elevator doors opened.

Bree rushed out onto the observation platform of the Washington Monument, some five hundred and fifty-four feet above the National Mall. She carried a chattering US Park Service Police radio, tuned to a frequency being used by all FBI, US Capitol Police, and DC Metro Police personnel rapidly responding to the situation.

She had a pair of binoculars lent to her by the officers guarding the closed monument. Balking at her initial demand to be let in, they had given her a hard time while checking her story.

Then the sirens had started wailing from all angles, and their commander came back with direct orders to open the monument and let her ride to the top. Bree had lost eight minutes in the process, but pushed that frustration to the back of her mind. They had fifty minutes to find the bomb.

Bree went straight to the high slit windows cut in the west wall of the monument, and peered through the binoculars toward the Lincoln Memorial and the long, rectangular pool that reflected its image and that of the Washington Monument. When she'd started to run toward the towering limestone obelisk, she'd hoped to get high enough to catch sight of someone fleeing the Mall or acting strangely.

But too much time had passed. The bomber would have beat feet, gotten as far away as possible, wouldn't he? That was the logical thought, but Bree wondered if he might be the kind of sicko to stick around, admire his explosive handiwork.

Even at this early hour there were scores of people running, walking, and riding on the paths that crisscrossed the Mall and paralleled the reflecting pool. Others were standing as if transfixed by the chorus of sirens coming closer and closer.

Bree pivoted, strode across the observation deck to the east wall where she could look out toward the US Capitol, and triggered the radio mic.

"This is Metro CoD Stone," she said, scanning the open park between the Smithsonian museums. "I can see hundreds of people still on the Mall, and who knows how many more that I can't see because of the trees. Move officers to 17th, 15th, Madison Drive Northwest, Jefferson Drive Southwest, Ohio Drive Southwest, and 7th Northwest, 4th Northwest, and 3rd Northwest. Work civilian evacuation from the middle of the Mall to the north and south. Keep it quick and orderly. We don't want to cause panic."

"Roger that, Chief," the dispatcher came back.

Bree waited until she heard the dispatcher call out her orders, then said, "Block all traffic through the Mall north and south and Constitution and Independence Avenues from 3rd to Ohio."

"That's already been ordered, Chief," the dispatcher said.

"Status of K-9 and bomb squads?"

"FBI, Metro, and Park Police K-9s en route, but traffic's snarling. Metro's ETA on 15th is two minutes. Bomb squads say five minutes out, but could be longer."

Longer? She cursed inwardly. Looked down at the flags fluttering and noted their direction and stiffness.

She triggered the mic again. "Tell all K-9 patrols that the wind here is south-southwest, maybe ten miles an hour. They'll want to work from northeast angles."

"Roger that," the dispatcher said.

Bree checked her watch. 7:41. They had forty-five minutes to find and defuse the IED.

Gazing out, her mind racing, Bree realized she knew something about the bomber. He or she had used the term IED, Improvised Explosive Device, not bomb. IED was a US military term. Was the bomber ex-military? Current military?

Then again, Bree had seen and heard the term often enough on news and media reports. But why would a civilian use that term instead of bomb? Why be so specific?

Her phone rang. Chief Michaels.

"Because of your unique location and perspective, we're giving you overall command of the situation, Chief," he said by way of greeting. "K-9, bomb, and tactical squads will operate at your call after advising you of the options."

Bree didn't miss a beat. "FBI and Capitol Hill?"

"Waiting on your orders."

"Thank you for the confidence, sir."

"Prove it," he said, and hung up.

For the next six minutes, as she monitored radio chatter, Bree roamed back and forth, looking east and west, seeing cruiser after cruiser turn sideways to block access to Constitution and Independence Avenues where they ran parallel to the Mall.

At 7:49, twenty-one minutes after the bomber's phone call, mounted police appeared and cantered their horses the length of the Mall, shouting to everyone to leave the quickest way possible. Other patrol cars cruised Independence, Constitution, and Madison, using their bullhorns to spur the evacuation.

Despite Bree's hope for calm, the police horses and bullhorns were clearly seeding panic. Joggers turned and sprinted north and south off the Mall. Fathers grabbed their kids and ran. Moms pushed baby carriages helter-skelter. Tourists poured like ants out of the Lincoln Memorial and left the Vietnam and World War II Memorials in droves.

Bree kept the binoculars pressed tight to her eyes, looking for someone lingering, someone wanting a last look at the spot where the bomb was stashed, or positioned to remotely detonate the device.

But she saw no one that set off alarm bells.

The son of a bitch is gone, she thought. *Long gone.*

CHAPTER 3

THE BOMB DOGS did not appear until 7:59 a.m., delayed by traffic caused by closing the Mall during rush hour. They had twenty-seven minutes to find the device, and Bree was fighting off a panic that threatened to freeze her.

She was in charge. What if something went wrong? What if the device went off?

As quick as the question popped into her mind, Bree squashed it. *Breathe.* The officers and agents converging on the Mall were outstanding, the best. *You're leading superior people,* she thought. *Trust them to do their jobs, and advise you well, and you'll be confident in your decisions.*

The Mall was almost empty when handlers released twelve German shepherds at intervals along Constitution Avenue from the west lawn of the Capitol to the Lincoln Memorial. Bree watched the dogs roam into the wind in big loops, noses up, sniffing out scents as their handlers tried to keep pace.

A minute passed and then two. On the radio, bomb squad leaders from the four law enforcement agencies announced their teams' arrivals at positions along Independence Avenue, now empty save for cruisers with blue lights flashing.

At 8:02, Bree was looking west toward the Capitol when one of the FBI's shepherds slowed, circled, and then sat by a trash bin along a pathway west of 7th Street, almost directly south of the National Sculpture Museum.

"K-9 Pablo says he's got a package," the dog's handler said over the radio.

Bree closed her eyes. They'd found it with what, twenty-four minutes to spare?

"Back K-9 Pablo off," Bree said. "Bomb squads move to his location."

The FBI and Capitol Hill Police bomb squads were closest. Tactical vans raced east along Monroe from 3rd, and west from 15th, stopping a block away from the trash bin at 8:04. They had twenty-two minutes to neutralize the threat.

Agents and officers in full bomb gear piled out of the vans. Two FBI bomb experts walked within fifty yards of the trash can before releasing an Andros Mark V-A1, a four-wheel-drive robot that rolled right up next to it bearing electronic sensors and cameras.

"We have a timed device," one of the agents said, within seconds. "Repeat, we have a timed device."

"Evidence of cellular linkage?" another radioed back.

"Negative."

Special Agent Peggy Denton, the FBI bomb squad commander, called for heavy mats and blankets made of fire-retardant Nomex materials stuffed with sliced-up tire rubber. Four agents and five Capitol Hill police officers carried the mats and blankets toward the trash can.

Bree's breath caught in her throat when they got within ten feet. If the bomber had a remote trigger on the IED, which was not cell phone driven…

But without hesitation, the bomb team showed exceptional courage. They went to the trash can and laid two bomb mats over it, and then a bomb blanket that draped over the entire can down to the sidewalk. The agents and officers moved back quickly, yanking off their hooded visors, and Bree sighed with relief.

It was 8:11. Fifteen minutes to spare.

"Job well done," Bree said into the radio, and suddenly felt weak and tired.

She sat down against the wall and closed her eyes, her fingers playing with her wedding ring, an old habit, until she thought to call her husband, Alex. She not only wanted, but *needed* to hear his voice.

After four rings, she realized that he was probably with a patient.

"Alex Cross," his voice mail said. "Leave your message at the beep."

"Hey, baby," she said, fighting down a surge of emotion. "I'm okay. I was running on the Mall and…"

Her radio squawked. "Command, this is Metro K-9 Handler Krauss. K-9 Rebel has alerted. Exterior trash bin, women's public restroom immediately southwest of Constitution Gardens Pond."

"Shit," Bree said, got to her feet, and ran to the opposite window as she ordered the officer and his dog back. She saw them trotting north toward open ground and heard the sirens of the other two bomb squads rushing to the new site.

Were there more IEDs? Bree wondered. All set to go off at 8:26?

It was 8:18 as the tactical vans skidded to a stop well back from the restroom. If the bomb was timed to go off at 8:26, they had eight minutes. As before, officers and agents in heavy protective gear and visors poured out of the vans.

There was brief radio chatter regarding tactics before Denton said, "Command, I recommend we move straight to the bomb mats and blankets. No time for the robot."

"No other options?" Bree said.

"We let it blow."

8:19. Seven minutes.

"Mats and blankets," Bree said. She now spotted police and news helicopters hovering outside the no-fly zone that covered much of the Mall, and all of the White House grounds to the north.

"Command, we have a Caucasian male in camo gear on the west Mall," an officer called.

Bree swung the binoculars and spotted him. The man was wearing filthy military desert fatigues, dancing in circles and shouting at the sky, on the lawn north of the Ash Woods. Officers ran toward him, shouting at him to get down.

Bree focused her binoculars on the man. Tall, lanky, bearded, grimy, with matted dark hair and wild eyes, he saw them coming and took off toward the reflecting pool. Before they could catch him he darted through the trees, across a path, and jumped into the pool.

He waded fast toward the center of the pool, heading almost

directly toward the bomb squads and the restrooms. The water was well above his knees when he stopped, reached into his pants pocket, and slipped out a Glock pistol.

"Gun!" she barked into the radio. "Repeat, suspect in reflecting pool is armed."

The police and FBI agents closing on the pool all had their weapons drawn now, shouting at the man to drop his pistol even as the bomb teams approached the restrooms north of the reflecting pool.

The man ignored the warnings. He sat down in the water, which came up to his chest. Holding the Glock overhead, he released the clip, which fell and disappeared below the surface. He ran the action next and ejected the round from the chamber before expertly stripping the weapon down to its components. Every bit of the gun was in pieces and sunk in under thirty seconds.

The officers were in the pool with him now, wading toward him, training their weapons on him, when he flopped back and disappeared into the water.

What the hell is that guy doing? Bree thought. She turned her attention back to the restroom and the first four members of the bomb squad who were close, maybe twelve feet from the second trash can, preparing to lay down the first mat.

She glanced at her watch. 8:23. Three minutes to spare.

She exhaled with relief as the bomb experts lifted the mat over the can—and the IED exploded in a brilliant, fiery red and yellow flash.

CHAPTER 4

THIRTY-FOUR-YEAR-OLD Kate Williams was curled up in the fetal position in the overstuffed chair opposite me, in the basement office where I'd been seeing patients since being suspended from DC Metro five months before.

"I'll end up killing myself, Dr. Cross," Kate said. "Probably not today or tomorrow. But it's going to happen. I've known that since I was nine years old."

Her voice was flat, her expression showing the anger, fear, and despair that her tone didn't betray. Tears welled and slipped from eyes that would not meet mine.

I took her threat seriously. From her records, I knew some of the damage she'd done to herself already. Kate's teeth were stained from drug abuse. Her dirty blond hair was as thin and brittle as straw, and she wore a long-sleeve Electric Daisy Carnival T-shirt to hide evidence of cutting.

"Is that when it started?" I asked. "When you were nine?"

Kate wiped at her eyes furiously. "You know, I'm not talking about it anymore. Digging around back there never helps. Just pushes me to pull the plug on sobriety, on everything, sooner."

I set my notepad aside, sat forward with my palms up and said, "I'm just trying to understand your history clearly, Kate."

She crossed her arms. "And I'm just trying to hang on, Doc. The court ordered me here as a term of my probation, otherwise I gotta tell you, I'd be a no-show."

This was our second session together. The first hadn't gone much better.

For a few moments I studied her slouched posture and the way she used her thumbnail to dig at the raw cuticles around her fingers, and I knew I was going to have to change the dynamic in the room if I was to get through to her.

There was another seat beside Kate I usually reserved for couples therapy, but I got up and sat in it so that I was roughly her mirror image, side by side. I let that physical change settle in her. At first she seemed threatened, shifting away from me. I said nothing and waited until she lifted her head to look at me.

"What do you want?"

"To help, if I can. To do that I have to see the world the way you see it."

"So, what, you sit next to me and expect to see the world the way I do?"

I ignored the caustic tone, and said, "I sit next to you rather than confront you, and maybe you give me a glimpse of your world."

Kate sat back, looked away from me, and said nothing for ten, then fifteen deep, ragged breaths.

"Yes, nine," she said at last. "Just before my tenth birthday."

"You knew him?"

"My Uncle Bert, my mom's sister's husband," she said. "I had to go live with them after my mom died."

"That's brutal. I'm sorry to hear that. You must have been terrified, betrayed by someone you trusted."

Kate looked at me and spoke bitterly. "It wasn't a betrayal. It was a robbery, armed robbery. None of that slow 'grooming' you hear about. Six months after I got there, my Aunt Meg went to visit friends for the weekend. Uncle Bert got drunk and came into my bedroom carrying a hunting knife and a bottle. He threatened me with the knife, told me he'd cut my throat if I ever said a thing. Then he pinned me facedown and…"

I could see it in my head and felt sickened. "You tell anyone?"

"Who would believe me? Uncle Bert just so happened to be the sheriff. Aunt Meg idolized him, the piece of shit."

"How long did the abuse go on?"

"Until I ran away. Sixteen."

"Your aunt never suspected?"

Kate shrugged and finally looked over at me. "When I was a little, little girl, I loved to sing with my mom in the church choir. My aunt was in a choir, too, and until Uncle Bert came into my room, singing with her was the only thing that made me happy. I could forget things, become part of something."

She was blinking, staring off now, and I saw the muscles in her neck constrict.

"And after Uncle Bert?"

Kate cleared her throat, said in a soft rasp, "I never sang in tune again. Just couldn't hold a note for the life of me. Aunt Meg could never figure that one out."

"She never knew?"

"She was a good soul in her way. She didn't deserve to know."

"You weren't at fault, you know," I said. "You didn't cause the abuse."

Kate looked over at me angrily. "But I could have stopped it, Dr. Cross. I could have done what I wanted to do: snatch that Buck knife off the nightstand when he was done with me and lying there all drowsy drunk. I could have sunk the knife in his chest, but I didn't. I tried, but I just couldn't do it."

Kate broke down then, and sobbed. "What kind of coward was I?"

CHAPTER 5

WHEN KATE WILLIAMS left my office twenty minutes later, I was wondering if my tactics had done any good. She'd opened up, and that was positive. But right after she called herself a coward, she clammed up tight again, said she hated thinking about those times—they made her cravings for the pipe and the bottle more intense.

"See you at our next appointment?" I asked before she went out the basement door.

Kate hesitated, but then nodded. "Got no choice, right?"

"Judge wants it, but I hope *you* come to want it. This is a safe place, Kate, no judgments. Opinion only if you ask for it."

Her eyes roamed to my face, saw I was sincere. "Okay then, next time."

I'd no sooner shut the door than my cell phone buzzed in my office. I ran and grabbed it on the fourth buzz, seeing Bree was calling for a second time.

"You already showered and off to work?" I said.

"I never made it home," she said in a strained voice. "You haven't heard?"

"No. I've been in a session the past—"

"Someone put two bombs on the National Mall, Alex. Michaels put me in command up on the Washington Monument where I could see everything. We got one neutralized before it exploded at 8:26. But I made a decision to send a bomb team to neutralize the second IED versus checking it first with a robot. When they were close, at 8:23, it went off. They're okay because of the mats and the suits, but it's a wonder they weren't killed."

"Jesus," I said. "How are you?"

"Shaken," she said. "I haven't sent men in to get bombed before."

I winced. "I can't imagine, baby. What's Michaels saying?"

"He has my back. Denton recommended the attempt. We had seven minutes, so I accepted her recommendation."

"How did you know you had seven minutes?"

"The bomber told me. He called my cell to warn me that an IED was supposed to go off at 8:26 a.m."

"Why you?"

"No idea. But he had my private number."

"No suspects?"

"We have a suspect in custody," she said, and told me about a man who'd waded into the reflecting pool before dismantling his pistol. "We want you to come in and talk to him ASAP."

"Uh, I'm suspended pending trial."

"Mahoney's taken the lead. He wants you there, and Michaels will never know."

"Okay," I said uncertainly. "But I'm stacked with patients until two."

There was a pause before Bree said, "Two bombs on the National Mall, Alex?"

Even though she wasn't there with me, I held up my free hand in surrender. "You're right. No argument. Where do you want me and when?"

"FBI building, ASAP. Bring me a change of clothes?"

"Absolutely," I said, grabbing a pen to scribble notes on what she wanted.

So much for my suspension.

CHAPTER 6

I RACED UPSTAIRS, told Nana Mama I wouldn't be picking up my younger son, Ali, after school, got Bree's clothes and basic toiletries in an overnight bag, and called a car through Uber that arrived in just a few minutes. The driver said traffic was finally starting to move, as the police opened up the roads. I spent most of the ride calling patients to cancel appointments.

When I finished, I closed my eyes and shifted my thinking from the call of psychotherapy back to the craft of investigation, a craft that until five months before had consumed most of my adult life in six years with the Bureau's Behavioral Science Unit, and fourteen on and off with DC Metro's major cases team.

When I opened my eyes, it felt like I'd put on an old and familiar set of clothes and picked up tools that I could have used blindfolded. I have to admit, I felt full of renewed purpose when we pulled up in front of the J. Edgar Hoover Building.

Still in her running gear, Bree was on the sidewalk waiting for me with Special Agent in Charge Ned Mahoney, my old partner at the Bureau. As usual, he wore a dark Brooks Brothers suit, starched white shirt, and repp tie. Both he and Bree looked big-time stressed. I climbed out, thanked the driver, and hugged and kissed Bree before shaking Ned's hand.

Bree took the overnight bag, checked it, and smiled at me, then Ned. "There's somewhere I can shower and change inside?"

"Women's locker room," Ned said. "I'll get you a pass."

"Perfect," she said, and we started up the steps to the front entrance.

"What do we know about the guy in the reflecting pool?" I said.

Ned preferred to wait until we were inside and upstairs in a conference room, close to the interrogation room where they were holding retired Marine Master Gunnery Sergeant Timothy Chorey. Ned told us Chorey had done almost three full tours of duty in the Middle East, two in Iraq during the surge and one in Afghanistan during the big pullout. Two months shy of the end of that third tour, Chorey sustained a head injury due to an IED explosion in Helmand Province.

The bomb killed two of Chorey's men, rattled his brain, and damaged his inner ears. He spent time in a US military hospital in Wiesbaden, Germany before transferring to Bethesda Naval Hospital, where the neurological effects of the blast eased, but did not entirely disappear.

Chorey was granted a medical discharge nearly four years before he waded into the reflecting pool. He left Bethesda with bilateral hearing aids, determined to go to school on the GI bill.

"'His behavior seems erratic at best,'" I said, reading from a VA doctor's notes taken on a walk-in visit a year after he left Bethesda. "'Patient reports he has lost apartment, left school, can't sleep. Headaches, nausea are common.'"

"That's it. Chorey basically vanishes after that appointment," Mahoney said. "He goes underground for three years and surfaces to put bombs on the National Mall."

"If he's your bomber, Ned."

"He's the guy, Alex. Master gunnery sergeants like Chorey wear a bomb insignia on their left lapel, for Christ's sake. This guy may not have triggered the explosion, but he was involved, Alex. He ran from police, ignored their repeated orders, and was diverting attention from the bomb squad when that IED went off. And he hasn't said a word since we've had him in custody."

"Explosives residue on him?"

Mahoney grimaced. "No, but he could have worn gloves, and the techs say his dunk in the reflecting pool could have removed whatever traces there might have been."

"No lawyer?"

"Not yet, and he hasn't asked for one. He hasn't said anything, in fact."

"Mirandized?"

"Most definitely. Second they pulled him out of the water."

"Okay," I said, shutting the file. "Let me see if he'll talk to me."

CHAPTER 7

AS SOON AS Bree returned after a shower and a change of clothes, I went into the interrogation room alone. My first task was to build trust, and see what Chorey might tell me of his own volition.

Wearing an orange prison jumpsuit, Chorey sat in a chair bolted to the floor, gazing intently at his grimy hands folded on the tabletop and the handcuffs that bound his wrists. A heavy leather belt encircled his waist, with steel hoops attached to chains welded to the legs of the chair.

If he saw me enter, he ignored me. Not a flicker of reaction passed over his face. His entire being seemed focused on his hands and wrists, as if they held some great secret that calmed and fascinated him.

He was, as Bree had described him, six-foot-three, rail thin, with dull brown dreadlocks, a sparse beard over drawn skin, and dark bags under his eyes, which were still gazing, barely blinking. He stank of body odor and cheap booze.

"Mr. Chorey?" I said.

He didn't react.

"Gunny?"

Nothing. His eyes closed.

I was about to take the seat in front of him, and shake the table so he'd open his eyes and at least acknowledge my presence. But then something dawned on me, and I eased to his side, studying him more closely.

I went around behind him and clapped my hands softly. Chorey didn't react. I clapped them loudly and he didn't startle, but instead slightly cocked his head as if wondering if that sound was real.

"He's almost stone deaf," I said to the mirror. "That's why he wasn't responding to officers' orders. And hate to say it, Ned, but it jeopardizes the Miranda."

Chorey opened his eyes and saw me in the mirror. He startled, squinted, and twisted around to look up at me. I held up my hands and smiled. He didn't smile back.

I went around the table, took another chair, and got out a legal pad and pen from my bag.

I wrote, "Master Gunnery Sergeant Chorey, my name is Alex Cross. Can you hear with your hearing aids?"

Chorey brought his head close over the tablet when I spun it. He blinked, shrugged, squinted at me and in a weird, hollow nasal voice said, "I don't know."

"Did you have them in when you went in the reflecting pool?" I wrote.

"Been two and a half years since I've had them. I think. Time goes by and…"

He stared off into the middle distance.

"What happened to them?"

"I got drunk, heard voices and that damn ringing in my head, and I don't know, I think I crushed them with a rock."

"Get rid of the voices and the ringing?"

He laughed. "Only if I kept drinking."

"Would it help if we got headphones and an amplifier for you?"

"I don't know. Why am I here? Is it that big a deal to protest in Washington? I've seen films of hundreds of peaceful protesters in that reflecting pool back in the sixties. Hell, they were in it in *Forrest Gump,* right? Jenny was, anyway."

I smiled because he was right. Before I could scribble my response, a knock came at the door. An FBI tech entered with headphones, amplifier, and a microphone.

The tech put the headphones on Chorey, and turned on the amp. He turned the sound halfway up, and told me to speak. Chorey shook his head at each hello. It wasn't until the amp was at ninety percent of capacity that he brightened.

"I heard it. Can it go louder?"

The tech said, "At a certain point it could further damage your ears."

Chorey snorted and said, "I already know what the silence is like."

The tech shrugged and turned the volume up again.

"Can you hear me?" I asked.

Both eyebrows rose and he said, "Huh, yeah, I heard that in my right ear."

I set down my pen and leaned closer to the microphone the tech had set up on the table. "Going in the water, dismantling your weapon, you did that as a protest?"

"Destroying my weapon as protest. Beating swords into ploughshares, and baptizing myself in the pool of forgiveness. It was supposed to be a new beginning."

He said this with earnestness, conviction even.

"You ran from the police."

"I ran from shapes chasing me," Chorey said. "My eyesight sucks now, except right up close. You can check."

"What about the bombs?" I asked. "The IEDs?"

Chorey twitched at the word bombs, but then appeared genuinely baffled.

"IEDs?" he said. "What IEDs?"

CHAPTER 8

FORTY MINUTES LATER, I entered the observation booth overlooking the interrogation room where Chorey was still in restraints, sweating and moaning with his eyes closed. Ned Mahoney's arms were crossed.

"You believe him?" Mahoney asked.

"Most of it," I said. "You saw his hands there at the end. I'd say it would be impossible for him to build a bomb."

"Your wife saw him dismantle a Glock in under thirty seconds," Mahoney said.

"Once it's unloaded, a gun's no threat. Building a bomb, you can cross wires and blow yourself to kingdom come. Besides, you heard him, he's got an alibi."

"Bree's checking it."

"Doc," Chorey moaned in the interrogation room. "I need some help."

"I'd like to get him to a detox," I said.

"Not happening until we get a firm—"

The observation booth door opened. Bree came in.

"The supervisor at the Central Union Mission vouches for him," she said. "Chorey slept there last night, and left with the other men at 7:30. The super remembered because he tried to convince Chorey to stay for services, but Chorey said he had to go make a protest."

Mahoney said, "So what? He leaves the mission, picks up premade bombs, goes to the Mall, and—"

"The timing's wrong, Ned," Bree insisted. "The bomber called me at 7:26 and again at 7:28, after he'd planted the bombs. The Mission supervisor said he was with Chorey between 7:20 and 7:30. During that time Chorey never asked for or used a phone, because he's, well, deaf. He left the mission on foot."

"The supervisor know about the gun?"

She nodded. "Chorey evidently turned it in whenever he came off the street to spend the night."

In the interrogation room, Chorey rocked in his chair. "C'mon. Please, Doc. I got the sickness, man. The creepy-crawly sickness."

"He's not your bomber," I said.

"He could be a diversion," Mahoney said. "Part of the conspiracy. Besides, he had a loaded weapon in a national park, which is a federal offense. The Park Police will want him for that."

"The Park Police can get him for that once he's dry. They'll know exactly where he is, should they decide to press charges. Or you can send him to the federal holding facility in Alexandria, which is ill-equipped to handle someone with advanced delirium tremens, and you risk him dying before he can get clean."

The FBI agent squinted one eye at me. "You should have been a lawyer, Alex."

"Just my professional opinion on a vet who has had a tough go of things."

Mahoney hesitated, but then said, "Take him to rehab."

"Thanks, Ned," I said, and shook his hand.

Mahoney shook Bree's hand, too, saying, "Before I forget, Chief Stone, you impressed a lot of people this morning. Word's gotten around how cool you were under pressure."

She looked uncomfortable at the praise and gestured at me. "You live long enough with this man and his grandmother, you can handle anything thrown your way."

He laughed. "I can see that. Especially with Nana Mama."

Bree and I lingered in the hallway. She was returning to DC Metro headquarters to brief Chief Michaels, and to buy a second phone.

"I'm proud of you, too," I said, and kissed her.

"Thanks. I just wish we'd been able to get the mats on that second bomb before…it will be interesting to see if it was a radio-controlled detonation."

"I'm sure Quantico's on it."

"See you at dinner?" she said, as I went back to the interrogation room door. "Nana Mama said she's creating a masterpiece."

"How could I miss that?"

Bree blew me a kiss, turned, and walked away.

I watched her go for a moment, more in love than ever. Then I turned the door handle and went inside, where retired Marine Gunnery Officer Tim Chorey continued to suffer for his country.

CHAPTER 9

I GOT HOME around seven to find Bree sitting on the front porch, looking as frazzled as I felt.

"Welcome home," she said, raising a mug. "Want a beer?"

I sat down beside her and said, "Half a glass."

She set the mug down, reached down by her side and came up with a second mug and a growler from Blue Jacket, a new brewery in a formerly industrial area in southwest DC.

"Goldfinch," Bree said. "A Belgian blond ale. It's good. Nana bought it."

She poured me half a mug and I sipped it, loving the cold, almost lemony flavor. "Hey, that *is* good."

We sat in silence for several minutes, listening to the street, and to the rattle of kitchen utensils from inside.

"Tough day all around," Bree said.

"Especially for you," I said, and reached out my hand.

She took it and smiled. "This is enough."

I smiled and said, "It is, isn't it?"

"All I could want."

I focused on that. Not on the memories of how sick poor Chorey had gotten before I could get him admitted into the detox unit. How he'd refused to wear the hearing device or read my words after a while, retreating from the world and what it had done to him in the surest way he knew how.

"Dinner!" Nana Mama called.

Bree squeezed my hand, and we went inside. My ninety-something grandmother was making magic at the stove when we entered the kitchen.

"Whatever it is, it smells great," I said, thinking there was curry involved.

"It always smells great when Nana Mama's manning the stove," said Jannie, my sixteen-year-old daughter, as she carried covered dishes from the counter to the table.

"Smells weird to me," said Ali, my almost nine-year-old, who was already sitting at the table, studying an iPad. "Is it tofu? I hate tofu."

"As you've told me every day since the last time we had it," my grandmother said.

"Is it?"

"Not even close," she said, pushing her glasses up her nose on the way to the table. "No electronic devices at the dinner table, young man."

Ali groaned. "It's not a game, Nana. It's homework."

"And this is dinnertime," I said.

He sighed, closed the cover, and put the tablet on a shelf behind him.

"Good," Nana Mama said, smiling. "A little drumroll, please?"

Jannie started tapping her fingers against the tabletop. I joined in, and so did Bree and Ali.

"*Top Chef* judges," my grandmother said. "I give you fresh

Alaskan halibut in a sauce of sweet onions, elephant garlic, Belgian blond beer, and dashes of cumin, cilantro, and curry."

She popped off the lid. Sumptuous odors steamed out and swept my mind off my day. As we scooped jasmine rice and ladled the halibut onto our plates, I could tell Bree had managed to put her day aside as well.

The halibut was delicious, and Nana Mama's delicate sauce made it all the better. I had seconds. So did everyone else.

The fuller I got, however, the more my thoughts drifted back to Chorey. Those thoughts must have shown on my face. My grandmother said, "Something not right with your meal, Alex?"

"No, ma'am," I said. "I'd order that dish in a fancy restaurant."

"Then what? Your trial?"

I refused to give that a second thought. I said, "No, there was this veteran Bree and I dealt with today. He suffered a head injury and lost most of his hearing in an explosion in Afghanistan. He lives in shelters and on the streets now."

Ali said, "Dad, why does America treat its combat veterans so poorly?"

"We do not," Jannie said.

"Yes, we do," Ali said. "I read it on the Internet."

"Don't take everything on the Internet as gospel truth," Nana Mama said.

"No," he insisted. "There's like a really high suicide rate when they come home."

"That's true," Bree said.

Ali said, "And a lot of them live through getting blown up but they're never right again. And their families have to take care of them, and they don't know how."

"I've heard that, too," my grandmother said.

"There's help for them, but not enough, given what they've been through," I said. "We brought the guy today to the VA hospital. Took a while, but they got him in detox to get clean. The problem is what's going to happen when he's discharged."

"He'll probably be homeless again," Ali said.

"Unless I can figure out a way to help him."

My grandmother made a *tsk* noise. "Don't you have enough on your plate already? Helping your attorneys prepare your defense? Seeing patients? Being a husband and father?"

Her tone surprised me. "Nana, you always taught us to help others in need."

"Long as you see to your own needs first. You can't do real good in the world if you don't take care of yourself."

"She's right," Bree said later in our bathroom, after we'd cleaned the kitchen and seen the rest of the family to bed. "You can't be everything to everyone, Alex."

"I know that," I said. "I just…"

"What?"

"There's something about Chorey, how lost he is, how abandoned he's been, hearing nothing, seeing little. It just got to me, makes me want to do something."

"My hopeless idealist," Bree said, hugging me. "I love you for it."

I hugged her back, kissed her and said, "You're everything to me, you know."

CHAPTER 10

AT THE MENTAL health clinic of the Veterans Affairs Medical Center in northeast DC, in an outpatient room drenched in morning sun, a shaggy and shabbily dressed man in his early forties chortled bitterly.

"Thank you," he sneered, in a falsetto voice. "Thank you for your service."

He shifted in his wheelchair and relaxed into a deeper, natural drawl that sounded like west Texas. "I freaking hate that more than anything, you know? Can you hear me folks? Can I get an aye?"

Around the circle, several of the other men and women, sitting in metal folding chairs, nodded, with a chorus of *Aye*.

The group facilitator adjusted his glasses. "Why would you hate someone showing you gratitude for your military service, Thomas?"

Thomas threw up his arms. His left hand and half the forearm were gone. Both of his legs were amputated above the knees.

"Gratitude for what, Jones?" Thomas said. "How do they know what I did before I lost two drumsticks and a wing? That's the hypocrisy. Most of the ones who wanna run up and tell you how much they appreciate your service? They never served."

"And that makes you angry?" Jones said.

"Hell, yeah, it does. Many countries in the freaking world have some kind of mandatory public service. People who don't serve their country got no skin in the game far as I'm concerned. They don't give a damn enough about our nation to defend it, or to improve it, or to lose limbs for it. They try to bury their guilt about their free ride in life by shaking my good hand, and thanking me for my service."

He looked like he wanted to spit, but didn't.

"Why did you enlist?" Jones asked. "Patriotism?"

Thomas threw back his head to laugh. "Oh, God. Hell, no."

Some of the others in the group looked at him stonily. The rest smiled or laughed with him.

"So why?" Jones said.

Thomas hardened. He said, "I figured the Army was a way out of East Jesus. A chance to get training, get the GI Bill, go to college. Instead I get shipped to pissed-off towelhead town. I mean, would anyone volunteer to go to the Middle East with a gun if the government offered college to someone who worked in schools, sweeping floors instead of getting shot? I think not. No freaking way."

"Damn straight," said Griffith, a big black man with a prosthetic leg. "You're willing to whack 'em and stack 'em, they'll pay for a PhD. You wanna do good, they pay jack shit. You tell 'em, Thomas. Tell 'em like it is."

"If you don't, I will," said Mickey, who sat between Griffith and Thomas.

Jones glanced at the clock on the wall and said, "Not today, Mickey. We've gone over our time already."

Mickey shook his head angrily and said, "You know they tried to do that to Ronald Reagan, shut off his microphone so folks wouldn't hear him before the election. Reagan wouldn't let them, said he paid for the microphone. Well, I paid, Jones. We all paid. Every one of us has paid and paid, so you are not taking our microphone away."

The psychologist cocked his head. "Afraid I have no choice, Mickey. There's another group coming in ten minutes."

Mickey might have pushed his luck, seen if he could get a rise out of the shrink, something he enjoyed doing. But he felt satisfied that day. He decided to give Jones a break.

Mickey waited until the psychologist left the room before rising from his chair, saying, "The powerful never want to hear the truth."

"You got that right, son," said Thomas, raising his remaining hand to high-five Mickey's.

"Scares them," said Keene, a scrawny guy in his twenties, paralyzed and riding in a computerized wheelchair. "Just like Jack Nicholson said to Tom Cruise: they can't handle the truth."

"I'm still gonna speak truth to power," Mickey said. "Make them learn the lessons at gut level, know what I'm saying?"

"You know it," said Thomas. "Get an ice cream before you go home, Mick?"

Mickey wouldn't meet Thomas's gaze. "Stuff to take care of, old man. Next time?"

Thomas studied him. "Sure, Mick. You good?"

"Top notch."

They bumped fists. Mickey turned to leave.

"Give 'em hell out there, Mickey," Keene called after him.

Mickey looked back at the men in the wheelchairs, and felt filled with purpose.

"Every day soldiers," he said. "Every goddamned day."

CHAPTER 11

MICKEY LEFT THE VA through the north entrance and climbed aboard the D8 Metro bus bound for Union Station. Always sensitive to pity or suspicion, he was happy that not one rider looked his way as he showed his ride card to the driver, and walked to an empty seat diagonally across from the rear exit. His favorite spot.

Mickey could see virtually everyone on the bus from that position. As he'd been taught a long time ago, to stay alive you made sure you could watch your six as well as your nine, twelve, and three.

In his mind he heard a gruff voice say, *"Understand your situation, soldier, and then deal with it as it is, not as you want it to be. If it's not as you want it to be, then fix it, goddamnit. Identify the weakness, and be the change for the better."*

Damn straight, Hawkes, Mickey thought. *Damn straight.*

The doors sighed shut. The bus began to roll.

Mickey liked buses. No one really noticed you on a bus, especially this bus.

The inflicted and the wounded were a dime a dozen on the D8, the Hospital Center Line. Cancer patients. Alzheimer's patients.

Head injuries. Amputees. They all rode it. He was just a bit player in the traveling freak show.

Which is why Mickey left the bus at K and 8th, and walked over to Christopher's Grooming Lounge on H.

A burly barber with a lumberjack beard turned from the cash register and gave his client change. He saw Mickey and grinned.

"Hey, Mick! Where you been, brother?"

"Out and about, Fatz. You clean me up?"

"Shit, what's a Fatz for, right? You sit right here."

When Mickey got out of the chair twenty minutes later, his wispy beard was gone and his cheeks were fresh and straight-razor smooth. His hair was six inches shorter, swept back, and sprayed in place.

"There," Fatz said. "You look somewhere between a hipster and a preppie."

"Right down the middle," Mickey said, turning his head. "I like it."

He gave Fatz a nice tip and promised to return sooner rather than later. The barber hugged him, said, "I got your back. I'll always have your back."

"Thanks, Fatz."

"You're a good dude, remember that."

"I try," Mickey said, gave him a high five, and left.

He walked the six blocks to the Capitol Self Storage facility at 3rd and N Streets, and went inside to a small unit, where he unlocked and rolled up the door. Stepping inside, he pulled the door down and switched on the light.

Six minutes later, Mickey emerged. Gone were the dirty denim jeans, the canvas coat, and the ragged Nikes, replaced by khakis, a lightly used blue windbreaker sporting the embroidered logo of a golf academy in Scottsdale, Arizona, and a pair of virtually new ASICS cross-trainers. It was remarkable what you could find in a Goodwill store these days.

Mickey put on a wide-brim white baseball cap and a pair of cheap sunglasses. Around his waist, he wore a black fanny pack with a water bottle in a holder. Around his neck hung an old Nikon film camera with no film inside.

There, he thought as he locked the unit, I could be any Joe Jackass come to town to see the sights.

Mickey left the storage facility and walked south, aware of the fanny pack, the water bottle, and the camera, and doing his best to contain his excitement. Be chill, brother. Stroll, man. What would Hawkes say? *Be who you're supposed to be.* You're Joe Jackass on va-cay. All the time in the world.

Fifteen minutes later, Mickey boarded the DC Circulator bus at Union Station with a slew of tourists. He stood in the aisle near the rear exit, holding the strap as the bus rolled down Louisiana Avenue.

He got off at the third stop, 7th Street, walked around the block, noted the increased police presence on the Mall, and re-turned to wait for the next bus to arrive. He boarded it, found a spot as close as he could to the rear exit and rode it until the eighth stop, the Martin Luther King, Jr. Memorial.

He got off. It was 11 a.m.

Seventeen minutes later, Mickey re-boarded the Circulator at the ninth stop, Lincoln Memorial. Taking his usual position by the rear exit, Mickey felt lighter, freed, as if he'd left things in his past, on the verge of a brighter future.

He waited to get off until the fourteenth stop, National Air and Space Museum. While tourists poured out the door after him, he dug in his pants pocket and came up with a burner phone. He walked away from the knot of people trying to get into the museum and thumbed speed dial.

"Yes?" the woman said.

"Chief Stone?" Mickey said, trying to make his voice soft and low. "It's your worst nightmare again."

CHAPTER 12

BREE SLAPPED THE bubble on the roof, hit the sirens, and said, "Hold on, Alex."

I braced my feet on the passenger side. She glanced in her side view and stomped on the gas.

We squealed out of 5th Street, ran the red light at Pennsylvania, and headed toward the Mall with Chief Stone calling the shots over a handheld radio.

"He says it's at the Korean War Memorial, but clear the MLK and Lincoln Memorials, too," she said. "Close Ohio Drive and Independence Avenue Southwest. I want to know the second those five are clear. Am I clear?"

"Yes, Chief," the dispatcher said.

"Call IT," she said. "Find out if they got a trace on the call that just—"

Her cell phone started ringing. She glanced down, said, "Forget it, they're calling me."

Cradling the radio mike, she snatched up her cell, said, "Chief Stone. Did you get it?"

Bree listened and said, "How much damn time do they need?"

A pause, then, "You'd think in this day and age, it would be a hell of a lot less, but okay. If there's a next time I'll try to keep him talking."

Hanging up and letting her phone plop in her lap, she let out a sigh of exasperation. "A minute ten at a minimum to hone in on an on-going cell signal. He spoke to me for twenty-one seconds."

"They have no idea where he is?"

"Somewhere in DC but they can't pinpoint the call. And even if they could, he has to be using a burner."

"You'd think," I said.

Six minutes later, Bree threw the car in park near the Ash Woods on Independence Avenue.

"You should stay here until you've got Mahoney at your side."

"Agreed," I said. "Be safe."

She kissed me and said, "I'll let the pros take care of the dangerous stuff."

I watched her get out and walk toward the traffic barrier closing off the west end of the National Mall. She couldn't be seen bringing me into a Metro investigation while I was on suspension.

Mahoney, however, could bring me in as a consultant. I left the car a few minutes later when he arrived with the FBI's bomb squad and a dog team of three.

The wind was out of the southeast, so Mahoney sent the dogs between the Lincoln Memorial and Korean War Veterans Memorial, a dramatic, triangular space with nineteen steel statues of larger than life soldiers on patrol, some emerging from a loose grove of trees and others in the open, walking across strips of granite and low-growing juniper.

The FBI dog handlers spread out and released the bomb sniffers. Muzzles up, panting for scent, they cast into the wind toward the statues. Back and forth they ran, coursing through the trees and the steel patrol soldiers. I stood beside Bree, looking around to spot my favorite part of the memorial: three statues crouched around a campfire, set on a granite slab inscribed with THE FORGOTTEN WAR.

"C'mon," Bree said in a low voice. "Find it."

At the northeast end of the memorial, two of the dogs circled a low, dark wall that read FREEDOM IS NOT FREE. They returned to their handlers waiting on the walkway. The third shepherd took a longer loop downwind of the MLK Memorial before trotting back to his handler and the others.

"Rio and Ben are not picking up anything here," a handler said on the radio. "And Kelsey wasn't smelling anything at MLK. We can run the Lincoln if you want us to."

"Yes," Bree said. "Better safe than sorry."

Mahoney said, "This the boy who cried wolf?"

"An effective tactic," I said. "Gets us all worked up, calls us to action. He probably gets a kick out of—"

The bomb exploded behind us.

CHAPTER 13

WE DOVE TO the ground and covered our heads. Bits of gravel rained down on my back. When it stopped, I lifted my head to see a thin plume of charcoal-gray smoke rising to the right of a walkway that led toward King's Memorial.

"Jesus," Mahoney said, getting up and dusting his suit off. "How'd we miss that?"

Bree, rattled but fine, said, "The dogs were just through there."

The lead dog handler shook his head in bewilderment. "If there was a bomb they would have smelled it."

"Well, they didn't," Mahoney snapped, before calling for a forensics team to gather the bomb debris for analysis.

We all put on blue hospital booties and moved toward the explosion site, everyone seeming jittery and uncertain. Yesterday he'd put two bombs on the National Mall. If the dogs didn't smell the first one, couldn't there be another?

No more than a foot across and five inches deep, the smoking crater was two feet off the pedestrian walkway, on the other side of a slack black chain fence. The bomb had been hidden under a low juniper, now charred and broken.

A mangled, burnt metal casing lay on the ground several feet away.

"Looks like a camera body," Bree said. "Or what used to be one."

That spooked me. How many tourists in DC carry a camera? It would never be noticed, at least not while the bomber was carrying it. He was smart. He was creative. But something about the explosion bothered me.

"It didn't do a lot of damage," I said. "I mean, it could have been bigger, made more of a statement."

"He wounded two agents yesterday," Bree said.

"I'm not discounting that. It just seems like this should have been an escalation."

"Or at least two bombs," Mahoney said.

"Exactly."

Before Bree could reply, one of the dog handlers yelled. He'd found something on the north side of the memorial.

"Is your dog on scent?" Mahoney shouted as we hurried toward them.

"No," the handler said when we got close. "I saw it in that clear trash bag there, a black fanny pack."

Bree triggered her radio and said, "Bring the bomb team up."

Within five minutes, FBI bomb squad commander Peggy Denton had arrived. We watched her iPad screen, showing the Andros robot's camera feed and monitoring several electronic sensors. She shook her head. "We're not picking up on a radio or cell phone. No timer, either. We can X-ray it."

Mahoney nodded. Another tense three minutes passed while they moved a portable X-ray into position and looked inside the fanny pack. Aside from a water bottle and a shirt, there was an irregular rectangular item roughly three inches long, two inches wide, and two thick.

"Too wide for a Snickers bar," I said. "Brownie?"

"Too dense for either of them," Denton said. "Can't see any triggering device, no blasting caps, or booby trap lines."

"Your call," Mahoney said.

The commander put on her hooded visor, walked the thirty yards to the garbage and retrieved the fanny pack. She unzipped it, reached in and pulled out the object, which was loosely wrapped in dull-green wax paper.

"Shit," Denton said through her radio headset. "I need a blast can here, ASAP."

Another of the bomb squad agents hurried toward Denton with a heavy steel box.

"What's going on?" Bree asked.

"It's C-4 type plastic explosive," Denton radioed back as her partner opened the box's lid. She set the bomb material inside and screwed the lid shut. "Yugoslavian Semtex by the markings on the wrapper."

"Why didn't the dogs smell it?" I asked. "Isn't there something added to plastic explosives so they can be detected?"

"They're called taggants," Denton said, taking off her hood and visor, and coming back over. "I suspect this C-4 is old. Pre-1980, before taggants were required under international law."

Bree shook her head. "Yesterday, the dogs smelled the bombs.

Why make just one bomb out of it, but not four? And why leave the uncharged C-4 at all?"

"My guess is he left it as a warning," I said. "He used plastic explosives with taggant the first time, but that game's over. He's saying we can't sniff him out now. He's saying he can bomb us at will."

CHAPTER 14

TENSE DAYS PASSED without a phone call from the bomber. Bree was under pressure from Chief Michaels. Mahoney was dealing with the FBI director.

The only break came from the FBI crime lab confirming that the explosive used in the third bomb was pre-1980 Yugoslavian C-4, and that the triggering devices—all timers—were sophisticated. The work of an experienced hand.

I did what I could to help Mahoney between seeing patients, including Kate Williams, who showed up five minutes early for a mid-morning appointment. I took it as a good sign. But if I thought Kate was ready to grab hold of the life preserver, and I certainly hoped she was, I was mistaken.

"Let's talk about life after you ran away," I said, sitting down with my chair positioned at a non-confrontational angle.

"Let's not," Kate said. "None of that matters. We both know why we're here."

"Fair enough," I said, pausing to consider how best to proceed.

In situations like this, I would ordinarily ask a lot of questions about documents in her files, watching her body language for clues to her deeper story. Indicators of stress and tension—the inability to maintain eye contact, say, or the habitual flexing of a hand—are often sure signals of deeper troubles.

But I'd had difficulty reading Kate's body language, which shouted so loud of defeat that very little else was getting through. I decided to change things up.

"Okay, no questions about the past today. Let's talk about the future."

Kate sighed. "What future?"

"The future comes every second."

"With every shallow breath."

I read defiance and despair in her body language, but continued, "If none of this had happened to you, what would your future look like? Your ideal future, I mean?"

She didn't dismiss the question, but pondered it. She said, "I think I'd still be in, rising through the ranks."

"You liked the Army."

"I loved the Army."

"Why?"

"Until the end it was a good place for me. I do better with rules."

"Sergeant," I said, glancing at her file. "Two tours. Impressive."

"I was good. And then I wasn't."

"When you were good, where did you see yourself going in the Army?"

I thought I'd gotten through a crack, but she shut it down. She said, "They discharged me, Dr. Cross. Dreaming about something that can never happen is not healthy."

She watched me like a chess player looking for an indication of my next move.

Should I ask her to imagine a future for someone else? Or prompt her to take the conversation in a new direction? Before I could decide, Kate decided for me.

"Are you investigating the IEDs?" she asked. "On the Mall? I saw a news story the other night. Your wife was there, and I thought I saw you in the background."

"I was there, but I can't talk about it beyond what you've heard," I said. "Why?"

She stiffened. "Familiar ground, I guess."

I grasped some of the implication, but her body said there was more.

"Care to explain?"

Struggling, she finally said, "I know them. They're like rats. Digging in the dirt. Hoping you'll happen by."

"The bombers?"

Kate took on a far-off look. It seemed she was seeing terrible things, her face twitching with repressed emotion.

"Stinking sand rats," she said softly. "They only come out at night, Doc. That's a good thing to remember, the sand rats and the camel spiders only come out at night."

The alarm on my phone buzzed, and I almost swore because our hour was nearly up. I felt like we were just getting somewhere. By the time I silenced the alarm, Kate had come back from her dark place and saw my frustration.

"Don't worry about it, Doc," she said, smiling sadly as she stood. "You tried your best to crack the nut."

"You're not a nut."

She laughed sadly. "Oh, yes I am, Dr. Cross."

CHAPTER 15

WIPING AT TEARS, Mickey left the VA Medical Center and ran to catch the D8 Metro bus heading south. He barely made it, and wasn't surprised to find the bus virtually empty at this late hour.

Breathing hard, Mickey went to his favorite seat, barely glancing at the only two other passengers, an elderly woman with a cane and a heavyset man wearing blue work coveralls.

As the bus sighed into motion, Mickey felt tired, more tired than he'd been in weeks, months maybe. Rather than fight it all the way to Union Station, he pulled his baseball cap down over his eyes and drifted. Feeling the bus sway, hearing the rumble of the tires, he fell away to another time, in a place of war.

In his dreams, the sun was scorching. Mickey had buried himself in a foxhole as the Taliban mortared an advanced outpost in the mountains of Helmand Province, Afghanistan. Each blast came closer and closer. Rock and dirt fell and pinged off his helmet, smacked the back of his Kevlar battle vest, made him cringe and wince, wondering at each noise if his time was finally up.

"Where the Christ is that mother?" he heard a voice shout.

"Upper south hillside, two o'clock," another voice called back. "Three hundred vertical meters below the ridge."

"Can't find him," a gruffer voice yelled. "Gimme range!"

A third man yelled, "Sixteen hundred ninety-two meters."

"That ledge with the two bushes on the right?"

"Affirmative!"

"I got it. Just has to show himself."

A fourth voice shouted, "Smoke him, Hawkes! Turn the sumbitch inside out!"

The mortar attack had slowed to a stop. Mickey got up, the debris falling off his uniform as he spat out dust and poked his head out of his foxhole.

To his right about twenty yards, Hawkes was settled in behind the high-power scope of a .50-caliber Barrett sniper rifle. Muscular and bare-chested under his body armor, Hawkes had the stub of a cheap unlit cigar dangling from the corner of his lips.

"Take him out, Hawkes," Mickey yelled. "We got better places to be."

"We do not move until that good son of Allah shows his head," Hawkes shouted back, his head never leaving the scope.

"I wanna go home," Mickey said. "I want you to go home, too."

"We all wanna go home, kid," Hawkes said.

"I'm going surfing someday, Hawkes," Mickey said. "Learn to ride big waves."

"North Shore, baby," Hawkes said as if it were a daydream of his, too. "Banzai Pipeline. Sunset Beach and…Hey, there you are, Mr. Haji. Couldn't stand the suspense, could you? Had to see just how close you came with those last three mortars to blowing the infidels past paradise."

Hawkes flipped off the safety on the Barrett, and said, "Sending, boys."

Before anyone could reply, the .50-caliber rifle boomed and belched fire out the ported muzzle. In the shimmering heat Mickey swore he could see the contrail left by the bullet, ripping across space, sixteen hundred and ninety-two meters up the face of the mountain before it struck with deadly impact.

The other men started cheering. Hawkes came off the rifle finally, and looked over at Mickey with a big, shit-eating grin. "Now we can go home, kid."

Mickey felt someone shaking him, and he startled awake.

"Union Station," the bus driver said. "End of the line."

Mickey yawned, said, "Sorry, sir. Long day."

The driver said, "For all of us. You got somewhere to be?"

Mickey felt embarrassed to answer, but said, "My mom's. It's not far."

The driver stood aside for Mickey to go out the door. He went inside the bus terminal, following the signage toward the passenger trains and the Metro. Most of the shops inside Union Station were closed and dark, though there were still a fair number of passengers waiting for Amtrak rides.

Mickey acted cold, pulled his hoodie up to cover his face from the security cameras, and went to short-term lockers, where he used a key to retrieve a small book bag. He reached into the book bag to retrieve a greasy box of cold fried chicken from Popeye's. The last drumstick and wing tasted nice and spicy.

Mickey dropped the bones back in the box just as an overhead speaker blared: "Amtrak announces the Northeast Corridor Train to Boston, departing 10:10 on Track Four. All aboard!"

With the cardboard box in his hand, he fished in his pocket for the ticket, fell in with the crowd and moved toward the door to Track 4. He showed his ticket to the conductor, who scanned it with disinterest, waved him through, and reached for the ticket of the passenger behind him.

Going with the knot of passengers, Mickey walked through a short tunnel that led out onto the platform. He passed the dining car and several others before spotting a trash can affixed to a post two cars back from the engines.

He walked past it, never slowing as he dumped the greasy, fried chicken take-out box that held the bomb.

Then Mickey boarded the train and settled into a seat. His ticket said Baltimore, but he would get out at the first stop—New Carrollton—and catch the Metro back into the city, where he'd try to get a little sleep before making a call to Chief Stone.

CHAPTER 16

BREE'S PHONE JANGLED at five minutes to three in the morning.

I groaned and turned over, seeing her silhouette sitting up in bed.

"Bree Stone," she answered groggily.

Then she stiffened. Her free hand reached out and tapped me as she put the call on speaker.

"A city on edge," the voice purred. "A third bomb found. Fears of more to come."

The diction and tone of the bomber's voice was as Bree had described it. I couldn't tell if it was a man or a woman talking.

"Are there more to come?"

"Every day until people start to feel it in their bones," the bomber said. "Until there's a shift in their mind-set, so they understand what it feels like."

"What kind of shift? Feel like what?"

"Still don't get it, do you? Look in Union Station, Chief Stone. In a few hours it will be packed with commuters."

The connection died.

"Shit," Bree said. She threw back the covers and jumped out of bed, already making calls as she moved toward the closet.

I was up and tugging on clothes when central dispatch answered her call, and she started barking orders as she dressed.

"We have a credible bomb threat in Union Station," Bree said. "Call Metro Transit Police. Clear Union Station and set up a perimeter outside. Get dogs and bomb squads there ASAP. Alert Chief Michaels. Alert FBI SAC Mahoney. Alert Capitol Police. Alert the mayor, and Homeland Security. I'll be there in nine minutes, tops."

She stabbed the button to end the call and tugged on a blue sweatshirt emblazoned with METRO POLICE on the back. I was tying my shoes when she came out of the closet.

"What are you doing?"

"Going with you," I said. "Mahoney will be there soon enough."

Bree hesitated, but then nodded. "You can drive."

Eight minutes later I slammed on the brakes and parked in front of the flashing blue lights of two Capitol Hill Police cruisers blocking Massachusetts Avenue and 2nd Street in Northeast.

Bree jumped out, her badge up. "I'm Metro Chief Stone."

"FBI bomb squad and a Metro's K-9 unit just crossed North Capitol Street, heading toward the station, Chief," one officer said.

"The station clear?"

"Affirmative," another officer said. "The last of the cleaning crew just left."

Bree glanced at me, said, "Dr. Cross is an FBI consultant on these bombings. He'll be coming in with me."

The officers stood aside. We hurried along deserted Mass Avenue toward the now familiar vehicles of the FBI bomb squad, and two Metro K-9 teams parked out in front of the station. Three men walked toward us wearing workmen's coveralls.

"You with the cleaning crew?" I asked, stopping.

The men nodded. Bree said, "Catch up."

I asked them a few questions and found Bree at the back of the FBI's Bomb Squad vehicle, where Peggy Denton was suiting up.

"Do we have a deadline?" Denton asked.

"It wasn't put that way," Bree said. "Just a suggestion to look in Union Station because at six a.m. the station will be packed with commuters."

"Awful big place to sweep in two hours and twenty minutes," Denton said, checking her watch.

"You can narrow it down," I said.

"How's that?" Bree asked.

"Your bomber likes trash cans. Three of the four IEDs were in them. The cleaners I just spoke to said they were working from the front entrance north. They swept, vacuumed, and picked up trash bags in the main hall and on the first level of shops. Those garbage bags are in cleaning carts. Two are in the shopping hall and food court. One in the main hall. I'd take the dogs to those carts first, and then sweep the second floor of shops and the Amtrak ticketing and the train platforms. Metro station after that."

The FBI bomb squad commander looked to Bree. "That work, Chief?"

"It does," she said. "Thank you, Dr. Cross."

"Anytime," I said.

Ned Mahoney showed up, along with two FBI bomb-sniffing canines and the entire Metro bomb unit.

"We've got to stop meeting this way, Chief," Mahoney said, bleary-eyed and drinking a cup of Starbucks.

"Our secret's out," she said.

"He's escalating," I said. "The interval between attacks is getting shorter. Twenty-four hours between the first and the next two. And now fifteen hours since then?"

"Sounds right," Mahoney said, nodding. "How much time did he give us?"

"Two hours eighteen minutes," Bree said. "Six a.m."

Denton said, "If Dr. Cross is right and he hid it in a garbage can, we'll find it a lot sooner than that."

"Unless he's using Yugoslavian C-4 again," I said.

"Which is why we'll treat every garbage bag or can as if it's a live bomb."

The first dogs went inside at 3:39 a.m. We went in after the bomb squads entered, and stood in the dramatic vaulted main hall of the station, listening to the echoes of the dogs and their handlers.

None of the K-9s reacted to the garbage carts the cleaners had abandoned. But Denton prudently had them turned over, dumping the trash bags, which she covered with bomb mats.

She couldn't do that to every remaining trash bag in the station. Instead, she told her agents to don their protective cowls. They would retrieve every public garbage bag left in the rest of the building and put them in piles to be matted.

They cleared the second floor of the shops first. I noticed and pointed to a *Washington Post* newspaper box. The headlines read: A CITY ON EDGE. FEARS OF MORE TO COME.

"He was reading from the paper," Bree said.

"Following his own exploits," I said. "Enjoying himself."

The dogs cleared the Amtrak Hall.

"It has to be out on one of the platforms then," I told Bree and Mahoney. "The cleaners said they almost always do them last."

Mahoney ordered the search personnel onto the platforms. We went through a short tunnel to Platform 6 and watched as the German shepherds loped past dark trains, flanking Platforms 1 and 2 to our far left, going from garbage receptacle to garbage receptacle, sniffing at the open doors to the coach cars.

Bree checked her watch.

"We'll find it," she said. "There's only so many places he could have—"

The tracks to both sides of Platforms 4 and 5 were empty. There was nothing to block the brilliant flash of the bomb exploding in a trash can at Platform 4's far north end, or the blast that boxed our ears and forced us to our knees.

It was 4 a.m. on the dot.

CHAPTER 17

LATER THAT AFTERNOON, I opened the door to Kate Williams, who actually greeted me before going into my basement office. She took a seat before I offered it.

"How are you?" I asked, moving my chair to a non-threatening angle.

"Could be worse," she said.

"The headaches?"

"Come and go."

"Tell me about that day."

Kate stiffened. "That's the thing, Dr. Cross, I don't remember much of it. Getting your bell rung hard has a way of erasing things. You know?"

"Yes. What *do* you remember?"

She fidgeted. "Can we talk about something else today?"

I set my pen down. "Okay. What shall we talk about?"

"Your wife's a police chief?"

"Chief of detectives," I said.

"She's part of the IED investigation. I saw her on the news. You, too."

"The FBI's brought me in as a consultant."

Kate sat forward in her chair. "What happened in Union Station this morning?"

"Beyond what's on the news, Kate, I really can't talk about it."

"But I can help you," she said eagerly. "If there's one thing I know, it's IED bombers, Dr. Cross. How they think, how they act, what to look for, how to sniff them out. With or without dogs."

I tried not to look skeptical.

"It's what I did in Iraq," she said. "My team. We were assigned to guard supply convoys, but we were IED hunters, pure and simple."

Kate said her team, including a German shepherd named Brickhouse, rode in an RG-33 MMPV, a "Medium Mine Protected Vehicle" that often led convoys into hostile territory. Her job demanded she sit topside in a .50-caliber machine gun turret, scanning the road ahead for signs of ambush or possible IED emplacements.

"What did you look for?" I said. I noted how much her demeanor had changed.

"Any significant disturbance in the road surface, to start," she said. "Any large boxes or cans on the shoulder of the road or in the brush. Any culverts ahead? Any bridges? Loose wires hanging to soil level from power poles. Any spotters on rooftops watching us? Men or women hurrying away from the road with red dirt all over their robes? Were they using cell phones? Were they using binoculars? If it was night, were we picking up anything in infrared images? It's a long list that gradually added up to gut instinct."

I studied her a long moment, wondering if it was possible she was involved. The bomber's voice had been soft, androgynous. But I saw no deceit in Kate's body language, nothing but openness and honesty.

"C'mon, Dr. Cross," she said. "I can help you."

"All right," I sighed. "I can't tell you everything. But, yes, an IED went off in Union Station early this morning. No one was hurt. The bomb caused minimal damage."

"Radio controlled?"

"Timer."

That seemed to surprise her, but she shrugged. "He's not trying to hit a moving target, though, is he? What's the medium he's using? Fertilizer?"

I hesitated, but was intrigued by the line of questioning. "Plastic explosive."

"C-4. We saw that when they targeted bridges. Describe the placements?"

I told her that four of the five bombs had been found in trash cans, one buried beside a path between the Korean War and Martin Luther King Memorials.

"He's nervous," she said. "That's why he's using the trash cans. They're easy. Disguise it as something else, dump it, and walk on. How much power in the bombs?"

"You'd have to ask the guys at Quantico. They're analyzing what's left."

"But we're not talking significant damage here," she said. "There's no ball bearings or screws wrapped around the C-4 to cause maximum mayhem."

"Not that I've heard."

She stared off. "That's when they're out for big blood. How's he warning you?"

We hadn't revealed that the bomber had been calling Bree directly, so I said, "Warning us?"

Kate cocked her head. "Every time a bomb's gone off, police and FBI have been on the scene, actively looking for a bomb. You had to have been warned."

"I can't talk specifics."

"Any Allahu Akbar, jihad stuff?"

"Not that I know of."

"That was another thing I was always tuned in to. I learned enough Arabic to look for jihadi phrases spray painted near IEDs."

"Really?"

"Oh, all the time," she said.

"There's been nothing along those lines."

Kate chewed on that. "He giving you any motivation?"

"Changing people's mind-set. Making them understand."

"You quoting him?"

"Yes."

She fell quiet for almost a minute and finally said, "He's no Middle Eastern terrorist, that's for sure."

I agreed with her, but asked, "How do you know?"

"Jihadists are in your face about why they're trying to blow you up," she said. "They'll take credit for it in the name of Allah or their chosen fanatic group. And the damage inflicted doesn't make sense to me. Rather than put five bombs out, why not use all that

C-4 and make a real statement? Wrap it in bolts, washers, and nuts, and get it somewhere crowded, like the Boston Marathon bombers?"

That made sense, actually. "So what's the mind-set change he's after? What's he trying to make us understand?"

Kate bit at her lip. "I don't know. But I have the feeling if you answer those questions, Dr. Cross, you'll find your bomber."

CHAPTER 18

HEAVY RAIN FELL when Mickey left the VA hospital long after dark. As soon as he felt the drops lash his face, he let go of the emotion he'd been fighting to keep deep in his throat. He choked off two sobs but finally let tears flow. Who could tell he was crying in the rain anyway?

Certainly no one Mickey encountered between the hospital and the D8 bus stop. They were all bent over, hurrying for cover. He was alone on the bench when the Hospital Center bus pulled up.

Mickey got on and was dismayed to find his favorite seat by the rear entrance taken, by a big Latino guy he recognized. Like almost everyone riding the Hospital Center Line from the north end, he'd been chewed up by war and was always pissed off.

Mickey nodded to the man as he passed and took an empty spot two rows behind, intending to take his territory back as soon as the man left.

But the bus was warm, and Mickey was as tired and dismayed as he'd ever been. *What am I doing this for? Doesn't he understand? How can't he understand?*

Tears welled up again. Mickey wiped his sleeve frantically at them. He couldn't be seen crying here. Out in the rain was one thing, but not here.

Be a soldier, man, he thought as his eyes drifted shut. *Be a soldier.*

Mickey dozed and dreamed of scenes he had imagined many times. He felt tires hit potholes, and he was no longer in the bus, but deep in the back of a US military transport truck taking him away from the firebase for good, heading straight to Kandahar, then Kabul, and home.

"You happy, kid?" Hawkes asked. "Going stateside?"

Hawkes, the sniper, was sitting on the opposite bench, next to the tailgate, his Barrett rifle balanced between his legs, grinning like he'd just heard the best joke of all.

"Damn straight, I'm happy, Hawkes," Mickey said.

"You don't look it."

"No?" Mickey said. "I'm just nervous, that's all. We're so close, Hawkes, I can taste it. No more crazy mofos in turbans lobbing mortars. Leave this shit behind for good. Go home and just…what are you going to do when you get home, Hawkes?"

Hawkes threw back his head and laughed, from deep in his belly. "Kiss my wife and play with my little boy, Mickey."

"He'll be happy his daddy's home," Mickey said. "That's so—"

Automatic weapons opened up from high in the rocks flanking the road.

"Ambush!" Hawkes shouted. "Get down, kid! Everyone get—"

Hawkes vanished in a roar and a blast of fire that knocked Mickey cold.

For what seemed an eternity, there was only darkness. Then neon light played on his eyelids, and someone shook his knee.

Mickey started, and awoke to see the Latino guy with the attitude staring down at him. "Union Station."

"Oh?" Mickey said. "Thanks."

He took his knapsack and left the bus, running to the terminal to get out of the rain. There were police officers all over the place, and dogs, and reporters. But not one of them paid Mickey any mind as he moved with the evening crowd toward the subway and train stations.

Avoiding the train or Metro platforms, Mickey instead cut through the main hall and out the front door. Four or five television news satellite vans were parked along Massachusetts Avenue, facing Union Station.

When the klieg lights went on, he almost spun around and went back inside. Instead he put up his hood and waited until two men much taller than him exited the station. He fell in almost beside them, within their shadows, until they were a full block east of the television lights.

Mickey left them and kept heading east past Stanton Park. He went to a brick-faced duplex row house on Lexington Place, and used a key to get inside as quietly as he could.

Television light flickered from a room down the hallway. He could hear a woman singing with a back-up band, really belting the song out, probably on one of those star search shows his mother loved, and he hoped the singing would be enough to cover his climb up the stairs.

But when he was almost at the top the song ended. His mother yelled drunkenly, "Mick, is that you?"

"Yes, Ma."

"I've been worried sick."

"Yes, Ma."

"There's left-over Popeye's in the fridge, you want it. And get me some ice."

"I'm tired, Ma," he said. "And I gotta be up early."

He didn't wait for a response but dashed up the stairs, around the bannister and into his room. He locked it and waited, listening for an indication of how drunk she was. A little plastered and she'd shrug it off. A lot plastered and she was likely to pound at his door and shriek curses at him.

A minute passed, and then two.

Mickey tossed his knapsack on the floor, took off his raincoat, and dug beneath his mattress, coming up with a dog-eared paperback book he'd bought online for twenty-two dollars. He'd read *A Practical Guide to Improvised Bomb Making* at least eight times in the past few months, but he climbed on the bed and returned to the chapter on radio-controlled explosives.

Mickey read for an hour, studying the diagrams until he understood how to build the triggering mechanism, and how best to trip it.

Glancing at the clock on his dresser, he stifled a yawn. It was eleven o'clock.

Opening a drawer in the nightstand, he retrieved one of six burner phones he'd bought online in a package deal from a dealer in Oklahoma. Then he called up the Voice Changer Plus App on his smartphone. Mickey started the burner, activated it with a paid-minutes card, and dialed Chief Bree Stone.

They're not listening, he thought as her phone rang. *Time to raise the volume.*

CHAPTER 19

BREE WAS FIGHTING to stay awake for the eleven o'clock news when her phone started buzzing and beeping in her purse. She struggled out of the easy chair in the front room at home, and said, "Mute it."

I thumbed the Mute button and said, "Speaker."

Nodding, Bree got her phone and answered the call.

The odd, soft, almost feminine voice spoke. "Chief Stone?"

"Who are you? What's your name?"

After a long pause, he said, "Nick. Nick the Avenger."

Bree glanced at me, pointed at her watch. I started timing. The FBI was monitoring and tracing all calls to her number. If she could keep him on the phone for just over a minute, they'd be able to locate him.

She said, "Nick, what's it going to take to stop the bombings?"

That question was part of a plan we'd talked about in anticipation of his next call. We both believed we needed to draw the bomber out, get him talking about more than just his next target.

After several moments, he said, "It's gonna take changes on Capitol Hill, Chief. Congress needs to get off its collective butt, and start treating the people who fight their wars right. Until they quit kicking vets in the balls, it's time for everyone to feel what vets have suffered, what they still suffer. I'd clear the Washington Monument if I were you."

The line went dead.

"Son of a bitch," I said. "Forty-four seconds."

We grabbed raincoats and headed out into the pouring rain. I drove. Bree started making calls to once again close off the National Mall, and summon sniffer dogs and bomb squads. Ned Mahoney called me as I turned onto Independence Avenue.

"You hear it?" he asked.

"Yes. The trace?"

"Bomber's within five miles of Capitol Hill. Closest we got."

"Any luck with the surveillance tapes from Union Station?"

"I have four agents watching footage from the twenty-four hours preceding the explosion, working backward from the actual blast. So far, nothing."

"Quantico?"

"Initial reports on the first two bombs came back," Mahoney said. "The detonators are simple, the kind you might see on an IED in the Middle East. But the explosive wasn't taggant-free C-4. That's why the dogs were able to locate them."

"So what was the explosive?"

"Black powder, like for muzzle loaders, but tricked out, made more powerful. A company out in Montana makes the stuff."

"So we can trace it?" Bree said.

"Not as easy as you think," Mahoney said. "There are no real restrictions on the stuff. You can order it from dozens of websites online, or buy it off the shelf at hunting and fishing stores. Surprising, but the company says they make and sell thousands of pounds of the stuff per year."

I thought out loud. "So he has knowledge of and access to a wide array of explosives. What kind of person would get that kind of knowledge and access? I mean to seek out and get the C-4?"

Mahoney said, "Money talks. You can buy nearly anything these days on the dark side of the internet."

"Or he's someone with real training, a military sapper. Or ex."

"You mean like a Marine master gunnery sergeant?"

"Tim Chorey's in detox," I said. I started to see blue lights ahead of us, and cruisers blocking access to the Washington Monument.

"No, he's not," Mahoney said. "I had someone check. Chorey walked out four days ago, within hours of you dropping him."

CHAPTER 20

DAWN CAME. THE rain had been torrential and relentless all night, hampering the search for the latest bomb, and the dark, low-hanging clouds above the Washington Monument showed no sign of clearing.

Bree and I were in our car, taking a break from the rain, listening to WTOP all-news radio and drinking coffee. I was only half paying attention to the newscast, covering the latest bomb threat and the likely effect on commuter traffic.

I was still brooding over Tim Chorey. On the drive over to detox, he'd told me he was ready for change. He was tired of the streets, tired of living in a soundless world, and tired of being blasted all the time. *Blasted.* It was the exact word he'd used.

Had the deaf veteran been playing me the entire time? I like to think of myself as a pretty shrewd judge of character, and an excellent reader of body language. I'd honestly believed Chorey, and I'd gone to bat for him.

The back door opened. Mahoney slid inside wearing an FBI rain slicker and ball cap. He pushed back the hood and said, "It's a monsoon out there."

"Anything?" I said.

"We're positive the inner monument is clear. But this rain's killing us. Really messes with the dogs' noses."

"And he could have used the pre-1980 C-4 again."

"True. Could also be he's abandoned his penchant for garbage cans as bomb sites. We've checked every one in a mile radius."

Bree said, "Are you hearing this?"

We looked at her. She turned up the radio, reporting on a veterans' appropriations bill stalled in the Senate. If the bill doesn't make it to the President's desk before Friday, there would be slashing of funds for dozens of critical veterans' programs across the board.

"You think this has something to do with it?" Mahoney said.

"He talked about Congress not treating vets right," she said. "Maybe this is his motivation. He knows this bill has to pass in four days, so he's pushing."

"But he never mentioned that specifically?" Mahoney said.

"No," Bree said. "He didn't."

"It's been seven hours since the call," I said. "Maybe there's no bomb this time. Maybe he's yanking our chain."

"What makes you think that?" Bree asked.

"It's a freebie. He gets us mobilized, on edge, and the media worked into another frenzy, and he doesn't have to use an ounce of plastic explosives to do it."

"Well, he's got me on edge," Mahoney said. "Six cups of coffee and two hours of sleep in the last twenty-four is not the way to better mental health."

"No, and neither is thinking Chorey's our guy," I said, looking over the backseat.

Mahoney started to stiffen, but I held up my palm. "The bomber hears just fine. Unless Chorey's had a cochlear implant, he's not who's been calling Bree. I read his medical files. There's no way he—"

Ned held up both hands. "Agreed, Alex. He's not the caller. But he could be the caller's partner."

I couldn't dispute that possibility. "Are you naming him a person of interest?"

"I'm supposed to have that conversation with the deputy director in about ten minutes," Mahoney said.

"You recommending it?" Bree asked.

"I'd be remiss if I didn't."

I stifled a yawn, and checked my watch.

"Patients?" Bree asked.

"Just one. Eight o'clock."

"You could cancel."

"I'll power through and get some sleep afterward."

Before she could reply, her cell phone rang.

"Here we go," she said, snatching it up, and answering it on speaker.

"I made a mistake," the soft, strange voice said. "Silly Avenger, I put that bomb in the Air and Space Museum."

CHAPTER 21

AT TWO MINUTES to eight, the bell at our basement door rang, and I snapped awake from dozing in my office. After leaving Bree and Ned on the Mall in front of the National Air and Space Museum, I'd come straight home and shut my eyes.

"Coming!" I called, then went in the bathroom to splash cold water in my face.

I opened the door. The rain had let up and Kate Williams was beaming at me.

"Were you at the scenes this morning?" she asked, sounding breathless and excited.

"All night," I said, following her toward my office.

"Oh? Well, I'm glad you didn't cancel, Dr. Cross. I think I found something, something about the bomber."

I closed my office door, feeling a headache coming on. "You know Kate, the FBI, Metro, Park Police, and Capitol Hill Police are working this pretty hard."

Her expression turned stony. "And you don't think I could come up with something the professionals couldn't?"

"I didn't say that."

"You implied it."

I rubbed at my temples, and took a seat. "If I did, I apologize. I haven't had much sleep. I've just found over the years that when amateurs get involved with cases as big as this one, they can find themselves working at odds with the authorities, and some get charged with obstruction."

Kate crossed her arms. "I am not an amateur. I hunted bombs and bombers on a daily basis for more than three years, Dr. Cross. I've been in on explosive charges as many times as or more than anyone on your bomb squads."

"I get it. But with bombs and bombers, there are protocols determined by people with bigger brains than mine, who—"

I was surprised when she suddenly burst into tears. "You don't get it, do you? I *have* to do this, Dr. Cross. I *have* to help. You asked me about that day I got hit? I missed something. I turned the wrong way and missed something, and four IEDs went off at once. When I woke up, three of my people were dead. Brickhouse was dead, too. I lived, and good friends and the sweetest dog I've ever known died, Dr. Cross. So do you want to hear what I have to say, or not?"

"I'm sorry," I said, holding out my hands. "Of course. What have you got?"

Kate dug in her raincoat pocket and came up with a tourist map of Washington, DC, which she unfolded and laid on the rug between us. Kneeling, she showed me where she'd marked and highlighted the bomb sites.

"Mall in front of the National Sculpture Museum," she said. "Constitution Gardens Pond. Korean War Memorial. Union Station. Washington Monument."

"False alarm there," I said.

"It doesn't matter," she said, before stabbing her finger at the map. "Air and Space Museum."

"I'm predicting a false alarm there as well."

"Like I said, it doesn't matter if bombs were there or not."

Ignoring the soft pounding at the back of my skull, I said, "Okay."

"What do they have in common?"

"They're all in and around the Mall?"

Reaching into her raincoat pocket again, she came up with a Metro transit map.

"They're also all on this city bus route that started up in 2015," she said. "The DC Circulator. It starts at Union Station and goes all around the monuments with stops that line up with the bombing sites."

Instantly alert, I sat forward and studied the transit map.

"See?" Kate said. "I'm telling you, Dr. Cross. Your bomber rides that bus."

CHAPTER 22

TWO DAYS PASSED without a call from the bomber.

The deadline for the veterans' appropriations bill loomed, with no sign that the IEDs on the National Mall were having an effect on Congressional gridlock. Senators on both sides of the aisle continued to maintain their support of veterans yet fight every effort to get the spending bill to the President's desk.

I'd told Mahoney and Bree about Kate Williams's theory that the bomber was using the DC Circulator, and they'd given it enough credence to have agents and detectives interview the route's drivers.

None of the drivers had noticed anything out of the ordinary. Then again, it was cherry blossom season. Even with the bombings and the threats, the Circulator continued to be packed with tourists.

In a meeting at FBI headquarters that Wednesday morning, Mahoney typed on his laptop, and said, "My agent missed it the first two times through, but he may have found something in the security video shot inside Union Station the night before the explosion. Look for the garbage can at center right."

The screen at the far end of the conference room lit and showed forty, maybe fifty people walking on platform four alongside an Amtrak train. The garbage can was blocked from view as passengers moved toward the last few cars.

"Any one of them could have planted it," Bree said when the footage stopped with the platform clear. "And there had to be other trains that used that platform earlier."

Mahoney said, "True, but watch the sequence again."

He backed the video up twenty-five seconds, saying, "Look for the one in the black hoodie carrying the book bag."

Bree and I studied the crowd, seeing several weary men and women in business suits, K Street–types working late, carrying briefcases and trudging along. Behind them walked a person of medium build, likely a male, wearing a black hoodie that was up, casting the face in shadows. His shoulders were hunched forward, his head down and turned, as if he knew the position of the cameras.

"Watch for the moment John Doe and the people in front and behind him go by the trash receptacle," Mahoney said.

It took them no more than two seconds to go by the trash bag, and I didn't catch what Mahoney was talking about. But Bree did.

"We can't see his left arm, but his shoulder moved, and there was a flash of yellow near the mouth of the trash can."

"Exactly," Mahoney said. He backed it up, froze the tape on that moment, and magnified the screen so we could see exactly what was being junked.

"Popeye's chicken?" I said.

"A take-out box for a five-piece dinner assortment," Mahoney said.

"Okay?" Bree said.

"Now look at this footage from eleven minutes earlier."

The screen jumped and showed the same person, wearing jeans and black shoes, hoodie up, face blocked from view, standing near some lockers, and a trash can. He was eating a drumstick from a yellow Popeye's box. He finished it, put the bone in the box, and then walked away when the Acela to Boston was called for boarding.

"That's our bomber," I said. "He could have trashed the box right there."

"Exactly," Mahoney said. "Why wait?"

Bree's phone and my phone buzzed almost simultaneously. I looked down at the text, and jumped to my feet. Bree did the same.

"What's going on?" Mahoney said.

"Someone called in a bomb threat to Jannie's high school," I said. Ignoring the fact that I was suspended from the force, I followed Bree to her squad car. We raced north through the city, sirens and lights flashing, to Benjamin Banneker Academic High School. We stopped at a patrol car blocking access to Sherman Avenue and Euclid Streets.

It was ten in the morning, almost hot, and though they were well removed from school property, the kids gathered on sidewalks and lawns looked anxious.

"Everyone's out?" Bree asked the principal, Sheila Jones, a woman we both liked and respected.

Jones nodded. "They know the drill. This has happened before, Chief Stone."

"Bomb scares?" I said.

"It's usually a student or a friend of a student who's behind on their studying before a big test. At least that's my theory, because nothing ever comes of it."

"Or hasn't yet," Bree said. I scanned the crowd of students for Jannie.

"Were there big tests coming up?" I said.

Jones frowned. "Not schoolwide tests. They just finished midterms."

"Dad?"

I turned to find Jannie had come up behind us. Looking very upset, she threw her arms around me and hugged tight.

"You okay, baby?"

She looked at me, shaking her head, on the verge of tears. "Don't you know?"

"Know what?"

"The threat, Dad. It was called in to me."

CHAPTER 23

LESS THAN THREE miles to the south, Kate Williams sat in the left side window seat three rows behind the driver of the DC Circulator bus, where she could study everyone who came aboard and yet not attract attention.

Kate herself had boarded at 6:30 a.m. Four hours of riding, on top of fourteen hours she'd spent on the bus line the day before, and twelve hours the day before that.

I don't care what I feel like, or how sore my butt gets, she thought, fighting off a yawn as the bus pulled over near the Vietnam Memorial. *Whatever it takes.*

She got off at the Vietnam Memorial to stretch her legs, use the public restroom, and buy a warm pretzel and a diet soda from one of the vendors along Constitution Avenue. Another Circulator bus would come along soon and she could resume her vigil.

He rides this bus line, Kate thought again, feeling irritated. *I'm sure of it.*

Dr. Cross had been interested enough to pass her suspicion along to the FBI and to his wife, but they'd decided against putting surveillance on the routes, relying on the recall of the bus drivers. She couldn't understand it.

That's just moronic. What do bus drivers know about bombers?

Eating her pretzel slowly, Kate scanned the steady stream of tourists heading toward the Vietnam Memorial. There seemed even fewer tourists out today than yesterday, when crowds were noticeably lighter than the day before. In the dwindling pool, she felt certain she'd spot the bomber at some point.

And she was confident a solid look would be enough. Kate had the ability to remember faces and recall them later, as in years later, even when the person had aged. Scientists called people with Kate's gift "super-recognizers."

The trait had helped her in Iraq. Unless the person was wearing a veil or a turban that obscured their features, she'd remember their faces should she see them again, especially in places where IEDs were actively in use.

Kate believed the skill would help her here. She kept combing the crowd, especially the people coming off the Circulator buses, recording faces, looking for twitches in their cheeks, or a slight hesitation when they passed the pair of police officers flanking the entrance to the walkway and the memorial.

Noticing that the hand of a woman her age shook visibly when she raised a coffee cup passing the cops, Kate focused on her face. Click.

She noted the excited expression of a young teenage boy coming off the next bus, in a blue school windbreaker with a hood. He was laughing and staring at his phone, watching a video no doubt. Pass.

Then she studied a red-faced, angry-looking old guy who got off, wearing a red felt vest festooned with military pins. Click.

A tall, lanky, bearded guy in filthy Army camo fatigues shuffled slowly toward her, heading west. He pushed a shopping cart filled with plastic bags and God only knew what else. Click.

As he came closer she saw his skin was smeared with grime. His dark hair was matted, and he had an odd wildness in his eyes, as if he were on drugs.

Click. Click.

A cop on Constitution Avenue lit up his siren for one whoop. It startled Kate, but the homeless vet seemed not to notice at all— as if he were one of those fanatics she knew all too well, the ones getting ready to kill or be killed.

Click. Click. Click.

There was something about him, something about that grocery cart. Maybe she'd been wrong. Maybe the bomber didn't use the bus line. Maybe he was just some homeless, off-the-radar guy, pushing a cart around filled with explosives.

Kate started to follow him, staying four or five people back. The tourists kept a wide berth as he moved resolutely west, and she understood why. He stunk bad.

This could be my guy, she thought.

Her smartphone vibrated in her pocket. Kate dug it out, still trailing the homeless man. She glanced at the screen, seeing a notification from Twitter. She'd set an alert for posts from a local news reporter to make sure she'd see any update on the DC bombings.

The tweet linked to a *Washington Post* story, D.C. HIGH SCHOOL UNDER BOMB THREAT. He asked, "The bomber again? Leaving the mall?"

Kate slowed her stride and clicked on the link, glancing at the homeless man's progress before reading the breaking story.

Benjamin Banneker High had been evacuated on a bomb threat twenty minutes earlier, she read. K-9 and bomb squads were on the scene. The bomber's call had gone to an unidentified student, who had notified school administrators and the police.

Banneker? Something about that nagged at her. She used Google maps to calculate the distance from her location to the school. Two point six miles, give or take.

Kate clocked the homeless vet, still shuffling west. The school wasn't that far, but there was no way that guy was walking two point six miles in twenty minutes, or even an hour or two. And she couldn't believe he owned a phone, much less used one to call in a threat.

Kate stopped, feeling doubt in her instincts for the first time, watching until she couldn't see him anymore. She turned away and headed back toward the Circulator bus stop. She knew the high school was far off the National Monuments bus route.

Maybe I'm wrong, she thought, the purposeful spirit of the last two days sinking. *Maybe I'm the moron.*

CHAPTER 24

BY THREE THAT afternoon, Benjamin Banneker had been cleared for after-hours activities. Like the threats to the Washington Monument and the Air and Space Museum, it appeared to be a false alarm.

Jannie described the caller as a guy with a deep, hoarse voice, who told her there was a bomb in the school and hung up. Bree and I debated the likelihood that the incident was linked to the National Mall bombings. Did we have a copycat at play?

Banneker was not far from the Mall, maybe two and a half miles, but what was the message here? There was symbolism in disrupting access to the national monuments to avenge the wrongs done to veterans. It sent a clear, if misguided, message. How did our daughter's charter high school fit into that?

Disturbingly, the caller had Jannie's phone number, and the Mall bomber had Bree's. We theorized that someone might have hacked into one or both of their phones, or downloaded their contact info from someone else. But when? And how?

These questions were still whirling around in my head early that evening when I boarded the DC Circulator Bus near the World War II Memorial. When I looked in and saw the person sitting three rows behind the driver, I smiled.

I paid the fare and took a seat next to Kate Williams, who stared straight ahead, looking like a poker player who's been up too long.

"Thought surveillance wasn't worth it," she said.

"I didn't say that. People over my pay grade make that decision." She didn't reply.

"You still think he rides this bus?"

"I'm here, aren't I?"

"How long have you been looking for him?"

Kate shrugged. "I don't know, forty? Forty-two hours total."

I gave her an appraising glance. "In the past four days?"

"Whatever it takes, Doc."

We pulled up to the Washington Monument stop, and I watched Kate studying each person who came on the bus. When they'd all paid their fares and taken their seats, I said, "What exactly are you looking for?"

"Their faces."

As we drove on, making a few stops over the next ten or fifteen minutes, Kate explained her innate skill. I'd heard of super-recognizing and its opposite—some people could remember every face they'd ever seen, and others could not remember even familiar faces.

"Any interesting faces so far?" I asked as we left the US Capitol stop.

"They're all interesting."

"No duplicates?"

"A few times, but they're usually tourists coming on and off, and I'll remember them from a few hours before."

"How about stand-outs? Someone who really hit you between the eyes?"

"You mean like my spider-sense?"

"Sure."

Kate tilted her head, thinking. "There was one, earlier today. But he wasn't on the bus. He was this homeless guy in Army fatigues, big crazy beard, pushing this grocery cart piled with his stuff in plastic bags, and he looked so…vacant…so…I don't know. More than drugs. Like he was unplugged. I mean, a cop lit up his siren maybe fifty feet from him, and the guy didn't startle, didn't even flinch. For some reason, seeing that, every alarm in my head started ringing."

Every alarm in my head started ringing as well. I asked her to describe the homeless guy in detail. As we pulled into the bus depot at Union Station, the end and beginning of the Circulator line, there was little doubt in my mind she was talking about Tim Chorey, the deaf vet who'd dismantled his Glock and submerged himself in the reflecting pool the day of the first bombing.

I didn't tell that to Kate, though. She said, "I've had enough for today. Think I'll catch a cab, head home from here."

"I'll get off here, too," I said, glancing at my watch. "A walk over the hill will do me some good."

Night had fallen during our ride. As we exited, a bus lumbered and sighed into the parking bay beside ours. The digital sign above the windshield blinked from D8—HOSPITAL CENTER LINE SOUTHBOUND to UNION STATION.

"Good night, Dr. Cross," Kate said, shaking my hand. "I appreciate you thinking enough of my theory to check it out."

"A good idea is a good idea," I said, and happened to glance over her shoulder at the sign on the other bus, now emptying of riders. The direction had changed.

D8—HOSPITAL CENTER LINE NORTHBOUND, it blinked. VETERANS AFFAIRS MEDICAL CENTER.

CHAPTER 25

I WISHED KATE Williams a good night and watched her walk off. Then I climbed on the empty Hospital Line bus. The driver, who looked to be in his fifties, was drinking coffee from a thermos, an egg-salad sandwich in cellophane in his lap. I noted his name, Gordon Light, posted at the front of the bus.

I identified myself as a consultant with the FBI, which he met with skepticism. "And how do I know you're not messing with me?"

"I can give you the private phone number of the special agent in charge of the bombing investigation," I said. "His name's Ned Mahoney."

He shifted in his seat. "I gotta be out of here in ten minutes. What do you want?"

Light turned out to be a nice guy. Asked about the people who rode the Hospital Center Line, Light said that during the day, in addition to the folks who lived along the route, you had sick people.

"Lots of them. Four big hospitals and a bunch of clinics on the line. That's why we got the wheelchair lift."

"Veterans?"

"Lots of them, too. You know, lost their arms and legs. Or their eyes. Or worse, their... you know."

I got it. "How do you know that?"

"It's in everything about them, man," Light said quietly. "They look so damn humiliated. Can't even pick their heads up. I feel so bad for those boys. And for the families, you know?"

"Lot of family members with them? The patients, I mean."

"You know, with all the non-vets stopping at Children's or Washington Hospital and the National Rehab, half and half maybe? Some relatives are very loyal, and you recognize them. There's this one couple. He's in a wheelchair, and there's his sister right behind him every time they get on."

"So you got regulars?"

"Oh, yeah," he said, taking a bite of the sandwich. "But they'll come and go. Very few stick around forever."

"Sure," I said. "You must hear things driving."

Light swallowed before letting out a laugh. "You wouldn't believe the things I've heard! What people say out loud in public, as if I wasn't even there. Make my mother blush."

"Ever hear any of the vets talking trash about the government? Congress?"

His laugh this time sounded bitter. "All the damn time."

"Anyone in particular?"

He thought about that. "Well, they all do it. One snafu after another for the vets, you know. But there's this one guy rides once or twice a week. He's got nothing but piss and venom to say about the whole lot of them at the VA and up on the Hill. How the Capitol should explode."

"He said that?"

"Yup, a week, maybe two ago. You bet."

"You got a name for him?"

Light pursed his lips, shook his head. "Not that I've ever heard."

"But you'd recognize him?"

"He stands out. Half his face got chewed up by an IED."

CHAPTER 26

AT 8:30 THE next morning, Bree and I were at the front entrance of Veterans Affairs Medical Center. We went straight to the plastic surgery unit, asked for the chief resident, and soon found ourselves in the office of Dr. Richard Stetson.

We explained who we were looking for. Stetson began to explain the various reasons he couldn't help us, starting with doctor-patient privilege, not to mention the HIPAA laws.

"We have reason to believe he may be involved in the Mall bombings," Bree interrupted. "We have reason to believe that he is doing this because of Congressional gridlock over the veterans' bill."

Stetson frowned. "If it's the man I'm thinking of, this is surprising. Stunning even. As for the gridlock, I condemn the bomber's tactics, obviously, but the fact is that most of the programs in this building will shut down if that bill doesn't cross the President's desk. He's not the only one with a grudge."

"And if his next bomb kills someone?" I said. "Isn't that against the Hippocratic oath—first do no harm? We need your help."

Bree said, "We'll find him sooner or later. If we find him sooner, we save lives."

The doctor thought for a beat, then said, "You didn't hear this from me."

"Of course not."

"I think the angry vet you're talking about is named Juan Nico Vincente."

Stetson would not give us Vincente's address or any of his records without a subpoena, but he did say the veteran had survived a brutal IED explosion in Afghanistan, and suffered from head trauma and post-traumatic stress.

"He come to see you often?" I asked.

"Far as my area is concerned, there's nothing more I can do for him. But he's in the building a few times a week, sees a whole menu of docs and therapists. Hang out in the lobby long enough, I'm sure he'll walk by."

As we left the hospital, Bree was already running Vincente's name through a law-enforcement database. He was on full disability from the Army and had several priors for drunk and disorderly, incidents occurring at bars around his government-subsidized apartment in northeast DC. We drove there, to a brick building off Kansas Avenue.

Mahoney met us out front.

"You really think this is our guy?" Mahoney said.

"By all accounts, he's a very angry dude," Bree said. "And he'll probably get hurt big-time if the veterans' bill doesn't go through."

Vincente lived on the fifth floor at the rear of the building. Most apartment complexes clear out during the day, with people at work and children at school. But with many residents of this building on disability, we heard televisions and radios blaring, and people talking and laughing.

But not behind Vincente's front door. Before we could knock, we heard him ranting: "Senator Pussy, you evil, lying, son of a bitch! You never served! I swear I will come up there, get my rotted face in yours, and show you what this is all about! Right before I stick my KA-BAR up your asshole!"

CHAPTER 27

WE ALL GLANCED at one another.

"That works," Mahoney said, and knocked at the door.

"Go away," Vincente yelled. "Whoever the hell you are, go away."

"FBI, Mr. Vincente," Mahoney said. "Open up."

Before we heard footsteps inside Vincente's place, a few doors to our left and right opened, revealing residents peeking out at us. Vincente's door creaked as if he'd put both hands on it. The light filtering through his peephole darkened.

Mahoney had his ID and badge up. So did Bree.

"What's this all about?" Vincente said.

"Open or we break the door down, Mr. Vincente."

"Jesus," Vincente slurred.

Deadbolts threw back. The door opened, and a barefoot, narrow-shouldered man in gray sweatpants and a Washington Nationals jersey peered out at us with bloodshot eyes. It was hard not to look away.

From scalp to jawline, the entire left side of his head was badly disfigured. The scarring on his face was ridged and webbed, as if the skin of many ducks feet had been sewn over his flesh.

He seemed amused at our reactions.

"Can we come in, sir?" Mahoney asked.

"Sir?" Vincente said, and laughed bitterly, before throwing the door wide. "Sure. Why not? Come in. See how the Phantom of the Opera really lives."

We entered a pack rat's nest of books, magazines, newspapers, and vinyl records. Stuff was almost everywhere. On shelves and tables. On the floor along the bare walls. And stacked below a muted television screen, showing C-SPAN and the live feed from the US Senate floor.

Streaming across the bottom of the screen it said, DEBATE OVER SENATE BILL 1822, VETERANS' APPROPRIATIONS.

I noticed an open bottle of vodka and a glass pitcher of tomato juice on a crowded coffee table. The ashtray next to them reeked of marijuana.

Vincente threw up his hands. "You've basically seen it all. My bedroom's off limits."

Mahoney said, "Nothing's off limits if I think you have something to do with the bombings on the National Mall, Mr. Vincente."

"The what...?" He threw back his head and laughed again, louder and more caustic. "You think I got something to do with that? Oh, that'll seal it. Just put the dog-shit icing on the crap cake of my life, why don't you?"

Bree gestured at the screen. "You're following this debate pretty close."

"Wouldn't you if your income depended on it?" he said darkly. He reached for a half full Bloody Mary in a highball glass. "I decided to treat the floor debate like it was draft night for fantasy football leaguers. Right? Have a few Bloody M's. Scream at the screen, Senator Pussy, or whatever. No federal offense in that, is there, Agent Mahoney?"

I said, "You ride the Hospital Center bus, Mr. Vincente?"

"All the time."

"How about the Circulator? The Monuments bus?"

He shook his head. "They won't let someone like me ride the Circulator. Upsets the tourists. Don't believe me? I'll let you check my bus pass. It'll show you. I only use the D8."

"That would help," Mahoney said.

Vincente sighed. "Hope you got time. Gotta find my wallet in this mess."

"We got all day," Bree said.

He sighed again, and started ambling around, looking wobbly on his feet.

"We hear you get angry on the bus," Bree said, putting her hand on her service weapon.

Vincente took a sip of his Bloody Mary, and raised it to us with his back turned, still searching.

He squatted down and moved aside some record albums, saying, "From time to time, Chief Stone, I speak my mind forcefully. Last time I looked, that's still guaranteed under the Constitution I was maimed for."

Mahoney also put his hand on his weapon and said, "Even under the First Amendment, the FBI takes seriously any threat to bomb Congress."

Vincente chuckled, stood unsteadily, and turned. Both Bree and Mahoney tensed, but he was showing us a wallet in one hand and a Metro bus pass in the other.

"It was a turn of phrase," he said, holding out the pass to Mahoney. "I've had this for three years. It'll show I have never once been on the Circulator. And look at my record. I was a camp cook, ran the mess, not the armory in Kandahar. I honestly don't know the first thing about bombs. Other than they hurt like hell, and they screw you up for life."

CHAPTER 28

IT WAS ABNORMALLY chilly and drizzling when Mickey climbed aboard the Hospital Center bus, taking his favorite seat at the window toward the back. He readjusted his windbreaker and the hoodie and vest beneath it so that he could breathe easier.

He wanted to explode. All day, the Senators talked and talked, and did jack shit. That one over-educated idiot from Texas talked for hours and said nothing.

How can that be? That's gotta change. It's gonna change. And I'm gonna be the one to change it. They're gonna talk all night, right? I got all night, don't I?

Mickey had watched the floor debate from the first gavel, growing increasingly angry. As his bus left Union Station and headed north, he felt woozy and suddenly exhausted. Being angry for hours and days on end was draining. Knowing he'd need his energy, he closed his eyes and drifted off.

In Mickey's dreams, an elevator door opened, revealing a scary, antiseptic hallway inside Landstuhl Regional Medical Center next to the US air base at Ramstein, Germany. Men were moaning. Other men were crying. Outside a room, a priest was bent over in prayer with a woman.

The beautiful brunette woman next to Mickey trembled. She looked over at him, on the verge of tears. "I'm gonna need to hold your hand, Mick, or I swear to you I'll fall down."

"I won't let you," Mickey said, and took her hand.

He walked with her resolutely until they found the room number they'd been given at reception, and stopped. The door was closed.

"You want me to go in first?" he asked.

She shook her head. "It has to be me. He's expecting me."

She fumbled in her purse, came up with a nip bottle of vodka she'd bought in the duty free shop, and twisted off the cap.

"You don't need that."

"Oh, yes, I do," she said, and drank it down.

Dropping the empty in her purse, she turned the handle and pushed open the door into a room that held a single patient lying in bed and facing a screen showing CNN. He was in a body cast with a neck halo. Bandages swathed his head. His left arm was gone. Both lower legs were missing above the knee. His eyes were closed.

"Hawkes?" she said in a quavering voice. "It's me."

The man inside the bandages opened his eyes and rolled them her way. "Deb?"

He grunted it more than said it. His jaw was wired shut.

Deb started crying. Shoulders hunched, clutching her purse like a life preserver, she moved uncertainly toward the foot of the bed, where Hawkes could see her better. "I'm right here, baby. So is Mickey."

Mickey came into the room, feeling more frightened than any-thing. He waved at the legless creature inside the bandages and said, "Hi—"

Hawkes screamed. "Get him out! I told you not to bring him! Get him out, Deb!"

"But he's—"

"Get him out!" Hawkes screeched. Monitors began to buzz and whine in alarm.

Shocked, feeling rejected, Mickey started toward the door. Then the tears came and his own anger flared.

Mickey spun and shouted. "Why didn't you leave when you said you would? You left when you said you would, we never would have been blown up! Never!"

Somebody nudged him.

Mickey jerked awake, realized he'd been yelling in his sleep. He looked around, saw a kindly older man with a cane.

"Nightmare, son?" the old man said.

Mickey nodded, realizing how sweaty he felt under the wind-breaker, the hoodie, and the vest, and then how close he was to his stop. Glancing past the older man, he scanned a woman reading a magazine, while the six or seven other passengers at the far back of the bus stared off into space with work-glazed expressions.

Time to really wake them up, Mickey thought when the bus pulled over across from Veterans Affairs Medical Center. *This sol-dier's done fooling around.*

Already late and not wanting to miss any more of the evening meeting, Mickey got up, waited until the rear doors opened with a *whoosh,* and hurried off the bus.

He didn't notice that the woman reading the magazine was now staring after him. He didn't look back to see her get off the bus and trail him at a distance.

CHAPTER 29

ALI, JANNIE, AND I were waiting on Nana Mama to finish some last minute dinner preparations when my cell phone rang.

"Don't you dare," my grandmother said, shaking a wooden spoon at me. "I've been working on this meal since noon."

I held up my hands in surrender, let the call go to voice mail, and sniffed at delicious odors seeping out from under the lid of a large deep-sided pan.

"Smells great, Nana!" Ali said, reaching for the lid.

She gave him a gentle fanny swat with the spoon and said, "No peeking behind curtain number one."

My cell rang again, prompting a disapproving sniff from Nana. I pulled out the phone, expecting Bree to be calling. We had all been frustrated leaving Vincente's apartment earlier in the day. He'd looked good for the bomber going in, and not so good coming out. He seemed even more unlikely when Metro transit confirmed he'd never once ridden the Circulator, and the US Army confirmed he'd been a cook.

But it wasn't Bree on my caller ID. Kate Williams was looking for me.

"Dinner in five minutes," Nana said.

I walked out into the front hall. "Kate?"

"I think I've got him, Dr. Cross," she said breathlessly. "I'm sitting on the bomber."

"What? Where?"

"Veterans Affairs Medical Center. He's in a support group meeting for IED-wounded vets until seven-fifty. I figure you have until eight to meet me at the bus stop at Brookland–CUA."

The call ended. I stared at the phone.

Nana Mama called, "Dinner's ready."

"I'm sorry, Nana," I said, grabbing my rain coat. "I've gotta go."

Out the door and down the front stairs, I ran north in the pouring rain to Pennsylvania Avenue and hailed a cab. On the way I tried to reach Bree, but it kept going through to her voice mail.

I texted her what Kate had said, and that I was going to check it out. As smart and IED-savvy as my patient was, I wasn't holding out real hope that she'd somehow identified the bomber. But I wasn't going to ignore her, either.

In the rain, traffic was snarled, so I didn't climb out of a cab at the Brookland–CUA Metro Station until two minutes past eight. Kate Williams stood at the bus stop shelter, leaning against a Plexiglas wall, smoking a cigarette and perusing *People* magazine.

Seeing me, she stubbed the butt out, flipped it into a trash can, and smiled.

"Means a lot that you came," she said. She explained that she'd come back looking for me the night before and saw me in the D8 bus talking to Mr. Light.

Kate put two and two together, and spent most of the day riding the Circulator and the Hospital Center bus lines. Around six, she got on the Hospital Center bus at Union Station and saw a guy she recognized, sleeping in a seat near the back.

"I didn't think much of him, beyond the fact that I'd seen him down around the Vietnam Memorial," she said. "But when we got close to the hospital, he had some kind of nightmare, and yelled out something about getting blown up."

I said, "I'm sure there are lots of guys who ride this bus and have flashbacks."

"I'm sure they do," she said. "But they don't wear a blue rain jacket with a logo on the left chest that says…shit, here he comes. Half a block. Don't look. Put your hood up. If he's been watching the news, he'll recognize you."

The D8 bus pulled in.

"Get on before he does," Kate said. "You'll be behind him. Easier to control."

CHAPTER 30

I HESITATED, BUT only for a beat. If it really was the bomber, being positioned behind him could be a good thing, especially in a confined space.

I pivoted away and climbed aboard. Gordon Light was driving. He recognized me and started to say something, but I held a finger to my lips as I ran my Metro card over the reader. I headed toward the rear of the semi-crowded bus but stood instead of taking a seat, holding on to a strap facing the side windows. When the doors shut and we started to move, I lowered my hood and glanced around.

Kate was standing in the aisle ten feet forward of me. Her eyes met mine, and she slightly tilted her head toward a man wearing a dark blue windbreaker, hood up. He was looking out the window, giving me no view of his face.

The seat beside him was empty. So was the entire seat behind him.

Kate sat next to him, blocking his exit, which caused him to pivot his head to glance at her.

What the hell is she thinking? I groaned to myself. And what the hell was I thinking, coming on this wild-goose chase?

Because I could now see that under a mop of frizzy brown hair was a bored, pimply, teenage boy, who turned away from Kate when she opened her magazine. Her right hand left the magazine and gestured behind her at the empty seat.

I wanted to get off at the next exit and head home. Maybe Nana had saved me a plate. But when the bus slowed for a red light, I thought, *What the hell?* Kate had led me this far. I slipped into the seat behind them.

When the bus started rolling again, Kate shut her magazine and said, "I have a friend who goes to your school."

I kept a neutral expression. The kid didn't respond at first, then looked over at her.

"What's that?" he said, roused from thought.

"Benjamin Banneker High School," she said. "It's on your jacket."

"Oh," he said, without enthusiasm. "Yeah."

"She runs track. Jannie Cross. You know her?"

The kid gave her a sidelong glance. "She's in my chemistry class."

Chemistry and in Jannie's class. Now I was interested. Real interested.

"Nice girl, that Jannie," Kate said. "What's your name so I can tell her I met you?"

He hesitated, but then answered, "Mickey. Mickey Hawkes."

"Kate Williams. Nice to meet you, Mickey Hawkes," she said, and smiled.

We pulled over at a bus stop, and more people started to board.

Kate said, "Must have been scary there for a while yesterday."

"Scary?" Mickey said.

"You know. The bomb threat?"

His posture stiffened. He said, "Oh, that. It was more boring than scary. We stood there for hours, waiting to see the school explode. I should have gone home."

"So you were out there the entire time?"

"Yup. Like three solid hours."

"Huh," Kate said. She looked at him directly. "Mickey, it's weird. I'm one of these people who remembers every face they see. And I distinctly remember seeing you come off the Circulator bus at the Vietnam Memorial, maybe twenty minutes after the school was evacuated."

"What? No."

"Yes. You were wearing that same windbreaker. You were excited, and looking at your cell phone. Probably at the news that the school had been evacuated, after you called Jannie Cross with the bomb threat."

The kid locked up for two long beats, before turning fully toward her. He looked past her, over his shoulder to me. In a split second I saw recognition, fear, and resolution in his expression. This was our guy. *But he's just a kid,* I thought.

Twisting away from us, he lurched to his feet and stepped onto his seat, holding his cell phone high overhead.

"I'm wearing a bomb vest!" he shouted. "Do what I say, or everyone dies!"

CHAPTER 31

PASSENGERS BEGAN TO scream and scramble away from Mickey.

"Shut up and don't move!" the teen yelled, shaking the cell phone at them. "Everyone shut up and sit down, or I will kill us all right now!"

The few passengers on their feet slowly sank into seats, and the bus quieted, save for a few frightened whimpers.

"Good," the teenager said, and then called to Gordon Light. "No more stops, driver. Straight south now."

I wished I had a gun. Lacking that, I eased my phone from my coat pocket.

"Where are we going?" Kate Williams said.

"You'll see," Mickey said, his head swiveling all around.

He looked at me, then back toward the front. When he did, I moved my hands and phone forward toward the back of his seat where I hoped he couldn't see them. The second time his head swung away from me, I glanced down to text Bree and Mahoney: Bomber taken D-8 bus hostage. Headed south on—

"What are you doing?" Mickey yelled.

I looked up to see him glaring at me.

Unzipping his jacket and hoodie, he exposed the vest, festooned with wires leading into opaque green blocks of C-4 bulging from pocket sleeves.

"Do you think I'm kidding here?" he shrieked.

"Why are you doing this, Mickey?" I said, thumbing Send.

"You'll see why," he shouted. "Have a little patience. And keep your hands where I can see them."

I palmed my phone and rested my hands on my thighs. "Your game, Mickey."

Gordon Light yelled, "Almost to Union Station."

"Keep going," Mickey directed. "Take a left on Mass Ave."

He looked back at me. I said, "Pretty difficult to get old Yugoslavian C-4, Mickey."

He smiled. "Sometimes you just get lucky, Dr. Cross."

We reached Mass Ave, and Light took the left. Kate was studying Mickey intently. I looked out the windows, searching for the flashing lights and sirens I hoped would somehow appear. If Bree or Mahoney got the text, they knew we were on the Hospital Center Line heading south. Metrobus had GPS trackers on them, didn't they?

But other than the rain and the nearly deserted sidewalks, it looked like any other evening in the District of Columbia.

Mickey stepped over onto the seat in front of him, then jumped down in the aisle with his back to me. "Take a right!"

I punched 911 into my phone.

"I can't!" Gordon yelled. "It's one way there!"

"Do it, or your bus blows up!"

"911, what is your emergency?" I heard the woman say.

The driver slammed on his brakes and cut right through a small parking area off Mass Ave. The bus hit a curb with a jolt. People screamed. My chin hit the back of Kate's seat and I dropped my phone, which went skittering across the floor before the bus smashed down onto Northwest Drive along the boundary of the Capitol's grounds.

I was dazed for a moment, hearing cars honking and swerving to get out of the way of the bus, which went careening uphill. As I shook off the daze, Mickey moved forward toward Gordon Light, his cell phone held high.

Passengers shrank from him as he advanced, yelling, "Turn on the lights in here. Open your window. And take the next right, Driver. Go right on up to the barrier!"

"The next right? I can't! It's—"

"Do it!"

Mickey ran up beside the driver. Light glanced at the cell phone Mickey held before pressing a button that opened his window, and another that lit up the interior of the bus. He downshifted and swung the bus right, following the curve of a short spur road that led to a bunker-like guard shack and a solid-steel gate.

Ahead, through the windshield, I could see the lights of satellite media trucks blazing across the small plaza in front of the steps of the Senate. A Capitol Hill Police officer armed with an H&K submachine gun stepped out of the shack.

"What the hell are you doing!" she shouted at Gordon. "Back the hell up! This is a restricted—"

"I'm wearing a bomb!" Mickey Hawkes yelled. "And I'm going to explode it and kill you and all these people unless I get to talk to those senators. Right here. Right now."

CHAPTER 32

I RECOGNIZED THE officer—her last name was Larson. She hesitated until Mickey exposed the bomb vest again.

"Do it," Mickey said. "Call in there. And don't even think of trying to shoot me.

"I drop this phone, the IED goes off."

Officer Larson blinked and said, "Let's calm down a second here, son. I can't just call into the Senate. I wouldn't even know how."

"Bullshit."

"She's right, Mickey Hawkes," I called loudly, and got up.

He looked at me as I started past Kate. "Sit down, man."

I hesitated. Kate tugged on my pants leg. I looked down at her, and saw she wanted to tell me something.

"What?"

She glanced at Mickey and said, "Nothing."

Mickey had turned to the Capitol Hill cop. "Call your boss, lady. Or call his boss. I'm sure one of them knows how to contact the senators blocking the vets' bill."

"Is that what this is about?" I said, moving up the aisle.

"Sit down, or I blow this now!" he shouted at me.

I sat down seven rows from the front with my hands up.

Mickey looked back at Officer Larson, who hadn't moved.

"Call now!" he yelled. "Or do you want to explain how you could have stopped the bloodbath that's about to happen?"

Larson held up a hand, said, "Calm down, and I'll try to make the call."

I said, "Mickey, how about letting some of these people go while she tries?"

He glared at me. "Why would I do that?"

"To show your goodwill."

"There's no such thing as goodwill," Mickey said. "Why do you think I'm here?"

Larson backed through the door into the guard shack.

I said, "Mickey, why are you here?"

"I'll tell those senators."

"You could start with us," I said. "Convince us, maybe you convince them."

The teenager didn't look at me, but I could see him struggle. He said, "I'm saying this once, my way."

"You could—"

"Shut up, Dr. Cross!" he shouted. "I know what you're trying to do! I've seen what all you goddamned shrinks try to do!"

Officer Larson emerged from the security bunker. I looked out the windows and saw the silhouettes of armed officers racing from all directions to surround the bus.

She said, "Mickey, I can't call the senators."

"You can't?" he screamed. "Or you won't?"

Larson said, "I don't make these kinds of calls, Mickey. But there's no way we're going to let a senator anywhere near you and your bomb."

His jaw clenched. He looked out the windshield, and back at the cop.

"Get them on the Senate steps then. And give me a bullhorn."

Larson started to shake her head, but I yelled, "Call, Officer. See if it's possible."

I was standing again. Larson could see me through the windows. She hesitated, but then nodded. "I'll ask, Dr. Cross."

When she disappeared back inside the bunker, I said, "If you get your chance to talk to them, Mickey, you'll let us go?"

He shook his head and said, "I want to see some action."

Before I could reply, Larson exited the bunker again. "I'm sorry, Mickey, but they won't allow it."

His jaw tensed again as he struggled for another option. But then he straightened and gave Larson a sorry look. "I guess I have to make a different kind of statement then, don't I?"

He held up the cell phone, and looked back at me. "Sorry I had to hack into Jannie's phone, Dr. Cross. I always liked her."

I saw flickers of anger, fear, and despair in his face. I'd seen the same in Kate Williams's face when we first met. I understood he was suicidal.

"Don't, Mickey!" I said.

"Too late," Mickey said. He moved his thumb to the screen.

CHAPTER 33

THERE WAS A flash of brilliant light, and I started to duck—but then I saw it was behind Mickey. For a moment the kid was silhouetted there.

I felt sure there would be a blast. We were going to die.

Then Kate Williams stood and yelled, "The bullhorn's behind you, Mickey!"

The teen looked confused, then glanced over his shoulder through the windshield. There were news cameramen running toward the bus, klieg lights flaring in the rain, and satellite trucks following.

"Go, Mickey!" Kate shouted. "Before they figure it out!"

Mickey stared at her as they shared an understanding that eluded me, then addressed Gordon Light. "Open the door!"

The driver pushed a button. The front and rear doors whooshed open. Mickey looked at us. "Sorry it had to come to this."

He climbed out.

I waited two seconds before I ran forward, saying, "Everyone out the back, and move away. Now."

The other passengers lunged for the rear exit. I went out the front door, and watched Mickey Hawkes go toward the barrier that blocked access to the Capitol, his jacket open, exposing the vest.

Officer Larson was aiming her rifle at him. "Not a step further, Mickey."

He stopped at the thick, solid steel barrier, which came up to the bottom of the vest, and stood there squinting as the cameras and lights came within yards and formed in a ragged semicircle facing him. Kate climbed from the bus and stood by me.

"You should get out of here," I said.

"No," she said. "It's all right."

One of the journalists shouted, "Who are you?"

"What do you want to tell the senators?" another cried.

We watched silently, transfixed. Mickey put one hand on the bomb vest and showed them the cell phone with the other.

"My name is Michael Hawkes," he said in a wavering, emotional voice. "I am seventeen years old. When I was eight, my father, my hero and my best friend, was blown up by an IED on his ride back to Kabul to muster out of the Special Forces for good."

"Shit," Kate said under her breath.

"Maybe he should have died," Mickey went on. "Most of the time he says he should have. He lost both legs and an arm, and suffered a closed head injury. When I went with my mother to see him at the hospital in Germany, he wouldn't let me into his room."

His shoulders heaved, and I knew he was crying. "My dad said to forget him. He told my mom the same thing. But I wouldn't forget my dad. No matter how many times he swore at me, no matter how many times he told me to never come back, I went to see him in every hospital he's lived in since the explosion."

Mickey paused, and looked around at Officer Larson, who had lowered her gun.

He glanced over at us. I nodded. Kate said, "Keep going. You're doing fine."

Mickey turned back to the cameras, and said, "I finally started to get through to my dad two years ago. There are daily support group meetings for IED survivors and their families at Veterans Affairs Medical Center. I go every day I can because I want to be there for my father, and because it's the only way I really get to see him when he doesn't get angry, and it's the only way he stays sane, and…"

His voice cracked as he said, "If I don't…"

Mickey looked at the sky, coughed, and cleared his throat before pointing toward the Senate.

"The politicians in there owe my dad," he said. "They made a promise that if he risked his life for his nation, his nation would stand by him. They made a promise that his nation would not forget him, that his grateful nation would help and provide for him."

Mickey took a deep breath, and said, "But those senators in there aren't standing by their promises, and they're not standing by my father. They've forgotten him, and every other vet. They've forgotten to be grateful to those who served. If they don't pass this bill tonight, the funding for veterans stops. The VA hospitals shut down. The programs halt. The help my dad needs is gone. The help every wounded warrior in the country needs is gone. And I…I can't let that happen."

He paused and then said in a strong voice, "Pass the bill, senators, or I'll blow myself up, and the blood's on your hands."

CHAPTER 34

THE RAIN PICKED up. So did the wind. And so did the pressure on Mickey Hawkes to give up his demands and surrender.

But Mickey stood resolute at the gate, holding his cell phone and staring beyond the cameras at the lights burning over the steps of the Senate. I didn't like his tactics a bit, and yet the more I watched him, the more I admired his guts and conviction.

Bree arrived ten minutes into the standoff, Ned Mahoney a few minutes later. She'd watched Mickey's speech streaming on her phone, and told us the cable news networks were going crazy with the story. It was irresistible, a David versus Goliath showdown, the teen versus Congress.

"What can we do?" she asked, peeking around me to look at Mickey.

"We can wait him out," I said. "There's been no vote yet."

Mickey's mother, Deborah Hawkes, a disheveled-looking woman in her early forties, arrived on the scene shortly after nine, climbing from a patrol car that had been dispatched to her apartment blocks away. She appeared not only frantic, but possibly drunk.

"Mick!" she yelled when Ned Mahoney led her up alongside the bus. "Oh, my God! What the hell do you think you're doing?"

He ignored her.

"Mickey!" she shouted. "You answer me, now."

The teen never turned toward her. "I'm doing what you wouldn't, Ma. I'm helping Dad, and every vet like him."

She started to sob quietly. "He left me," she said. "He left you, too."

"I wouldn't let him leave me," Mickey said. "That's the difference between us."

The cameras caught all of it. According to the live updates Bree was watching, the phones in senators' offices were ringing off the hook with calls from vets and families, urging them to pass the bill.

Apparently, Mickey's threat was echoing in the Senate. For supporters of the bill, he was the dramatic proof they needed to argue that lack of support for veterans had gone too far.

The senators opposed to passage called Mickey a terrorist and a blackmailer.

"They do this after every big war, you know," Mickey shouted at the cameras around 10 p.m. "Congress gets all gung ho to spend to fight. But when it's time to take care of the vets, they claim poverty because of how much they spent on the war. It happened after the Revolutionary War, the Civil War, World War I, and World War II.

"The Vietnam vets? They got screwed, too. So did the ones who fought in Desert Storm. And now it's happening all over again for the soldiers who served in Iraq and Afghanistan. When is this going to stop? When are they going to fulfill their promises?"

A cheer went up from behind the bus, back out on Northeast Drive where a crowd—many of them veterans, it seemed—had gathered to lend Mickey support.

At 10:20, we heard that debate over the veterans' bill had been closed. An up or down vote was underway. Fifteen minutes after that, with the ongoing vote leaning 44–40 against passage, a panel van parked on Northeast Drive. Thomas Hawkes rolled out the back in a motorized wheelchair.

Officer Larson led him around the security bunker, lowered the steel barrier, and let Hawkes wheel toward his son.

"Jesus, Mickey," Hawkes said. "You sure know how to cause a shit storm."

Mickey smiled, but his jaw was trembling. "I learned from the best."

"No, son, I think you've got me beat by a long shot."

Mickey didn't reply.

"You gonna blow yourself up?"

A long moment passed before Mickey answered, "If I have to."

Hawkes looked pained and used his remaining arm to bring his wheelchair closer.

"I don't want you to," he said, quiet but forceful. "I want you to stay in this world. And…I'm sorry for all the times I pushed you away. I need you, Mick."

Mickey started crying again, but stood still.

"You hear me?" his father said. "The whole goddamned world needs men like you, willing to take a stand. A warrior if there ever was one."

Back by the road, claps and whistles of approval went up from the crowd, many of whom were also watching live updates on their smartphones.

Mickey wiped at his tears, and looked over his shoulder at Kate Williams, who shook her head ever so slightly.

"Give up, Mick," his mother called. "I promise, I'll be better. We'll be better."

"Listen to her," Hawkes said. "We both need you in our lives. And we both can change things, if you'll just—"

Suddenly a shout rang out from one of the broadcast journalists. "Passed! It passed by two votes!"

"You did it, Mickey!"

The kid hung his head and leaned on the barrier, sobbing. His father wheeled toward him while his mother tried to get around Mahoney, who held her back.

"Not until my people have defused that vest," he said.

"Don't worry about it," Kate said, wiping tears from her eyes. "There's no bomb."

Bree, Mahoney, and I all said, *"What?"*

"Sorry, Doc," she said, laughing and shaking her head. "I know a real IED when I see one, and I knew right away he was wearing a fake. That hot-shit, nerves-of-steel kid just bluffed the whole goddamned thing!"

CHAPTER 35

TWO DAYS LATER, in the early evening, I was helping Nana Mama set the table for six. The aromas wafting from the oven were heavenly. Painfully hungry, I wished I'd eaten a bigger lunch.

"What time did you say dinner was?" Nana said.

"Six-thirty."

My grandmother nodded and checked her watch. It was just shy of six. "That'll be fine then. I'll start the jasmine rice, and you can finish up here?"

"Seeing how you put this together on short notice, I'd be happy to."

That pleased her. She opened the oven to take a peek at the lamb shanks, bone in, braising in the oven. It smelled so good my stomach growled.

"I heard that," Bree said, and laughed as she came into the kitchen.

"The whole neighborhood heard it," Nana Mama chuckled.

"It's your fault," I said. "My stomach's just reacting to your latest masterpiece."

That pleased her even more. I saw her smile as she put the rice into a cooker. Bree gave me a kiss and picked up the napkins.

"Good day?" I said.

She thought about it and said, "Yeah, you know, it was. The pressure was off, and I could think about something other than the bomber."

"Mickey's story shaking out?"

Bree cocked her head and pursed her lips, but nodded. "So far, but he broke about fifty different laws. He can't get around that, even if he is a juvenile."

"They're making him sound awful sympathetic in the media," I said.

She shrugged. "They're focused on the mitigating circumstances."

"What does that mean?" Nana said.

Bree explained the latest: Mickey Hawkes had cooperated fully since his arrest. Kate Williams had been absolutely right that there was no bomb in his vest.

The "plastic explosive blocks" he carried were actually large chunks of colored wax. The wiring was nonsensical, connected to no timer or triggering device whatsoever. Kate had recognized the wiring issues immediately, but wanted to see what Mickey was going to do with a fake vest.

Once the veterans' bill had passed the Senate, bound for the President's desk, Mickey Hawkes had surrendered. As he was led off the Capitol grounds in handcuffs, the crowd of vets on Constitution Avenue and Northeast Drive broke into cheers and applause.

"I watch the news. He's got popular opinion on his side," Nana

Mama allowed. "But he did set off three bombs, and that plastic explosive at the Korean Memorial. And he did blackmail the Senate."

She wasn't wrong, but it wasn't the whole story. It turned out that the bombs on the Mall were made from muzzle-loader black powder, tamped into thick cardboard tubes and wrapped in duct tape. With no ball bearings or screws inside, they were basically large firecrackers.

Mickey had told Ned Mahoney that he found the small chunk of plastic explosive material buried in a locker sent back from US Special Forces in Afghanistan, shortly after the IED explosion that took his father's arm and legs.

Mickey had done enough research to know that the small amount of C-4 could not do any significant damage—so he decided to leave it at the Korean Memorial to raise the stakes, making us believe he had access to unscented plastic explosives.

My grandmother seemed unconvinced.

"We were stumped on this, too, Nana," Bree said.

I said, "But you have to hand it to him. He actually got Congress to *act*."

"Pigs fly every once in a while," Nana said.

"What?" Ali said, looking puzzled as he came into the kitchen. "They do not."

"It's just an expression," sighed Jannie, who followed him, looking at her phone mid-texting. "It means that miracles can happen."

The doorbell rang.

"I'll get it," I said, pausing to give Jannie a hug. "No phone at the table. No phone behind the wheel."

She scrunched up her nose, but put her phone in her pocket. "A deal's a deal."

"Thank you for remembering," I said, and gave her a kiss on the cheek.

Ali said, "I can't believe she's getting a car just for controlling her texting!"

As I was leaving the kitchen, Jannie said, "Maybe you'll believe it when you need a ride."

The doorbell rang again. I hustled down the front hall and opened it to Kate Williams.

"Welcome!" I said.

"Not too early?"

"Right on time. I hope you're hungry for a home-cooked meal."

Kate smiled. "It's been a long time. It smells outstanding! I'm just happy to be invited, Dr. Cross."

"Upstairs, I'm Alex. And you do look happy."

Kate stopped in the hallway, grinning and lowering her voice. "I probably shouldn't be telling you this, but I got a call from the lab at Quantico this morning. There's a slot open in TEDAC, the Terrorist Explosive Device Analytical Center. They want me to interview for it!"

"Wow. That is great news! How did that happen?"

"I'm not sure. Maybe your friend? Agent Mahoney?"

"I'll ask him if you want."

"No, no, it doesn't matter. I'm just...I can see a way forward now, Dr....Alex, and I'm grateful."

"You deserve it. Want to meet the rest of my family?"

"I'd like that. But…I wanted to say thank you. For all the help you've given me."

"Glad I could help, Kate," I said. I smiled, and gestured toward the kitchen.

Following her, remembering the near-suicidal woman who'd sat down in my office not two weeks before, I couldn't help thinking—maybe that suspension wasn't such a bad thing. Sometimes miracles really do happen.

THE
MEDICAL
EXAMINER

A WOMEN'S MURDER CLUB STORY

JAMES PATTERSON

WITH **MAXINE PAETRO**

PROLOGUE

INSPECTOR RICHARD CONKLIN WAS conducting what should have been a straightforward interview with a female victim. The woman was the only known witness to a homicide.

But Mrs. Joan Murphy, the subject, was not making Conklin's job any easier. She was understandably distraught, traumatized, and possibly a bit squirrelly. As a result, she'd taken the interview straight off road, through the deep woods, and directly over a cliff.

She'd seen nothing. She couldn't remember anything. And she didn't understand why she was being interviewed by a cop in the first place.

"Why am I even here?"

The question made Conklin immediately wonder: *What is she hiding?*

They were in a hospital room at St. Francis Memorial. Mrs. Murphy was reclining in a bed with a sling around her right arm. She was in her mid-forties and was highly agitated. Her face was so tightly drawn that Conklin thought she might have had too much cosmetic surgery. Either that, or this was what the aftereffects of a near-death experience looked like.

Currently, Mrs. Murphy was shooting looks around the hospital room as if she were about to bolt through the window. It reminded Conklin of that viral video of the deer who'd wandered into a convenience store, then leapt over the cash register and the pretzel rack before finally crashing through the plateglass windows.

"Mrs. Murphy," he said.

"Call me Joan."

A nurse came through the door, saying, "How are we feeling, Mrs. Murphy? Open up for me, please." She stuck a thermometer under Mrs. Murphy's tongue, and after a minute, she read the numbers and made a note on the chart.

"Everything's normal," she said, brightly.

Conklin thought, *Easy for you to say.*

He turned back to the woman in the bed and said, "Joan, it kills me to see you so upset. I fully comprehend that getting shot, especially under your conditions, would shake anyone up. That's why I hope you understand that I have to find out what happened to you."

Mrs. Murphy was not a suspect. She was not under arrest. Conklin had assured her that if she asked him to leave the room, he would do it. No problem.

But that wasn't what he wanted. He wanted to understand the circumstances that had victimized this woman and had killed the man who had been found with her.

He had to figure out what kind of case it was so he could nab the culprit.

"Don't worry. I'm not afraid of you, Richard," Joan told him, looking past him and out the window. "It's everything you've told me that's upsetting me. I don't remember having a dead body beside me. I don't remember much of anything, but I do think I would remember that. Honestly, I don't think it even happened."

She shook her head desperately and the tears flew off her cheeks. She dropped her chin to her chest and her shoulders heaved with sobs.

Conklin reached for a box of tissues and offered them to his disconsolate subject, who was melting down in front of him.

He inched his chair closer to the bed and said, "Joan, please try to understand. It did happen. We have the body. Do you want to see him?"

She plucked a tissue from the box, patted her eyes, and blew her nose.

"Must I?"

Conklin said, "I think it would be best. It might jog your memory. Look, I'll stay with you and you can lean on me."

"And then you'll drive me straight home?"

"I sure will. I'll even put the sirens on."

FORTY-EIGHT HOURS EARLIER

CHAPTER 1

CINDY THOMAS, SENIOR CRIME reporter at the *San Francisco Chronicle,* breezed through the front door of Susie's Café. She threaded her way through the raucous crowd in the front room, past the steel drum band and the crowded bar, and headed down the corridor to the back room. It was packed to the walls with the Saturday-night dinner set.

She saw an empty booth and a recently vacated table, and asked a busboy for help as she shoved the table up against the booth.

"How many people are coming?" he asked her.

"Six," she told him. "I hope the kitchen doesn't run out of the mango chicken. That's our favorite."

Four of the six were herself and her closest friends in the Women's Murder Club. The other members were Lindsay Boxer, Homicide, SFPD; Claire Washburn, chief medical examiner; and Yuki Castellano, assistant DA. Tonight, the two additional seats would be for Lindsay's husband, Joe Molinari, and Cindy's own beloved fiancé, Rich Conklin. Rich was also Lindsay's partner on the job.

It had been a joke when Cindy dubbed the four of them the

Women's Murder Club years ago, but the name had stuck because they liked it. The girls regularly gathered at Susie's, their clubhouse, in order to vent, brainstorm, and fill up on spicy Caribbean food and draft beer. It was nice to go with the "don't worry, be happy" flow every once in a while.

Laughs were definitely on the menu tonight.

Lindsay had been pulling double shifts at her high-stress job, and recently had been put on a harrowing assignment with the antiterrorism task force. Her husband, Joe Molinari, was still recovering from injuries he'd received in a terrorist bombing related to that very case.

That was probably why Lindsay's sister offered to take their little girl, Julie, home with her and her own little girls for the week. Everything was all set. Lindsay and Joe were leaving in the morning for a well-earned vacation in Mendocino, a small-town escape 150 miles north of San Francisco.

Cindy was excited for them. She ordered beer and chips for the table and had settled into the banquette when Lindsay and Joe arrived. They all hugged, and then the tall blond cop and her hunky husband slid into the booth.

Lindsay said, "I think I'm going to fall asleep in the car and then stay in bed for the entire week. It's inevitable."

Joe put an arm around Lindsay, pulled her close, and said, "If that's the case, there will be no complaints from me."

"All righhhht," said Cindy. Beer was poured into frosted mugs, and Cindy made the first toast. "To rain," she said. "Gentle, pattering rain and no Wi-Fi reception."

"Let's drink to that," said Lindsay.

Glass clinked, Lindsay gulped some beer, and after setting down her mug, she asked Cindy, "You sure you're up to taking care of Martha? She's used to being the boss, you know."

Lindsay was referring to her family's best dog friend, an aging border collie who had pulled a tendon and was under doctor's orders for bed rest.

"I think I can handle it. After all, I, too, am used to being the boss," Cindy said with a wink.

"You? Bossy? You must be joking," said Lindsay.

Cindy was known to be more pit bull than pussycat. She and Lindsay were still snickering about it when Claire Washburn arrived.

Claire emphatically endorsed Lindsay's upcoming week of R & R. She slid into the booth next to her, saying, "I know I'm going to miss you to death, but I'm not going to call you. And I mean, no way, no how, not for any reason. Seriously. This week, nothing but radio silence, okay?"

Before Lindsay could answer, Rich Conklin arrived tableside, stepping on Claire's laugh line. He said hey to his friends and bent down to give Cindy a kiss as Yuki danced into the room, singing along with the Caribbean tune. Rich gave her the seat next to Cindy and pulled up a chair for himself.

Yuki ordered her first margarita of the evening, and the dinner orders went in after that. Even though the upbeat music was plinking loudly and laughter and applause made conversation challenging, Cindy felt a tremendous pleasure in this gathering of close friends. The gang was all here and the evening felt like a group hug. It was the kind of night out that she wanted to soak up and remember forever.

She wouldn't change a thing.

CHAPTER 2

ON MONDAY MORNING, CLAIRE arrived at the medical examiner's office—her office—at ten before eight.

As she walked through the reception room, she was still transitioning from her home to her work mindset. Her thoughts hopscotched from the pressure of back-to-school week with her youngest kiddo, her grumpy husband, who was looking toward early retirement, and the transmission fluid she needed for her car. Not to mention the strong coffee and donut she needed to help her shift her own gears.

She had just hung her coat behind her door when Dr. Harrison, the on-call ME handling the night shift, knocked on the door frame to her office.

"Morning, Bernard. What's the latest?" she asked her number two.

"First, we had a bad accident on the freeway at around midnight last night," he told her. "A car jumped the median and T-boned a family that was coming home from grandma's house. There were three fatalities. One of the children is in the emergency room."

"Oh, damn."

"Fifteen minutes after we'd admitted the car crash victims, two more fatalities came in. It's all in here," he said, waggling a folder containing a sheaf of notes. "I was able to get through two of the freeway postmortems and left the rest for you."

"So you've left three patients for me, you're saying?"

"You don't get paid the big bucks for the easy jobs."

She smiled at their inside joke. There were no big bucks to be found in civil service, but Claire loved what she did. She wouldn't have it any other way.

Dr. H. kept filling her in. "Bunny's here, and so is Mallory. Greg is running late, and I have a headache the size of a beach ball."

"Go home," she told him. "Take an aspirin and get some sleep."

"Don't have to tell me twice, Doc," he said. "Watch out for my vapor trail."

He handed his notes to Claire. She took them with her to the kitchenette, where she poured coffee, snagged the one chocolate donut in the box, and ate her second breakfast at the small square table. Her two assistants, Bunny Ellis and Mallory Keane, came in and took turns filling her in on the horrible car crash.

Bunny's eyes were welling up as she said, "One's just a little kid, Doctor. He's only eight."

Claire said, "I know, I know, Bunny. We never get used to the kids."

Then Claire gowned up and went into the cool room with

Bunny at her elbow. Mallory trailed close behind them. Claire opened the refrigerator drawer that contained the remains of the young boy. He should have been getting on a school bus next week.

"I'm so sorry, Sean Morrison," Claire said to the dead child. "I know a lot of people are going to miss you terribly."

She turned to Bunny and asked, "Are his parents here?"

"Dr. H. did the posts on his mom and dad. His sister is at Metro in serious condition."

"And the driver?" Claire asked.

"Drunk, and texting while driving. He just walked away. From what I heard, there was hardly a scratch on him."

Bunny wheeled a stretcher over to young Sean's drawer. As she helped Claire lift the child's body, they heard a sound that was part moan, part shriek.

"Bunny? What the hell was that?"

"It wasn't me. Could it have been the wheels squeaking, maybe?"

Claire turned around and asked, "Mallory? Was that you?"

"What? No. I didn't hear nothing, and I didn't say nothing either."

The three women stood very still. When they were sure they heard only the sounds of their own breathing, they resumed moving the little boy's body to the gurney.

But then there was another moan, and this time it was followed by a fit of coughing. Together, Claire and Bunny converged on the second level of shelves, four feet off the floor.

Mallory pointed to the drawer at the far end. Claire pulled on the handle—and jumped back.

The body bag inside the drawer was moving.

Claire screamed, surprising herself, and after that, she stepped up and pulled down the body bag zipper. A bloody arm protruded from the bag. A body stirred within and then spoke.

"What kind of nightmare is this?"

CHAPTER 3

THAT MORNING, CINDY OPENED the front door to Lindsay and Joe's airy three-bedroom apartment on Lake Street.

Martha was lying in the living room next to Joe's big chair, where she had a clear view of the doorway. As soon as she saw Cindy, she got to her feet and, with her tail wagging, trotted over to her. It took a couple of tries for Martha to get up onto her hind legs, so Cindy bent down to hug her and hold her up.

"Hey, Sweet Martha. Howsa good girl? Wanna go for a walk?"

Cindy grabbed a paper bag from the counter, found the collar and leash on a hook by the door, and took Martha for a slow but productive stroll on 12th Street. She knew there wasn't very much traffic there, so it'd be a safe route for the two of them.

While they were walking, Cindy talked to Martha, reciting two headlines for a story she had to turn in in the next hour. She asked her which one she liked better, but Martha was noncommittal. After Martha did her business and Cindy bagged it, the duo returned to Lindsay's apartment.

Cindy was pouring dog chow into Martha's bowl, concentrating so she didn't get kibble all over the floor, when the phone rang. She knew it was going to be Lindsay, checking on her. Ha! She reached for the phone.

"Linds?"

"No, it's Claire. Oh, damn it to hell! Sorry, Cindy. I just speed-dialed Lindsay. I forgot. Force of habit."

Cindy kept the phone to her ear as she filled Martha's water bowl in the sink. When Claire explained why she had called, Cindy almost dropped the phone. She shut off the water to make sure that she'd heard her friend correctly.

"Say that again?"

Then Cindy said, "What? Ha. Good one, Claire."

Claire's voice came over the earpiece—loud. "I'm not making this up. Look, I've got to go."

Cindy said, "I'm on my way. Jesus, Claire. I'm coming."

"No, Cindy."

"Yes, Claire. I'm ten minutes away."

CHAPTER 4

THE WOMAN WHO HAD been logged into the morgue as deceased helped Claire and her assistants get her own body out of the bag. She moved into a sitting position inside the drawer. This, whatever it was, was very, very disturbing. In all her years as a medical examiner, Claire had never seen anything like it. The body in front of her had literally come back from the dead.

Was this a prank? A mistake? A true zombie?

She said, "Bunny, get my kit. Mallory, call an ambulance."

The woman sitting in the drawer was naked, and blood was smeared all over her body. She was holding her left arm at her elbow and was wincing in pain.

Claire said, "My name is Dr. Washburn. May I help you? What hurts? Okay, now. Here we go."

Claire peeled the woman's hand away from her shoulder and saw a gunshot wound that went from the front straight through to the back. It was called a through-and-through. Because the woman was able to move her arm, it looked as though no bones had been broken. Thank goodness.

She asked, "Can you tell me your name?"

"I should wake up now," said the woman in the drawer. "This has to be a dream. This is a nightmare for the ages."

"You're in the medical examiner's office. You're going to be fine," Claire said. "We're going to get you off of that skinny little bed, right now."

Claire was still shocked that the woman in the drawer was alive, but she was starting to get some perspective. This wasn't the first time in history that a convincingly dead person had revived himself or herself inside a morgue—or a coffin. There were cases in the nineteenth century where people overdosed on barbiturates and were presumed dead, even though they had, instead, fallen into a deathlike state. Some of the time, they "came back to life" before burial.

Claire wondered if there was a modern drug affecting the woman in front of her, but then she remembered that there was a condition called catalepsy.

Could the bloody woman have that disorder?

Claire knew that people who suffer from catalepsy go into a dead-not-dead state, with slow breathing and a weak pulse. Their muscles go rigid, and sometimes they lose sensation in their body. Claire recalled from something she had read long ago that catalepsy could be triggered by disease, certain drugs, or traumatic shock. And if the "undead" was cooled down— for instance, by being stored inside a morgue's cold room—the brain would remain functional until death took over or the person awoke.

In today's high-tech medical environment, it would be hard to mistake catalepsy for death. But this woman appeared to be an exception to the rule.

The patient was clearly not dead.

CHAPTER 5

THE WOMAN IN THE drawer stretched out her good arm, and Claire and Bunny helped her to a standing position.

Claire's spot assessment was that this poor thing was middle-aged and bone-thin. She'd been shot and was lucky to be breathing.

Claire also saw that another bullet had grazed her hip. Like the shot to her shoulder, it wasn't life-threatening.

Would this lady's good luck continue? Or would bad luck send her back in the drawer?

Bunny and Mallory helped the woman onto a stretcher and pulled a sheet up to her shoulders while Claire checked her vitals. The woman was breathing without assistance. Her pulse was slow, but her heart was beating regularly. Her wounds weren't bleeding and she had spoken, which is always a good sign.

Claire put her stethoscope away, and the woman's eyelids suddenly flew open. The woman drew back, afraid. It was as though she'd forgotten she'd been awake just moments ago.

"Who are you?" she gasped. "Where am I?"

Claire introduced herself again and ordered someone to get water. Then she asked, "What's your name?"

"My name?"

After a few long seconds, the woman said, "I'm Joan Murphy. Did you say this is a morgue? What am I doing here?"

"I was hoping you could tell me, Miss Murphy."

"Call me Joan. My shoulder. It hurts."

"Actually, medically, that's a good sign. You took a bullet, Joan, so it's natural for your body to be reacting to the pain. Do you know who shot you?"

"What day is it?" Joan asked.

"Monday. It's about eight thirty in the morning."

"So yesterday was Sunday?"

"That's right."

"Well, I woke up in my own house. I had breakfast and watched the news shows with my husband—my husband. Someone has to call Robert."

"Of course. We will. Right away."

Joan Murphy recited numbers and Mallory wrote them down.

Then Claire said to her patient, "Joan, an ambulance is on the way. You need emergency medical attention and I'm not equipped to do that for you here."

"If I could just get dressed," said Joan.

Just then, the swinging doors to the autopsy suite blew wide open.

And here was Cindy, as promised. She was breathing hard

as she hurried over to Claire and the woman lying on the stretcher.

"I'm Cindy Thomas," she said to the patient. "I hope you're feeling better. What an ordeal, right?"

Then Cindy turned to Claire and said, "What did I miss?"

"I don't remember anything," said Joan Murphy. "But obviously, I was murdered. Well, it was attempted murder, I suppose. That's all I know."

CHAPTER 6

THE IRREPRESSIBLE CINDY THOMAS had just breathlessly materialized in Claire Washburn's autopsy suite, and Claire wasn't pleased. Not in the slightest.

Claire said, "Seriously, Cindy? Didn't I say no?"

She was planning to spin her friend around and march her straight out when the doors to the ambulance bay banged open.

Bunny shouted to the EMTs, "Hurry. She's in there."

The EMTs burst into the cold room with a stretcher in tow.

"What have we got, Doctor?" asked an EMT. The name W. Watson was appliqued on his shirt.

Claire said to Watson, "This is Mrs. Murphy."

"Hello," Joan said. "The rumors of my demise have been wildly exaggerated."

Watson cracked a smile.

"She was brought in just after midnight," Claire continued. "She has a gunshot wound to the shoulder and a bullet graze on her hip. She revived on her own fifteen minutes ago and needs emergency care ASAP."

Watson said, "You're not kidding."

Mallory went to Mrs. Murphy and patted her hand.

"I left a message for your husband," she said. "I told him you were on the way to Saint Francis Memorial Hospital."

"How ya doing, Mrs. Murphy?" EMT Watson asked. "We're going to give you a nice smooth ride. And we'll get there faster than a speeding bullet." Then the EMTs helped the gunshot victim onto their gurney and wheeled her out to the ambulance.

The doors closed behind them and the wail of sirens sounded down the road as Bunny entered the autopsy suite holding a brown paper bag that was sealed with red tape. "Dr. Washburn, I opened this to see what it was. I think the handbag inside belongs to Mrs. Murphy."

Only fifteen minutes had passed since the patient formerly assumed to be a corpse had called out to Claire's team for help.

"Leave the bag here," Claire said. "Right now, I'm calling the cops."

As Bunny did as she was told, Claire saw Cindy eyeing the large paper bag on the stretcher recently vacated by Mrs. Murphy.

Without any discernible hesitation, Cindy opened it up and peered inside. Then she pulled out a handsome red leather handbag, opened it, and began laying its contents on the stretcher.

Claire said, "Cindy. What the hell are you doing?"

"I'm just taking a quick peek. It's in my nature. I'm an investigative reporter, remember?"

Claire said, "Thanks for the news flash. Listen to me. I disavow all knowledge of what you're doing. You know full well the contents of that bag are off-limits and off the record. By tampering with them, you could mess up a case against the shooter. Do you hear me?"

But Cindy took Claire's disavowal as a yellow light, not a red one. She listed the contents of the bag out loud as she emptied the capacious interior and the many pockets. "Here's her wallet, Claire. The driver's license belongs to our not-actually-departed Joan, and the picture matches the woman we just met. She lives on El Camino Del Mar in Seacliff. She has five credit cards in here and a buncha receipts.

"Wow. Look at her makeup kit, Claire. I've seen ads for this stuff. The makeup is infused with stem cells tailored to your own DNA. Well, so they say, anyway. I, on the other hand, say it's expensive. Lots of brushes and sponges, and okay, enough with the makeup.

"She's also got a photo in the glassine sleeve behind the driver's license. It's a picture of Joan and a man who could be her husband."

Cindy let out a low whistle. "This man is handsome."

Then she flipped the plastic sleeve over and read the inscription, "Robert and me, Cannes, second honeymoon, 2016."

Robert appeared to be ten years younger than Joan, at least. He was very good-looking. Dark hair, tall and built, a definite ten. He looked like Tom Selleck when he was Magnum, PI.

Cindy said, "Claire, look at this picture of Joan and her husband, Robert."

"Nope. You're going to get us in trouble with the law."

Cindy said, "I'm wearing gloves. Look." She wiggled her fingers.

"No harm done, Claire. Okay, I've been through everything, every pocket and every secret zippered section. A woman with a four-thousand-dollar handbag would have jewelry, but Joan wasn't wearing any jewelry and there wasn't a single piece in her bag, either. But look at what she's wearing in the photo. Diamonds on her fingers, encircling both wrists, and draped around her throat. That pendant alone has to be eight carats. Maybe even bigger."

"Hey, Girl Reporter," Claire said, "put it all back like you found it. Seal the paper bag. I'm going to wash my hands. Be back in two minutes."

"Got it."

Claire went into the kitchenette and picked up the notes from last night's intake that Dr. H. had left her. She ran her finger down the list of deceased. There were the three car-crash victims. Two on the list were checked off with appended death certificates. Dr. H. had also listed the two who came in after them.

Female, Joan Murphy. Male, John Doe.

Two people had been brought in by the van at the same time. John Doe was in the drawer next to Joan Murphy.

Dr. H. had done a cursory external exam and had written notes:

White female, 45, Joan Murphy, non-fatal gunshot to right shoulder. Flesh wound on hip. COD, pending. John Doe, white male, approx. age 35-40, two shots to the back and one to the left arm. COD, gunshot to the heart. MOD, homicide.

Claire closed the folder and dropped it off in her office. Then she returned to the autopsy suite where Cindy was replacing the tape on the bag of Joan Murphy's possessions.

Claire said, "Cin, as much as I love you, you really have to go. I've got work to do, and honestly, you can't know any of this until next of kin is notified and we've got a green light for speaking to the press."

"I understand. I'm outta here," Cindy said. "I'll talk to you later."

Claire was about to open John Doe's drawer when Greg, the receptionist, called out to her from the front desk.

"Dr. Washburn. Inspector Richard Conklin called. He said to tell you that he wants to see the John Doe."

"Call him back and tell him that now is fine."

CHAPTER 7

WHEN RICH CONKLIN WOKE up earlier that morning, he reached for Cindy—but her side of the bed was empty. And it wasn't even warm anymore.

It took him a few minutes to remember that she was dog-sitting for Lindsay. He smiled. It had been sweet of her not to wake him up.

Rich got moving. He showered, dressed, ate buttered toast over the sink, and washed it down with a Yoo-hoo. He started up his old Bronco on the first try and then made the drive to the Hall of Justice, where he worked in the Southern Station, Homicide Division. He was parking his car a block away from the Hall on Harriet Street when he got a call from Claire. She filled him in on the bizarre happenings in her office.

"I'll punch in at work and get back to you," he said.

It was eight thirty when Conklin entered the squad room. Lieutenant Jackson Brady was inside his office, which was located at the back corner of the bullpen. Conklin crossed the room and knocked on the glass office door. Brady waved him in.

Brady was a veteran of Miami vice and homicide, and had taken over the command of this squad when Warren Jacobi moved up to chief. Conklin thought that in some ways, it was a waste of talent to keep Brady behind the desk, but he was an excellent CO. He was direct, smart, and unafraid. Brady was also Rich's friend, but during work hours, he was all business.

Conklin took a chair opposite Brady and said, "Lieu, I got a call from the ME. Two bodies came in last night. Both had gunshot wounds. One of them is a John Doe. The other is a female who resumed breathing and started talking while she was inside the body bag."

"Christ. What did you just say? The female victim wasn't really dead? Did I hear that correctly?"

"Yup. Her name is Joan Murphy and she's on the way to Saint Francis. I'd like to be on the case."

Brady said, "Let me see who caught it last night."

Conklin looked out the window, watching the traffic on the freeway as Brady's fingers tapped on the keyboard.

"Okay. Okay," Brady said. "Summing it up here, it seems like it was a madhouse in the morgue last night. There was a car crash with three fatalities. Then, this case came in. It started with a 911 call from the Warwick Hotel. A housekeeper went into room 321 to turn down the bed and found two dead bodies in it."

Conklin muttered, "Holy shit."

Brady continued his summary.

"Sergeant Chi got a search warrant and met Detectives Sackowitz and Linden at the hotel. Room three twenty-one was registered to Joan Murphy, who lives locally, over in Seacliff. Murphy's body was completely naked on the bed. She had a gunshot wound to the right shoulder and another that had grazed her hip. She was covered with blood and had no detectable vital signs. Hear that, Conklin? Not breathing. No heartbeat."

"Unreal," said Conklin. "Keep going."

Brady said, "Continuing. The male victim is in the morgue and isn't talking or breathing. He's white, in his thirties, and was also found naked and lying on top of the female. There was no wallet, no ID to be found. He was wearing a wedding band. The male vic took three shots, two to the back, one in the left arm. The murder weapon wasn't found."

Brady took a slug of coffee and then went on.

"Sackowitz and Linden waited for the wagon to arrive. ME techs pronounced both victims DOA. Sac and Linden started a canvass in the hotel. They'll look at surveillance video and do the interviews, et cetera, but I agree with you that they could use help."

Conklin said, "Good to hear that. My desk is clean, Brady. Use me."

Brady said, "I don't have anyone free to partner up with you."

"It's just for a few days, Lieu."

Brady said, "Should be okay, I'm thinkin', since Joan Murphy can probably ID the doer. I'm betting the shooter was the wife of the John Doe. Stay on Murphy and get her story."

Brady lifted his icy blue eyes from the computer and turned them on Conklin.

"We're going to need you to use your famous charm when

you interview Miss Murphy, Conklin. This is a sticky situation. We don't want her to sue the city for taking her to the morgue before her time."

"I'll do my best."

Conklin went back to his desk and downloaded the notes from Sac and Linden. Then he called Claire's office, leaving a message with her receptionist.

He said, "Greg, tell Dr. Washburn I'm on the case. I want to see the John Doe, ASAP."

CHAPTER 8

CONKLIN MADE THE SHORT walk from the back exit from the Hall of Justice lobby, along the breezeway to the ME's office in under two minutes. He was thinking about this murky case of a dead woman who was not actually dead, and a John Doe who was gunned down in flagrante delicto.

Conklin reviewed Sackowitz's case notes one more time. He'd written that no weapon had been found at the scene of the crime and that the John Doe's wallet was missing. He and Linden were still working the hotel angle, trying to get an ID on the dead man.

If they could figure out who the John Doe was, they might be able to learn why he was shot in the first place.

Was the John Doe the target? That would make Joan Murphy a victim of circumstance. And why hadn't the shooter finished off Joan Murphy? She had witnessed the crime, after all. Had the shooter assumed that she was dead?

Could be.

According to the reports, she'd been covered with blood, both hers and the John Doe's. Her muscles had gone rigid. Her breathing and pulse had hardly been there, and were so delicate that they'd become undetectable. Apparently, neither the cops nor the ME techs had ever seen anything like this before, and Murphy's deathlike state had fooled them all. How scary was that?

Conklin pulled open the double glass doors to the ME's office as another question popped into his head. Why hadn't anyone heard the shots?

But he shook his head, clearing out his mind. There were several people waiting in the reception area to see Claire: some were cops, others legal aides and administrators who worked at the Hall. He needed to get control of this situation before it got out of hand.

The receptionist knew Conklin, so as soon as he saw him he said, "She's waiting for you, Inspector. Go on in."

Conklin knew his way around the ME's office and took the main corridor, which led to the autopsy suite in the back.

Claire was gowned and masked. Her assistants were backing her up as she worked on the postmortem assessment of a young boy with a visible head injury. She saw Conklin come in and covered the child with a sheet. Then she shucked her gloves and put on a clean pair. She picked up a large brown paper bag from an empty table and said, "Let's go into my office, Richie."

As he stood with her in her office, Conklin watched Claire open the paper bag on her desk and take out the large, blood-red leather handbag with what looked to be expensive stitching and details.

Claire said, "This purse belongs to Joan. I also have bags of her clothes and those belonging to the John Doe. But let's look at the contents of her handbag first."

She began taking items out of the handbag. There was a nice-looking wallet, a makeup case, keys, and an assortment of other commonplace items.

"This is a pricey bag," Claire told Conklin. "It appears that Mrs. Murphy is a woman of means."

She handed over the wallet. Conklin opened it and looked through the contents.

Claire said, "Look at this."

She was pointing to a photograph under plastic of a man and woman at a resort, their backs to the ocean. Claire flipped the sleeve over, and Conklin read the inscription. "Robert and Me, Cannes, Second Honeymoon, 2016."

Claire said, "Notice the necklace Joan is wearing in the photograph. That pendant is a helluva big diamond. There is a similar enormous rock in her engagement ring, and the wedding band is encrusted with other precious stones. Look at all the glittering bangle bracelets. Joan clearly likes her diamonds."

"A girl's best friend, right?"

"That's what they say. But, Richie, no jewelry was found on her person or in her bag."

"She was robbed."

"That's my first guess."

Conklin made notes, then said, "What do you say, Claire? Can you introduce me to Mr. Doe?"

"I'm dying to meet the man myself," said Claire.

They walked back to the autopsy suite and Claire pulled open the drawer next to the one that had been vacated recently by Joan Murphy.

Conklin found the unknown man to be as described. He was a white male who seemed to be in his thirties. He had a slight paunch and a lot of chest hair. From his conservative haircut and manicure, Conklin guessed that the guy was some sort of businessman. He looked like he could be a sales executive of some sort.

Conklin told Claire what Sackowitz had put in his case notes. "He was found naked, lying on the naked body of Mrs. Murphy."

Claire said, "That seems right. Looks to me like he took the first two shots to his back. Then, he probably turned to face the shooter and that's when he got this one to the underside of his biceps. It went through the muscle and into the chest. That could have been the slug that stopped his heart forever."

Conklin said, "So, who do we think was the shooter? Mrs. Doe? Did she get someone to let her into the room so she could kill her husband? It's a logical explanation. An obvious one. Or could it have been Mr. Murphy, who killed the man cuckolding him? Is that why his wife was spared?

"And if the motive was a domestic beef," Conklin continued, "why take the jewelry? Was it staging, to make the shooting look like a robbery?"

Claire listened as Conklin continued theorizing out loud. He said, "Or was it, in fact, a robbery? A stranger gets into the room or he was waiting in the room. He gets the loot and John Doe's wallet. But why didn't he give Mrs. Murphy a shot to the head so she couldn't testify? Was he convinced she was dead?"

Claire cut off his musings, saying, "Here's my theory. Anyone would have been convinced that that woman, Joan Murphy, died in that hotel room. You see, there's an unusual condition called 'catalepsy.' If this is that condition, it's my first experience with it. I know that death is a many-part process. Different parts of the body cease at different times. Skin lives for twenty-four hours after a person dies, for instance.

"So, catalepsy is a nervous condition that looks like death even though it's an attenuated slow-down. If Mrs. Murphy had not been refrigerated overnight, she would have suffered brain death and she would have died."

"Okay, so what causes catalepsy?"

"Could be a number of things. Parkinson's disease, epilepsy, cocaine withdrawal. It can be a side effect of an antipsychotic. And one of the most common causes can be traumatic shock."

Conklin said, "She had to be pretty traumatized, all right. You think her memory will ever come back?"

Claire shrugged and said, "It's possible. Let me know, will you? I can't really explain it, but I feel somewhat attached to Joan. I want to know what happened to her and why."

CHAPTER 9

CONKLIN CAME THROUGH THE gate to the Homicide squad room and went directly to the small island made up of two facing desks—his and Lindsay's—and a side chair.

He grabbed his desk phone and called St. Francis Memorial. He was shunted around to various bureaucrats until finally a head nurse told him that Mrs. Murphy was in stable condition and was currently having a CAT scan.

Conklin said he'd call back. He was glad to have time to do a background check on the miraculous Mrs. Murphy before meeting with her.

He booted up his computer and began opening the databases that were at his disposal at the police office. He learned that Joan Murphy, nee Tuttle, had been born in New York in 1972. Her mother had been an editor at a high-fashion magazine and her father was CEO of a business machine corporation. Joan had gone to private schools and had capped off her high school diploma with a degree in literature from Berkeley.

Murphy's first husband, Jared Knowles, was a well-regarded art director in Hollywood. Her second and current husband,

Robert Murphy, was a model and small-time actor who was born in 1986. Conklin did the quick math in his head. That made Robert fourteen years younger than his wife.

Joan had bought and paid for the Murphys' home prior to her marriage to Robert, and it had since been featured in multiple glossy style magazines. The Murphys were also pictured in many of the society columns and had a handful of celebrity friends. On the face of it, they seemed to have a pretty good quality of life.

Conklin stretched, taking a break. He texted Sackowitz, telling him he was going to interview Joan Murphy ASAP. After that, he scavenged the refrigerator in the break room and found a container of yogurt marked "Boxer." He grabbed the snack, knowing Lindsay wouldn't mind.

He ate at his desk and opened the criminal databases, finding zip, zero, and nada on Joan and Robert Murphy. They hadn't ever been in trouble with the law. No scandals, no shoplifting, no nothing.

Next, Conklin looked at all online photos he could find of this nice, upscale couple. What had happened to Joan? She seemed to have a decent life, but then one night she checks into a hotel room and entertains a man who isn't her husband. A shooter somehow gets into this hotel room and blows away the lover. Then that same assassin wings the millionairess and leaves her for dead.

And what had happened to Joan's jewelry? Had the whole thing been a pre-planned armed robbery? It was starting to look that way to Conklin. Maybe it hadn't been about the duplicitous relationship after all.

Suddenly, his desk phone rang, jerking him out of his thoughts.

The caller ID read SACKOWITZ.

"It's crazy that Joan Murphy is alive, right?" he said to the night-shift detective.

Sac said, "My thinking exactly. Who's the target here? Or was this a robbery that got out of control?"

Conklin said, "I've been wondering the same thing. Hopefully this interview helps us figure things out. Then, after I see Mrs. Murphy, I'm going to drive out to her home so I can talk to the husband. I'll let you know how it goes."

"Sounds like a plan. But be careful."

PRESENT TIME

CHAPTER 10

RICH CONKLIN HAD FINISHED his useless bedside interview with Joan Murphy, but before they could go to Claire Washburn's office, Joan had to be cleared to leave the hospital.

He called Cindy from the waiting room and left her a voice mail telling her that she shouldn't hold dinner for him. Minutes later, the attending physician came down the hallway to ask him to come with him to his patient's room.

Once he was standing at Joan's side, Dr. Kornacki turned to Conklin and said, "I want you to be my witness on this situation. I told Mrs. Murphy she should stay with us overnight, so that we could keep an eye on her for twenty-four hours at minimum."

Joan chirped, "And I said, 'No thanks, doctor. I'm fine now.' And I really, truly am. I'm ready to go home."

Kornacki said sternly, "There's a chance that you might relapse if you leave, but I can't force you to stay here. See your regular physician. Please do it tomorrow."

Joan plucked at the hospital-issue nightgown. "Detective, may I please have my clothing and other belongings back? I must have been wearing quite a bit of jewelry. I'm never without my engagement ring and mother's necklace."

Conklin ran his hand down the side of his face. "Unfortunately, Joan, we weren't able to locate your jewelry. And your clothing will need to stay with our team for now, for testing."

Joan sighed and said, "Doctor, may I borrow some scrubs? Either blue or green would be fine with me."

Conklin stood outside as Joan dressed and then he co-signed the "Against Medical Advice" release form. He watched as Joan submitted to the nurses, who were fussing around her as they seated her in a wheelchair.

He pushed Joan's chair out to his car. The foot well on the passenger side was filled with litter, and Joan sniffed in disgust when she saw it.

"Sorry," he said. "I can get that."

He gathered up the pile of fast-food wrappers and empty water bottles, and then placed it on the seat of the wheelchair. He walked the trash over to a garbage receptacle and returned the chair to the lobby.

He'd rarely worked a case as incomprehensible as this double homicide that only had one actual fatality. But he was determined to see it through to its conclusion. Whatever that might be.

When he and Joan were both in the car and buckled up, she said, "Richard, why not just drop me at home? We can shake hands and say good-bye. I'll write a note to your superior saying how good you have been to me. You have been very nice."

"Joan, there was a dead body of a man found in a bed with you. He has a family out there somewhere and they're never going to see him again. Someone killed him." He wanted to add, *Does that ring a bell?* but he bit down on the sarcasm. The last thing he wanted to do was drive his witness underground.

Joan said nothing in reply. She just looked out the window at rush hour traffic on Pine.

He continued, "We're going to make a quick stop at the medical examiner's office. Twenty minutes after that, you'll be home."

She said, "I know I said I would look at that man. But this isn't easy for me, Richard. I have really bad memories of that place."

"I know you do. But can you try to look at this a different way? Your unscheduled stop at the ME's office was a blip in the span of your life. Now you're alive and well, and you're helping out the San Francisco Police Department. For about two minutes, you're going to return to the site of a personal miracle."

She looked at him dubiously.

Rich gave her one of his beautiful smiles and said, "I'm not going to leave your side. You want the sirens, Joan? Or shall we just enjoy the ride?"

She let out a good laugh.

"Sirens," she said.

Conklin grinned at her.

He flipped on the sirens and the lights, and they headed

toward the medical examiner's office. He couldn't wait to reintroduce Joan to Mr. John Doe. He had absolutely no idea—couldn't even guess—what she would say or do when she looked at the man's dead body.

But he had a feeling her reaction was going to surprise him.

CHAPTER 11

CONKLIN DRAPED HIS WINDBREAKER around Joan Murphy's narrow shoulders and walked her from Harriet Street to the ME's office.

Claire was waiting for them at the open rear door. She gently placed her arm around Joan and told her how glad she was to see her.

"How's that shoulder? Are you feeling okay?" Claire asked.

"The pain pills are telling me that I feel just fine." Joan Murphy's smile faded as she looked around the autopsy suite. She stiffly walked with Claire and Richie into the cool room in the back. There, she took in the sight of the stacked stainless-steel drawers that were holding bodies of the dead.

Claire said cautiously, "Are you ready, Joan? I'm going to open the drawer now."

Joan Murphy shook her head and said, "I'm never going to be ready for this. But let's get it over with."

Claire slid the drawer open slowly. Wisps of brown hair peeked out over the top of the crisp sheet, followed by a long topographical stretch of white. The sight before them terminated with a man's knobby toes.

Claire carefully folded the sheet down below John Doe's chin.

Conklin stood beside Joan as she peered down at the dead man's blanched and chubby face. To Rich, the man's features were unremarkable. He looked like a typical suburban dad, the kind of guy who would watch out for the kids on the block, was handy around the house, and didn't fool around at the office.

Clearly, his appearance didn't square with the circumstances in which his body had been discovered.

Joan stared at the corpse for a long moment. Then she seemed almost indignant when she said, "I'm supposed to know this person?"

Conklin looked past Joan to Claire. Their eyes met. He said, "Joan, this is the man who was found dead, naked, and in bed with you in room three twenty-one at the Warwick. His wallet was stolen. We're trying to identify him and it's only a matter of time before we're successful. And we could do it faster and better if you can give us a name or a lead."

"Sorry to disappoint, Richard. I've never seen this man before, and honestly, I don't think I would even notice him if he walked by me on the street. He's not my type.

"Here's my theory," she continued, looking up at Conklin. "Somehow, both he and I were drugged, kidnapped, put into that bed, and shot. Maybe he was already dead. I was as good as dead, and maybe they didn't realize that I was still kicking. There's no other explanation."

Conklin stifled a laugh. He couldn't believe that Joan had

come up with the fantastic theory that somehow two people had been kidnapped and smuggled into the Warwick, where they were stripped, posed, and shot, in that order. For what purpose? To create a scandal?

Maybe to create a pulp fiction murder tableau for a book cover.

He arranged his features in a straight face. "But why would anyone do that to you?"

"How would I know? I don't have a criminal mind. And now, I'm ready to go home. Didn't you hear the doctor? I need to rest."

CHAPTER 12

CONKLIN HAD PROMISED TO bring Joan home and he kept his word. He walked her back to his car and drove them to Seacliff. The sun was going down and house lights winked on along Lake Street. Conklin turned right on 28th and took it to El Camino Del Mar. When he pulled into her neighborhood, he noticed that it was an upmarket, oceanside area dotted with large estates. Many of them had water views and private access to the shoreline. Joan was looking straight ahead, saying to him, "How am I going to explain all of this to Robert?"

"That you were found in bed with another man?"

"What? No. He'll believe me when I say that I was drugged and kidnapped. But I have to explain getting shot. Why would anyone shoot me? Maybe Robert got a call from the kidnapper. Maybe he had to pay ransom money or something. Did you think of that, Richard?"

Joan had some pretty crazy theories about her attempted murder, but this time, she had a point. Her husband hadn't reported his wife as missing. Could he have forked over a ransom payment while he was waiting for his wife's return?

Rich Conklin couldn't wait to see Robert Murphy's face when Joan came through the front door to her house—alive.

Maybe it would give him the final clue to crack this case.

CHAPTER 13

THE CLOSER THEY CAME to Joan's home on El Camino Del Mar, the more anxious Joan became. She tried to call her husband again, as Mallory had done when Joan had first woken up in the morgue, but the call went unanswered.

"I'm very frightened now," Joan said to Conklin. "What if we find him shot and lying dead on the floor? What if my kidnapping was part of a larger plot?"

"Everything's going to be okay, Joan. We'll investigate every piece of evidence we find. If a clue surfaces in your memory, you know where to reach me."

The brass house numbers were embedded in the gateposts that flanked the driveway leading to a handsome Mediterranean-style stucco house with a tiled roof. The gate was open, revealing manicured gardens inside the walls. Conklin pulled his car up the long driveway and parked it between a blue Mercedes XL sedan and a silver Bentley.

"Which one is Robert's car?" he asked Joan.

"The Mercedes. The Bentley is mine."

Conklin went around to the passenger side and helped Joan out of the car. He retrieved her handbag from the foot well and held it open for her while she searched inside it for her keys. When she found them, she handed the set to him.

They reached the front door, and Conklin unlocked it. He pushed the door open and said, "Stay here. I'll go in first to make sure everything is safe."

Conklin took three steps into the room, entering the foyer. Lights were on inside the house, but the security alarms weren't set.

He called out, "Mr. Murphy? This is the SFPD."

There was no answer. Conklin drew his gun and held it out, but he kept the muzzle pointing down. He walked through the foyer, which emptied into a spacious living area decorated with modern furnishings. The windows along the far wall looked out over lawns with topiary and a small pathway of stone steps. A large swimming pool was across the lawn and off to the right.

He called Mr. Murphy's name again as he rounded a corner. He heard music coming from outside the sliding glass doors, where a set of teak outdoor furniture faced the ocean.

A man stood up and turned to Conklin, holding a sheaf of paper in his hand. He was big, not just tall, but well-built and handsome. He was wearing what looked to be a cashmere half-zip sweater and expensive jeans. He showed no sign of injury.

Conklin said, "Mr. Murphy?"

The man said, "Who the hell are you? And how did you get into my house?"

"I'm Inspector Conklin, SFPD. I've brought your wife home from the hospital."

"Oh? I didn't know. Why was Joan in the hospital?"

"She was shot, Mr. Murphy. Let me go get her. I'll tell her that you're back here."

Conklin went back out to the front door and told Joan Murphy that her husband seemed fine. She smiled and then started to weep. Conklin holstered his gun and accompanied the frail woman, who was still wearing blue scrubs, paper slides, and an SFPD windbreaker.

When he saw Joan, her husband opened his arms and folded her in. He patted her back as she sobbed against his chest.

"I almost died, Robert. I almost died."

Conklin thought that Murphy's actions were warm, but his expression and his affect seemed to be a little distant. Conklin watched and listened as Joan gave Robert a shorthand version of the story as she knew it. *But why didn't Joan's husband seem shocked by the news?*

Joan told Robert that she had woken up in the morgue. Apparently she had been shot in the shoulder and had a wound on her hip as well, but she had no memory of being attacked. Thank goodness she had no broken bones. She just needed some TLC and rest.

There was no mention of the deceased John Doe.

Robert asked her where this had happened and she said, "At the Warwick, Robert. I was found in a hotel room, bloody and unconscious. The police thought I was dead! My jewelry was gone. That lovely pendant of my mother's. And oh, my God. My rings were taken, too."

"Why were you at the Warwick?"

"I have no idea how I got there, Robbie. I think that I was drugged and kidnapped."

"Drugged and kidnapped? My God, Joan. By whom?"

"That's my theory, but this kind man, Inspector Conklin, is going to figure out what happened and who is responsible."

"God, I hope so," Robert said as he hugged her close one more time. "We're going to take good care of you, dear."

From inside his embrace, Joan looked up at her husband and smiled.

"I'm going to change into my own comfortable clothes, Robert. I could use a drink. Tell Marjorie I'm very hungry. I have no idea when I last had a meal. I think I'd like chicken stew. That will fix me right up. Inspector, you're welcome to stay for dinner. I'll be right back."

When Joan had left the room, Conklin turned to Robert Murphy and said, "You mind answering a few questions for me?"

CHAPTER 14

MURPHY NODDED HIS HEAD and directed Conklin to a squared, taupe-colored chair. As Conklin sat down, Murphy took a seat in an identical chair that was situated at a right angle from him. Murphy did finger riffs on his knees, looking impatient and resigned.

Conklin said, "These are routine questions, Mr. Murphy. Your wife was shot and left for dead. So I'm going to need details of your movements over the last forty-eight hours."

Murphy said, "Right. I know this one. You think the husband did it."

Conklin said, "Not necessarily. Think of this as the way we clear the husband, Mr. Murphy."

Murphy sighed, raked back his hair with his fingers, and said, "I didn't leave the property all weekend and I haven't left it today, either. Marjorie Bright, our housekeeper and cook, can vouch for me. Our pool boy, Peter Carter, saw me Sunday morning when I went for a swim. Gotta stay fit, no? Peter lives in a cottage in the back. He has the weekends off, but he was there on Sunday."

Conklin said, "You seriously haven't left the house in two whole days?"

"Honestly, it's been longer than that. I have a part in a movie. It's a thriller called *Case Management.* Craig Noble is directing and I play Evan Slaughter, the lead detective. I've been reading and rehearsing my lines for these past couple days. Marjorie even helped me run through them. She usually does. Anyway, we start shooting next week."

Conklin asked, "Were you contacted by anyone demanding ransom for Joan's return?"

"What? No. Of course not. I would have called the police if that had happened."

Conklin said, "Can you think of any reason why someone might want to hurt Joan?"

"I doubt it. But she does have a strong personality. She always says what she thinks. She's on a lot of committees and charity boards. Wherever money and politics are involved, people can get pretty pissed off. Thankfully, Joan keeps me out of her business."

Conklin nodded, wondering, *Does this actor really think that murders spring from charity board decisions?* Both Joan and Robert had B-movie theories to real-life murder. It was just another clue that they might be hiding something.

Rich said, "Mr. Murphy, when your wife didn't come home Sunday night, weren't you worried about her?"

"As I said, Joan does what Joan wants to do. We don't question each other, Inspector. And if your next question is 'Do you love your wife?' the answer is 'I like her independence, her humor, and her intelligence.' And yes, I do love her as well."

"I have to ask you. Do you think your wife could be having an affair?"

Murphy gave Conklin a scathing look and said, "If she is having an affair, it would shock the hell out of me. We have a full and trusting relationship. Thank you for bringing her home safely. I'd like daily reports on your progress in finding the kidnapper."

Joan Murphy returned to the room in flowing garments, looking like an entirely different woman. She was relaxed. Beaming. Confident.

"Richard," she said. "You'll have dinner with us, right?"

"I wish I could, Joan. Maybe another time. But before I leave, I need a few moments with Marjorie."

CHAPTER 15

JOAN BROUGHT CONKLIN TO the kitchen, where he met with Marjorie Bright, a wiry, blue-eyed woman who was about sixty years old. She was dressed casually in dark pants and an untucked white shirt.

She dried her hands on a dish towel and checked on the contents of the oven. After Joan had left the room, she and Conklin sat down at the kitchen table.

Conklin asked some preliminary questions. How long had she worked for the Murphys? What did she think of them? Had she ever witnessed any arguments between the two of them?

Miss Bright told Conklin that she had worked for Miss Joan for thirteen years. She lived in a private suite on the third floor. She seemed happy with her job in the Murphys' home.

When Conklin asked if the couple fought, she shrugged and said, "I guess there's been some shouting over the last five years, but there's never been any violence. They have separate suites connected by a hallway on the second floor. Their lives are separate, mostly, but sometimes they'll entertain at home, vacation, and attend functions together. They live well in this house, and I do think they are in love."

Conklin asked, "Do you recall if Mr. Murphy was home on Sunday?"

"Yes, he was here. I'm off on Sundays, but my rooms overlook the front of the property and his car never moved. I saw him and Joan eating breakfast together on the patio on Sunday morning. Later that afternoon, Mr. Robert called up and asked if I could help him rehearse his lines. He's very talented, you know."

"Could you estimate the time that Mrs. Murphy left the house on Sunday?"

"No. Like I said, it was my day off, so I wasn't looking at the clock. Besides, she doesn't like to drive. She usually uses a car service, so I couldn't guess a time for you, since her car never left the driveway."

The housekeeper got the name and number of the service, and after Conklin thanked her, he returned to the sprawling drawing room and told the Murphys he'd be in touch as soon as his team had any kind of big break or lead in the case.

Once he got in the car, he called Cindy and talked to her as he drove home. They clicked off when Rich was on Kirkham with his apartment building in sight, and that's when his phone rang with another call.

It was Sackowitz.

"We've got an ID on our John Doe," Sac said. "His name's Samuel J. Alton and he's from San Bernardino. He's the senior VP in claims for Avantra Insurance. He's married, has three kids under twelve, and is a regular at the Warwick Hotel. On the first Sunday of every month, he comes to town for a Monday morning meeting at Avantra's main office on Beale Street."

"Interesting," said Conklin. "What are you thinking? Was Alton Joan's boyfriend? An attacker? A random hookup?"

"I'm going with boyfriend. We were able to get a look into the Warwick computer systems, and it turns out that Joan Murphy has a monthly reservation at the Warwick. And it's always on a Sunday night. The first Sunday in the month, in fact."

Conklin said, "I've got to agree with you then. Sounds like these two were having an ongoing affair. Yet Joan's husband tells me there's no chance in hell that his wife is stepping out on him. 'We have a full and trusting relationship,' he told me. And that's a direct quote."

"Gee," said Sac. "Could the husband be telling you a lie?"

Conklin laughed.

Sac said, "I'm going to drive to San Berdoo. I'll notify Mrs. Alton that her husband was shot to death in the arms of another woman. Then, I'm gonna go home and get drunk because that's going to be one hell of a conversation. You want to mention Samuel Alton's name to Joan Murphy? See what happens?"

"Oh, yeah, I do. The woman tells a fantastic story. Can't wait to hear what she comes up with this time."

CHAPTER 16

CINDY WAS AT LINDSAY and Joe's apartment Tuesday morning, drying Martha after their walk had gotten drowned out by an unexpected drenching rain.

Martha shook herself off, causing Cindy to shriek, "No!"

Martha, excited by her friend's response, put her paws on Cindy's shoulders and licked her face.

Cindy couldn't help laughing. Martha was showing good progress with her injury if she was already this mobile. That made Cindy pretty proud to have helped out her friend in need.

"What now, Miss Martha?" she lovingly asked the dog. "Are both of us going to have to get into a hot shower? Hmmmm? You know I have to wear these clothes to work."

Martha woofed. Cindy laughed again and said, "Copy that, Big Girl. Breakfast is coming right up."

Cindy was dumping dog food into a bowl when, of course, the phone rang. It was just like the other morning, only this time it really was Lindsay.

"Are you checking up on me?" Cindy teased.

"Of course not. Well, maybe I am, but just a little. Put Martha on the phone for me."

"Sure thing. Here ya go."

Cindy put the receiver near Martha's face as the dog gobbled down her beef stew with supplements. She could hear Lindsay talking to her dog, who stopped eating long enough to lick the phone. Cindy cracked up.

"I'm totally grossed out," she said to Lindsay. "By the way, it's not just raining here, it's a certified downpour. Your dog is wet. The phone is wet. I'm wet. And I'm about to rifle through your closet so I don't have to go to work in an outfit that's completely soaked."

Lindsay told her, "Go ahead. Be my guest. And take a selfie so I can see how my size ten clothing fits your itty-bitty size-four bod."

"Great idea. So, how's the vacation going?"

Lindsay's voice was as light as fluffy clouds in a blue sky. She told Cindy about their lovely room, the pleasure of "waking up with Joe and not having one damned thing to do. I'm eating actual meals at real tables."

Cindy laughed. "That's amazing. Take a selfie of that."

Lindsay asked if she was missing anything back home, and Cindy had the Joan Murphy story racked up and ready to roll. But at the last second, she held it back. Lindsay was with her hubby, and their baby was with Lindsay's sister. For the first time in a while, her friends were enjoying a nice hotel and room service. Lindsay deserved a clean break while she was on vacation.

"As far as I can tell, life goes on without you, Linds."

Lindsay laughed. Then she promptly told her to shut up and informed her friend that she was going back to bed.

They exchanged love-yous and hung up, and then Cindy picked up where she left off with her chores. It was funny how, even though she had known Martha forever, she felt her feelings toward the fluffy dog had deepened while taking care of her. This doggy was changing from just a typical cute dog to a close friend.

Cindy had been fighting Richie on the subject of having kids for a couple of years now. She wasn't ready for them. Yet he'd been ready since before he'd even met Cindy. At one point, the two of them had actually broken up over this very issue. Thank God they had been able to get past their differences and get back together.

Even though Cindy hadn't changed her position.

Still, being responsible for this old dog made Cindy think she might have some tiny maternal instinct inside her after all.

She threw the wet towels into the wash, left her shoes in the bathtub, and found a pair of Lindsay's sneakers in her closet. They were big, but they almost fit her. Then she dried her hair, and when her blond curls had sprung back into shape, she located a trench coat with a belt in the back of Lindsay's closet. She tried it on and decided it would work well enough.

Before she left the apartment, she called the girls and put them on a conference call.

"Lunch, anyone?"

Claire and Yuki were both in.

CHAPTER 17

CLAIRE STRIPPED OFF HER gown, mask, and gloves. She told her crew that she was going out for a quick lunch and that she would be back in an hour.

MacBain's, the bar and grill down the street from the Hall, was named for a heroic captain of the SFPD who was now deceased. His daughter, Sydney, owned the local watering hole. It specialized in a five-dollar burger-and-fries lunch and was generally packed from twelve noon to midnight with Hall of Justice workers.

Claire, Lindsay, and Yuki were card-carrying customers.

Cindy didn't work at the Hall but had her own card. It said Press on it, and Sydney MacBain was happy to have her business.

At a quarter past noon, the line of customers was trailing out the door, of course. Claire joined it and was greeted moments later by Yuki. The two friends grabbed each other into a big hug.

Yuki had just returned to the DA's office after a year of doing pro bono defense work and was charged up to be putting bad guys away. She had just lost a case of national and global proportions, and was eager to put it behind her by diving into the next one. And Claire had no doubt that her friend would do a phenomenal job on it.

Yuki said, "Tell me all about this woman who apparently came back from the dead in your morgue."

"I can only tell you because she's alive," said Claire. "And because Cindy isn't here."

Yuki drew an X over the breast pocket of her suit jacket with a finger, swearing to keep the secret.

So Claire told her. "The subject, who shall remain nameless, was found naked under the naked body of a man who was not her husband. He'd taken a few plugs to the back and one to the arm, and she had been shot a couple times, too. She appeared to be dead, but in fact was cataleptic."

"Is that like catatonic?"

Claire laughed. "Not at all."

Just then, there was a tap on Claire's shoulder.

She turned and was standing face-to-face with Cindy Thomas, the crime reporter. Her springy blond hair bounced and shook as she said, "Don't give me that off-the-record crap. I swear not to run anything until you say it's okay. Okay?"

Yuki said, "I feel like I've heard this pitch before."

The three friends threw their heads back as they laughed. Then the line moved forward and a table opened up inside. When they were settled at their table and had ordered their burgers and sparkling water, Claire told her friends the rest of the information that she knew about the case.

"The unnamed female's outfit was collected from the hotel

room and is with my team, currently undergoing testing. It's a two-piece Givenchy suit, a black button-down shirt, evening slacks, and high-heeled sandals. Also, she had *very* expensive undergarments. The kind that I can only afford in my dreams."

Cindy said to Claire, "You've been holding out on me."

Then she turned to Yuki and said, "So, here's the rest of it—as I was able to figure out." She cracked a sly grin.

"This naked man who was found lying on top of this unnamed female. Let's call her, well, let's call her, Joan—"

Claire shook her head and sighed.

The food arrived at the table, and after the ladies took a few bites, Cindy went on. "The naked man was shot dead and Joan was also hit by a couple of slugs. She appeared to be dead. Stonecold dead. But she was not. And based on the *very* expensive undergarments and the nakedness, it seems like she went to the hotel with recreation in mind."

Yuki said, "So are there any other theories besides the obvious? Do we know for certain that she was having an affair with the John Doe?"

Cindy said, "When I met her, she was just regaining consciousness. She told us that she had completely lost her memory."

"And it could be true," Claire told her friends. "She was out of it for six hours, at least. The refrigeration saved her life, but that's not to say she didn't lose a few memories. She needs a neurological workup and I hope she gets one."

"Or she could be lying," said Yuki. "You say she knew her

name but not what happened to her in that hotel room? That's pretty convenient, if you ask me."

Cindy put down her burger and pointed a French fry at her friend before she dipped it into a puddle of ketchup. "If you met her and talked with her, you'd believe her, Yuki."

"I'm a human lie detector," Yuki said sweetly. "I'll bet if I met her, I still wouldn't believe her. I'm pretty sure she's a very charming and skillful liar."

Claire sighed, looked down at her watch, and said, "I have time for a quick coffee if you do."

When she glanced back up at Cindy's face, she could tell that her friend had disappeared down a road of deep thought.

No doubt she was working on a story headlined "Dead Woman Walking."

CHAPTER 18

RICH CONKLIN WAS AT his desk in the squad room. He was doing a background check on the deceased, since he now had his name.

Samuel J. Alton had a negligible record. Twenty years before, when he was seventeen, he had been busted for selling pot at a beach party in LA. He'd pled guilty to the misdemeanor, got six months' probation, and paid a fine. It seemed he'd learned his lesson, though, because after that he hadn't gotten so much as a parking ticket.

But Sam Alton wasn't exactly a model citizen, because once a month he came to town, stayed at the Warwick, and apparently spent time with a very wealthy woman who had a home in an exclusive part of town. That woman always booked a room for the two of them. She also happened to have a husband. And he'd had a wife and kids.

Had last weekend's tryst gotten Sam Alton killed?

If so, by whom? How did the killer gain access to the room?

And if his death wasn't caused by a scorned spouse, what was the motive for the shooting?

Conklin opened a file of photos. Dr. H. had taken some at the scene, while Claire had taken the others. In Claire's pictures of the victim, he was resting on a metal table in her lab. She'd also included close-ups of the labels. Seeing Claire's careful, meticulous work made Conklin smile. She was very good at her job.

There was a second zip file containing photographs of Sam Alton's clothing that had been stowed away at the hotel.

The attached note from Dr. H. read:

See Joan Murphy's clothes as they were found in the room. No GSR on them. Same deal with John Doe's apparel. The clothing was neatly folded on a chair, jacket hung in the closet. Also no GSR. The lab has it all now and is processing for trace. We'll get who did this.

Rich stared at the pictures for a while. What the neatly hung and folded clothing told him was that these two people knew each other well. He saw no violence, but he didn't see any uncontrollable passion, either. It felt to him as though Joan and Samuel had been a couple for a while. He thought about the way Joan had stared at Alton's dead body.

What had she said? "I've never seen this man before."

And she had seemed indignant.

Her voice had been hard. Cold. Had it been full of guilty knowledge? Had she set Alton up to be killed? Or had she suffered brain damage that had resulted in memory loss while she was in that cataleptic state? Did she truly not remember her lover?

Conklin's cell phone vibrated. He looked at the caller ID and saw that it was Robert Murphy.

Rich answered the phone by simply saying his name, and Joan's husband replied, "This is Robert Murphy. Have you heard from Joan?"

"Not today. Why do you ask?"

"She's missing, Inspector. She slept in her bed last night, but both she and her car are gone now."

"Can you please give me the plate number?"

Murphy recited the numbers.

Conklin asked, "Is there a tracking device on her phone?"

"You've got me there. I don't have the slightest idea. Inspector, I'm worried about her. Especially in light of recent events."

Rich said, "I'll put out a lookout on her car and will let you know if I hear anything. If you hear from her in the meantime, please call me."

"I will."

Conklin hung up and then played the conversation back in his mind. Had Murphy been straight with him or was he acting? It seemed strange that he would be worried that Joan was missing for a few hours, even though he hadn't been ruffled when she'd been missing for almost twenty-four hours.

The alarm bells were going off in Conklin's head. Something just didn't add up.

What had happened to Joan?

Had she collapsed somewhere and gone into another cataleptic state? Had her husband killed her? Or perhaps she'd just gone somewhere to grieve for her dead lover because the memories from the shooting came back.

Whatever the reason, Rich wasn't going to chance it. He called Joan's number and left a message. "Joan, it's Rich Conklin," he said. "Please call me. I'm concerned for your safety."

CHAPTER 19

RICH WAS AT HIS desk when John Sackowitz dropped by and sat down in Lindsay's chair. Sac was a big man and was wearing a gray jacket, jeans, white shirt, and a weird pink tie.

Sac moved the desk lamp out of his way so he could look Conklin directly in the eye. Then he said, "Sam Alton's betrayed widow, Rachel, is in shock. It's nightmare city over at her house. God, I hate notifications. Did you get a chance to speak to Joan?"

"She's gone missing. That's according to her husband anyway. I'm heading out to Seacliff to tour the house and grounds. I'll call you later."

Sac stood up and said, "I've got some paperwork to do." He lumbered over to his desk across the room and began typing up his report.

Conklin turned off his desktop and waved good-bye to Sac.

A few minutes later, he was in his car and driving out to Seacliff when Brady called.

"Conklin, a dead body was found in an apartment building in West Portal. Welky was the first one on the scene, and an

ADA just brought him a search warrant. Welky found two IDs in the room and a wallet that belongs to Samuel J. Alton."

Seriously? There was no way Samuel J. Alton had died twice. *So who was this dead man with his wallet?*

Conklin made the excruciatingly slow drive to the middle-class, family-oriented neighborhood. He got stuck at the lights at both the entrance and exit of a three-block shopping district, and then, once he'd gotten free of that, he hit another traffic snarl on a block filled with homey bars and restaurants. Twenty minutes after leaving the Hall, he parked in front of an apartment building on West Portal Avenue, between a cruiser and the coroner's van. He hopped out of his car and headed toward the crime scene.

The building was a classic midcentury San Francisco–style home with five stories of gray stucco, arched windows, and a view of the West Portal Muni. A half dozen trees out front softened the lines of the building under a clear sky overhead. A light-rail car rattled by as Conklin entered the building. If he hadn't been summoned there on police duty, he would have never guessed that there had been a murder inside.

The old man behind the front desk pointed to the elevator behind him, then raised four fingers.

Fourth floor. Got it.

Conklin was met upstairs by the two beat cops who'd arrived on the scene first. Their names were Officers Calvin Welky and Mike Brown. Conklin signed the log, put on booties and gloves, and then walked into a clean, bright three-room apartment.

Welky said, "The manager, Mr. Wayne Murdock, said the apartment belongs to one Arthur O'Brien, an actor and probably a junkie. Murdock got a call from O'Brien's mother. She hadn't heard from her son in a couple of days. She said he wasn't returning her calls. Murdock went to the young man's residence, found his body here, and called it in."

Conklin looked around the living room. It was dominated by a fifty-two-inch TV. Across the room from it sat a nondescript brown couch. A set of weights took up one corner of the space. It looked to Conklin like this was a single man's apartment. There were no knickknacks or sentimental items breaking up the uniform brown color palette. But the most telling detail of all was the drug paraphernalia that was scattered across the coffee table.

Conklin noticed a stubby candle, a scorched spoon, a box of matches, and a flock of opaque glassine envelopes that were coated with white powder.

Conklin walked to the bedroom, stood in the doorway, and nodded to the two CSIs who were photographing the dead man. His body was lying in the center of the unmade bed.

Conklin said hello to Claire and Bunny, and then he took in the whole of the room. There were movie posters on the walls, a laundry bag by the window, a desk with an open laptop computer, and a knapsack up against the wall. His eyes went back to the dead man lying in a relaxed fetal position.

If you squinted, you could almost imagine that Arthur O'Brien was sleeping.

Conklin wished that he could shake the man to ask him some questions.

Who are you, bud? Why do you have Sam Alton's wallet?

CHAPTER 20

CLAIRE WASHBURN PHOTOGRAPHED THE deceased from every angle with her old Minolta camera while she and Bunny waited for Rich Conklin to arrive.

The dead man's real name was Arthur O'Brien. He was white and in his thirties, but since that's where his similarities to Samuel J. Alton ended, it was a wonder that he was in possession of Alton's identification.

Arthur O'Brien didn't have a double chin or love handles. He was as thin as a rail, and had spiky blond hair and a square diamond earring in one ear. He wore jeans and a long-sleeved blue knit shirt. One of his sleeves was rolled up, almost to the shoulder, revealing a length of rubber tubing knotted around his left biceps. The track marks that ran down his arm showed that this had not been his first time at the rodeo. The syringe was lying on the sheets about three inches from his right hand, and there was a puddle of vomit on a pillow.

Probable cause of death: suicide, most likely unintended.

Conklin came through the door. He pushed his hair out of his eyes, then checked out the room and the body. Then he said to her, "Don't commit yourself, but what are your thoughts?"

She said, "I'll send out the blood sample in the morning and do the post, but he's cold. On the face of it, he OD'd and I'd say he's been dead at least twenty-four hours."

Claire lifted up the dead man's shirt and pushed a thermometer into the skin above his liver. Then she waited a minute before reading it.

She said, "I'd estimate that this man's death occurred more than thirty hours ago. That means it happened early Monday morning."

"The wallet's over there," Welky told Conklin, pointing toward the dresser opposite the bed. Conklin walked over, picked it up, and took a look at its contents. Claire had already seen the wallet. It was good quality and was made from tan-colored calf's skin. The initials *SJA* were embossed in one corner.

Inside was Samuel Alton's driver's license. The photo on the identification card matched the face of the man who had been found dead in Joan Murphy's embrace.

"One twenty in cash in the billfold," said Welky, "along with four credit cards and a dozen business cards. Everything seems to belong to Samuel Alton, Avantra Insurance, San Bernardino. Inspector, there's also a backpack you'll want to see here."

Brown picked up the backpack that had been leaning against the wall and set it down on the desk. Claire left the deceased and went over to watch Conklin go through the contents of the bag.

He hefted it, undid the zipper, and said, "Call me crazy, but I'm feeling lucky."

Conklin put his hand into the backpack and removed the first item: a snub-nosed Smith & Wesson, small, what was known as a .38 Special. It held six bullets. He showed Claire the chamber. There was only one bullet left inside.

She thought, *The first three went into Alton's back and arm, and the last two went into Joan Murphy's shoulder and hip. That adds up.*

Conklin handed the weapon off to a CSI, saying, "That goes to ballistics right away, Boyd. It looks like it could be evidence in an active homicide case."

A few more items came out of the backpack, including a bag of chocolate chip cookies and an empty liter-sized Coke bottle with a hole in the bottom. Conklin held up the plastic bottle. He knew that on the street, this sort of thing was used as a suppressor. If a killer screwed the gun into the mouth of the bottle and fired, the bottle would silence the gunshot.

The next item in the bag was a gray T-shirt. Richie sniffed it and said, "Gunpowder."

He handed the shirt and the bottle off to Boyd. Then he put both hands into the bag and took out a red-patterned kerchief that was neatly folded into a bundle. He said, "This is so heavy, it almost feels like it's alive."

Claire saw that the object inside that kerchief was jointed and pointy. Maybe it wasn't one item, but a number of many small pieces wrapped up together. Conklin set the makeshift package down on the desk and turned to Wallace, the CSI who was holding the camera, saying, "Please shoot the hell out of this."

Rich opened the kerchief one fold at a time, exposing a pair of very sparkly earrings, two chunky rings, three diamond encrusted cuff-style bracelets, and a twenty-two-inch white metal chain necklace with a large diamond pendant.

He stared at the glittering array for a long moment. Maybe he was dazzled, thought Claire. Because it was dazzling.

"What do you think of this?" he said to her. "Is it a million dollars' worth of diamonds?"

Claire said, "If it all came from Cartier or Harry Winston, that batch could be worth multiples of that. But I know one thing for sure: those are Joan's jewels. I recognize most of it from that second honeymoon photo that was in her wallet. I'll bet she never expected to see these pieces again."

Conklin dug around in the main section of the backpack some more but came up empty-handed. Then he opened a zippered pocket in the front and took out a wallet. This one was slim, holding only one credit card and a driver's license. He showed Claire the photo on the license. It belonged to the man on the bed, Arthur O'Brien.

Claire said, "There's another pocket on the side there, Richie."

The pocket was tight and the fabric seemed to resist the insertion of his gloved fingers. Conklin persisted. At last, he pulled out a green plastic hotel key card.

He showed it to Claire and put it down on a corner of the desk. He asked Wallace to take a couple of shots of the card. On the center of the card were the words *Warwick Hotel*.

"Beautiful," he said to Claire. "Assuming the gun in the backpack killed Sam Alton, Arthur O'Brien has tied up all the loose ends and wrapped up the case against himself."

Claire nodded curtly as she handed off the pillowcase with the vomit on it. That's when she found the cell phone in the bedding. She held it up to Rich and said, "He might have even tied up that package with a bow on top," she said. "I wonder who Mr. O'Brien had been calling in the weeks before he died."

CHAPTER 21

CONKLIN MADE PHONE CALLS from his car as Claire supervised the transport of Arthur O'Brien's body and belongings into her van.

First he called John Sackowitz, and then he patched Brady into the call and told both of them what he knew.

He said, "It looks like O'Brien died from an accidental drug overdose. The deceased was in possession of a backpack that was a forensic lab's dream. There's a recently fired .38 with one slug left in the six-chamber cylinder and a street suppressor. Also, get this, we found a key card from the Warwick. I'm going to take a wild guess and say it opens room three twenty-one."

Sac and Brady were suitably impressed and excited.

Conklin kept going. He was on a roll.

"How'd he get the card? This, I don't know. But we have his cell phone. Maybe his call history will give up the other players in this thing. Oh, and to really seal the deal here," Conklin said, "Joan Murphy's diamonds were also in O'Brien's backpack. All of them, and they were nicely wrapped in a bandana. CSI found O'Brien's prints on all of it."

Brady said, "Good work, Inspector Conklin. Take a bow and the night off."

It was a quarter to six, so Conklin called Cindy and said, "I'll pick up a pizza." Then he sent her a phone kiss.

After that, he called Joan Murphy's phone and left a voice mail. "Joan, this is Rich Conklin. We've recovered your jewelry. There are about three pounds of diamonds here, including that pendant that I think belonged to your mother. Call me, please. We'll need you to identify it."

He clicked off and then spoke to the disconnected phone, "And by the way, Joan, I also need to talk to you about Sam Alton and Arthur O'Brien, both of whom are now deceased. You're starting to look like the center of a category 5 storm to me."

His phone buzzed.

It was Joan.

It was almost as if she'd heard him.

She said, "Hi, Richard. I'm doing all right. Keeping it together. I want to remind you that someone tried to murder me. I don't want to give this person another shot at it. You understand what I'm saying, don't you?"

"Where are you? Everyone's been worried about you. Robert called you in as a missing person."

"Never mind that. Look, Richard, the important thing is that I think I know who was behind all of this."

But then the phone went dead in his hand.

Conklin hit the Return Call button. He listened to the ringtone and got Joan's outgoing voice mail message.

"This is Joan. You know what to do."

Conklin said, "Call me back, Joan. Call me."

He got out of his car and walked over to Claire. She was shutting the back doors to the van.

"Joan just called me. She won't tell me where she is, but she said that she's staying out of harm's way. Then she hung up on me."

"Curiouser and curiouser," said Claire.

"Do you get the feeling," Rich asked Claire, "that she's making things harder for us on purpose? Why would she do that?"

CHAPTER 22

THAT NIGHT CINDY AND Rich got into bed before ten. It was an early night for them and that was a kind of blessing.

It was good to be home. Their apartment on Kirkham Street was small and cozy. They'd decorated it together so that it fit them like a hug.

Richie's arm was around Cindy, and she was wrapped around him with her cheek pressed to his chest. Streetlights sliced through the blinds, striping the walls and ceiling. Their alarm clocks were set. They each had glasses of water on their nightstands, and she had the extra blanket. Rich had the king-sized pillow behind his back.

And they had the luxury of these quiet hours to talk about their days. She loved listening to the sound of his voice.

Rich was telling her about Arthur O'Brien, the shooter who'd killed Samuel J. Alton and wounded Joan Murphy. He explained how Arthur had been the one to steal her jewelry, expose her affair, and then step off stage into the shadow of death.

"And after all this craziness about whodunnit and why," said Rich, "he keeps all the evidence in his backpack and leaves it for us to find."

"Careless," said Cindy. "It's basic hit man 101. The first thing you do is get rid of the gun."

"That's the thing, Cin. He was not a pro. Not even semi. Still, he got a key card, got an unregistered gun, shot two people, and ditched with the jewels. He got out of the hotel just like that. Shazam."

"It seems too neat," said Cindy. "How did a drug addict and occasional film extra get onto Joan and her jewels? Someone had to have put him up to it. If I had to guess, someone gave him a playbook."

"You're right. We downloaded the call log on his phone. We found a lot of stuff there, but at first look, nothing was incriminating. He called his mother regularly. He had a few friends, none of whom connected him to Alton or the Murphys. But then we found several calls to a burner phone in his call history. If he was given instructions, I bet it went through that phone. I'm thinking that if O'Brien was the shooter, he was supposed to cash in the jewels. But he flamed out before he could collect his check."

Cindy asked, "What's your next move?"

"Wait for the lab reports. Sam Alton's widow wants justice. The Murphys are out of it. Joan is alive. She has the jewelry plus a great story for all of her dinner parties, and a couple of decorative scars.

"I don't understand her," Rich continued. "I'd expect her to want me to catch the person who did this and killed Sam."

"That might be the snag," said Cindy. "Maybe she doesn't want to admit to having an affair with Sam."

"Sure. Maybe that would torpedo her marriage. But do you think that Robert doesn't know? Is he really so clueless? Or is he grilling her when the cops aren't there? Is that what's making her stick to her story? 'I was drugged and kidnapped and shot and I don't know who that hairy fat guy was who was found naked on top of me.'"

Cindy laughed and Rich joined her.

It was all so crazy.

But it was just the kind of mystery Cindy loved to solve.

CHAPTER 23

THE NEXT MORNING, CINDY and Rich said good-bye on the street and got into their cars. Rich headed to the Hall, and Cindy set her course toward Seacliff.

She didn't tell Rich where she was going. She knew what he would say. "You're poking into a police investigation. It's dangerous." Or words to that effect. Either way, it wouldn't be something she'd want to hear.

If she listened to Rich and some of her well-meaning friends, she'd be writing a fashion column. Or maybe pieces about local politics.

But she was a crime writer. Crime was not just her beat at the *Chronicle,* it was her passion. She'd written a bestselling true-crime book, sold two hundred fifty thousand copies in paperback, and had a standing offer from her publisher that he'd entertain any book ideas she might have. So, yeah.

And then she laughed out loud at the realization that she was justifying her job to herself.

She drove from her apartment through Golden Gate Park on Crossover Drive and then continued into the Richmond District toward Seacliff. She checked the house numbers on

El Camino Del Mar, a street populated with mansions and set back from the road. She slowed the car and took in the gateposts bracketing a stucco wall. This was the house. The iron gates were closed.

Cindy cruised past the house, slowing as she saw another break in the wall. This gate was also made of wrought iron, but it wasn't as wide. Only one car could fit through it at a time.

Cindy saw that there was a driveway beyond the gate. It seemed to be a service entrance, and it looked to her as though the gate had been left open.

Cindy drove farther down the road, parked her Acura on the verge, and got out. Since it was eight thirty in the morning, she had the street to herself, though she could hear the distant sound of a power tool up the road. It was either a chainsaw or blower. When one car came toward her, a Lexus with tinted windows, she busied herself on her phone until the car passed by.

Then, she crossed the road and walked directly to the service entrance gate.

Cindy pulled on the handle and the gate swung open. She slipped inside and carefully closed the gate behind her. She stopped in her tracks, looking around at the grassy lawns beyond the drive. There was a barnlike machine or tool shed to her left and beyond that a pathway of beckoning stone steps cut into a steep upward slope in the lawn.

Right now, she was "snooping," as it was called in the trade. But once she'd climbed those steps, it would no longer be fun and games. She'd have no believable excuse. It would be trespassing, plain and simple.

She stopped for a moment and put her game face on. Then she climbed up every one of those thirty steps. Technically, she wasn't breaking in. She was looking for someone to interview about a pretty interesting story that centered around a murder and the robbery of an impressive jewelry collection. If she got lucky, she'd run into Joan while she was wandering around the premises. And if she got really lucky, Joan would remember her from Claire's office.

She set out toward the pool house. It was a darling cottage with French doors that faced the pool.

Cindy reflected on what she knew about Joan. Joan had always been rich. She had owned this magnificent house before she met and married Robert Murphy, who, after all, might actually love her. And maybe she loves him, too. But anyone could make a case that something had gone horribly wrong in their marriage. That something may have caused two people to die.

Who'd done what to whom and why?

If the answer to those questions didn't make a good story, Cindy didn't know what would.

She was about to check on the pool house when a door on the side of the house opened and a man came striding toward her. He was wearing his glasses on a cord around his neck, and they bounced against his bare chest with every step he took. He wore cargo shorts, but he wasn't wearing any shoes.

And he was carrying a rifle.

A rifle that was pointed directly at Cindy's chest.

He barked, "What do you want?"

She put up her hands with her palms facing out and said, "Hold on, okay? I'm with the *Chronicle*. Joan knows me. I'm just gathering some background material on a story about the murder. Look. I have identification."

The guy looked crazy. She had opened her bag and started searching for her press pass when she heard the crack of a gunshot. Pieces of marble flew from the last stone steps in the pathway, and then with another crack, a sphere exploded at the top of a post.

Fear spiked through Cindy. She knew that words weren't going to help with this guy. He wasn't hearing her. He didn't care that she was unarmed and no threat to him. Keeping an eye on the bare-chested gunman, Cindy backed away, careful not to lose her footing on the steps below her.

But then he raised his gun and fired twice more.

Holy shit. This could not be happening. He was going to kill her, or at least give it his very best try.

Cindy knew from her experiences shooting a gun that it's a lot harder to hit a moving target than it seems on TV or in the movies. But that didn't mean that she wouldn't get shot.

As she ducked into a crouch and kept backing down the steps, her ankle turned—hard. She reached for something, anything, but she lost her balance. She made a last wild grab for another stone post, but it was too late.

Gravity was winning. She fell backward and wasn't able to

break her fall with her hands. Her head slammed against a step and her body kept rolling down, hitting stone tread after tread.

And as she completely lost consciousness before she stopped rolling on the ground, the shadow of the crazy man loomed over her.

CHAPTER 24

WHEN CLAIRE ANSWERED THE phone early that morning at the morgue, she immediately recognized the voice on the other end of the line. She asked, "Where are you, Joan?"

"About three minutes from your office, depending on the rush hour traffic. I stayed at the Intercontinental for a night. I just needed to be alone with my thoughts. Claire, I have an idea. Actually, can we talk about this in person? I'd like to invite you to breakfast at my house."

Claire genuinely liked Joan and loved to hear her laugh. She was curious about how her recovery was progressing. Not only that, but Joan was offering Claire an oceanside meal prepared by a gourmet chef plus a round-trip ride in the Bentley—and well, who could turn that down?

A few minutes later, Joan picked Claire up. As she drove them along Fell Street, she told Claire that she loved Robert.

Claire couldn't help thinking that there was going to be a *but* somewhere in Joan's story.

"I was smitten at first sight," said Joan. "He was bartending at the Redwood Room on Geary when I came in with a girl-friend from the library board. We were organizing a literary lecture series for kids. When Robert asked me to pick my poison, I told him to surprise me.

"He made me a drink, Claire, and called it a Robertini." Joan laughed and took a turn onto Stanyan Street. "I still don't know what was in it. It was layered in many colors and smelled like a garden in the rain. That's what it tasted like, too, but it had a secret punch at the end."

Claire was enjoying the romantic meet-cute story, but she was still waiting for the *but*.

"We started dating. He was very demonstrative and funny. He could do impressions, you know. His George W. Bush was hilarious, and his impression of me—my God." Joan laughed long and hard. "Maybe he'll do it for you. You won't believe how spot-on it is.

"But most important, I could tell Robbie anything and everything. I felt completely comfortable around him. I told him about my first marriage to Jared, and how the man I loved had turned out to be gay. That's when Robert said, 'I got news for you, Joanie. I play for that team, too.'"

Claire exhaled. So that was the *but*. She said, "And the two of you decided to get married anyway?"

"It worked for Judy Garland." Joan laughed. "Look, I love Robbie. He is handsome, don't you think?"

"Very."

"He's very talented, too. He can sing and dance. And he can act like that guy on NCIS. Mark Harmon."

"Impressive," said Claire.

Joan nodded and pulled the large silver Bentley up to the gates to her home. She held the remote out the window with her good arm, pressed the button on it, and the gates swung in. She drove up to the beautiful house and parked next to a Mercedes sedan.

"I got that for Robbie for our anniversary. The two of us have a good marriage." Joan turned off the car and faced Claire. "That's why I know that Robert didn't try to kill me, Claire. He doesn't want to be a widower. He's pretty obsessed with his image, and that title would make him seem old. Besides, he and I have nothing but good times. We don't fight. We have love and companionship. Honestly, that's all we need."

"And Samuel Alton?"

"Who? Say, is that coffee and something yummy I smell?"

Claire opened her car door and Joan reached over to the glove box with her bandaged arm. She took out a pistol.

Claire said, "Whoa. What's that for?"

Joan shrugged and said, "Someone tried to murder me, remember?" Then she grinned and started waving the gun like a rodeo clown as she took Claire around the side of the house and out to the patio.

Once they sat down at the table, Marjorie came out and said, "Welcome, Dr. Washburn. Would you like a mimosa to start?"

Claire said, "I'll have orange juice without the champagne, please. I have to go back to work after breakfast."

Joan was standing at the edge of the patio, sighting various objects on the property over the top of her gun, from the statuary to specimen trees to the birds. Each time she aimed her gun at something, she said, *"Pytoo, pytoo, pytoo."*

Claire said, "Joan? Is that thing loaded?"

Joan called back, "Of course it is. I've also got a license, if you're wondering, and I've gone out to the range to practice. You can never be too careful when you were almost murdered."

"Come sit down and give me that thing. I'll give it back after I leave, okay? It's just for my own safety, get me?"

"You're silly," Joan said, laughing, but she sat down and put the gun on the table. The muzzle was pointing in Claire's direction. Claire gently spun the gun so it was pointing toward the horizon.

She let out a small breath, but her heart kept beating wildly in her chest.

Marjorie brought out the breakfast. It was a mushroom and fines herbes frittata that smelled delicious and was paired with a side of oven-fresh warm bread. Claire's stomach rumbled, so she unfurled her napkin and placed it in her lap. She was just lifting her fork when she heard what sounded like a gunshot.

"What's that?" Claire asked.

Two more shots were fired.

"It's coming from the pool house. Damn it to hell!"

Then Joan grabbed the pistol and started to run.

CHAPTER 25

CLAIRE STOOD UP FAST. She knocked over a chair, hit the table with her hip, and scattered the contents of the dishes and the juice in the wineglasses. She started moving, doing her best to catch up to Joan. The woman was her age but slimmer, and even with her clipped wing, Joan was faster and more athletic than Claire.

She called out to her, "Joan, wait up!"

But Joan was not listening.

Claire huffed behind her, crossing the lawn. She saw a cottage to her left, a swimming pool, and a set of meandering stone stairs. There was a man standing at the top of it with a rifle. He had the gun sight up to his eye as he pointed it down the steps.

Joan yelled, "Peter! Peter, stop what you're doing! Right now!"

The man whom Joan called Peter was fit and bare-chested. A pair of glasses was hanging from the cord around his neck, and he was wearing a pair of khaki shorts. When he heard Joan calling him, he turned toward her, but only slightly. He hardly lowered the gun at all, maybe just a few degrees. And he certainly didn't drop it.

Joan was still holding her pistol. And she raised it and pointed it at Peter.

It was a standoff. But how long would it last?

Claire pictured the horrible scene that was about to happen in front of her.

But then she had an idea, albeit untested. She called out, using the most authoritative voice she had.

"Everyone freeze."

She heard a groaning noise coming from the edge of the steps, where Peter had pointed his rifle and had likely fired the three shots. It sounded almost human. Had he shot someone? Was that person lying down there?

"Peter," Joan called out from forty feet away. "You'd better put that gun down. I figured out what you did. I know that it was you all along. And if you drop that gun, we can talk about it."

Again, Peter lifted the gun sight to his eye. This time, he was aiming his rifle directly at Joan. But before he could squeeze off a shot, Joan fired.

Not once, but three times.

And the sound of the gun was not *pytoo, pytoo, pytoo*.

It was *BAM, BAM, BAM*.

The sound was deafening, and the aftershocks echoed off the exterior walls of the tiny cottage. Peter yelped, grabbed his gut, and went down to the ground. His body curled into a ball.

At that moment, a man came galloping across the lawn from the direction of the main house.

And he was screaming, "Peter, Peter! Oh, my God, Joan! You shot Peter!"

CHAPTER 26

CLAIRE HAD LEFT HER handbag at the breakfast table, which meant that she didn't have a phone on her.

Holy shit, she didn't have a phone.

She ran past Joan over to the man called Peter, who was on his back on the grass. The other man, whom Claire took to be Robert Murphy, was cradling Peter's head and pleading with him, asking him not to die.

A quick visual exam told Claire that Peter had taken a shot under his rib cage. The man was probably bleeding internally. He'd taken another bullet to his left thigh, which was spouting blood like a small fire hose.

Peter was conscious, and he seemed to be in excruciating pain. In between moans, he was gasping to Robert, "It had to be done. I had to do it."

What was he talking about?

Claire directed Robert to take off his belt so he could make a tourniquet above the bullet hole in Peter's thigh.

"Robert, cinch it and hold it tight. Good. I'm going to make sure an ambulance is on the way. Do not let him move. Do you hear me?"

Robert nodded. Tears were running down his cheeks. "He has PTSD. From a stint he did in Afghanistan."

"I don't understand."

"He freaks out sometimes. Jesus Christ. Peter."

Claire told Robert to try to keep Peter calm. Then she stood up to look for Joan.

And she saw her. Joan was walking back toward the house at a leisurely pace. She was still holding the gun at her side. She'd simply turned her back on the bloody, awful scene that had blown up in her own backyard. All because of the gunshots she'd fired.

But in Claire's opinion, Joan had shot Peter in self-defense. Those shots had saved her life and probably Claire's, too. She must be in shock. That was understandable. But now that a man's life was on the line, Joan had to snap out of it.

Claire yelled, "Joan! Call an ambulance!"

"Okay," said Joan. But she didn't quicken her pace. She just continued to stroll up the soft, grassy lawns toward the house.

"Joan, they don't call this a matter of life and death for no reason! If you don't hurry up, Peter could actually die!"

Joan turned and seemed to give Claire's words some thought. Then she shrugged her shoulders and said, "There's a landline in the pool house."

"Make the call," Claire said. "Damn it, Joan! Run!"

Claire's mind was reeling. She obviously couldn't count on Joan to do what needed to be done, and she didn't know if she could count on Robert to help her, either. Claire was surrounded by eccentrics when she needed an ambulance filled with professionals and a platoon of cops.

She went back to Robert and Peter. Robert had completely lost his cool. As far as Claire could tell, he wasn't acting. Clearly, he cared a lot about the man in his arms—and that man was currently pale, sweaty, and losing consciousness. She told Robert, "Joan is calling an ambulance." Honestly, she couldn't be confident that Joan had listened to her, but she hoped the news would calm Robert down.

Claire walked toward the street and looked out over a grassy hillock and the stone staircase that led toward the drive, the gates, and the street.

She was completely unprepared to see a woman's body sprawled out on the stairs, her head facing toward the bottom.

Oh, my God. Peter had killed someone.

Of course. She and Joan had heard shots at breakfast, and they had been fatal. Claire ran toward the body, and once she got closer, her heart almost stopped.

It couldn't be true, but it was.

The woman on the steps had a blond mop of curls and her entire outfit was baby blue. It was Cindy.

And she was lying motionless on the ground.

Please. Don't let her be dead.

CHAPTER 27

CLAIRE KNELT DOWN BESIDE her friend. There was blood at Cindy's temple. A head wound. But Claire could see the gentle rise and fall of Cindy's chest. Her friend was still breathing.

Claire felt her pulse. It was strong. *Thank you, Lord.*

"Cindy, can you hear me? It's me, Claire."

She gently turned Cindy's head and looked for the source of the blood. She was covered in it. It was running from her temple, down her neck, and into her sweater. Had Cindy been shot in the head?

But then Claire found it. Four inches behind the temple, at the back of her head, was a bloody gash. Not a hole. Claire parted Cindy's hair and saw that the laceration looked like it had been caused by Cindy's fall. She must have hit her head on the edge of a stone tread.

Claire put her hands on Cindy's shoulders.

"Cindy. It's Claire. Can you hear me?"

Cindy groaned and Claire said, "Thank you, God."

"Claire? What happened?"

"Put your arms around my neck."

Cindy reached up, and Claire helped her friend into a more

comfortable position. She sat her on a step, and leaned her back against the edge of the wall.

"How do you feel?"

"My head hurts. And I think I twisted my ankle."

"Aw, Cindy. I'm here. I'm here." Claire patted her friend's back.

Claire saw Cindy's handbag below the steps, lying on the grass. She ran down to get it, opened the hobo bag, and poured out the contents. She pawed through the litter of purse junk until she found it.

Cindy's cell phone. She checked the battery. The phone was charged.

Next, she dialed the radio room at the Hall and let out a breath of relief when she got the voice of dispatcher May Hess. May knew every cop in the Southern Station. And she knew everyone in the ME's office, as well. Claire was in good hands.

"May, this is Claire Washburn and I'm reporting an emergency. I need an ambulance pronto to 420 El Camino Del Mar. We've got a man bleeding out from multiple gunshots. And we have another victim here with a head injury. When I say pronto, I mean it. Get everyone moving at the speed of light."

When she clicked off with dispatch, Claire called Richie, cursing silently when the call went to voice mail. "Rich, I'm at Joan Murphy's house. Cindy is here. She's taken a fall and is a little shaken up, but she's going to be okay.

"Also, Rich, the pool boy who goes by the name of Peter was about to fire on Joan but she shot him first. Twice.

"An ambulance is on the way. Listen, Rich, I think Robert Murphy might be involved with Peter. And it seems that Peter may have knowledge of the Warwick Hotel shooting. He might tell you what he knows. But on the other hand, there's a good chance he might die. And soon."

CHAPTER 28

CLAIRE LISTENED FOR THE sound of sirens.

Only four minutes had passed since she'd called dispatch, but each minute was critical. She needed to get Peter into emergency care alive.

Robert was still cradling Peter's head in his lap. He was also holding his hand, stroking his hair, and telling him that he would be fine. But as the soothing words left his mouth, Robert shot a questioning look at Claire, looking for verification that Peter would survive.

She nodded but couldn't fully commit to her answer. The man's shorts were soaked with blood. Despite the tourniquet, Peter was hemorrhaging. He could very easily bleed out if help didn't arrive soon.

"The ambulance will be here in a minute. I'll be right over there with the other victim."

She walked back to the staircase where Cindy was reclining against the stone wall, breathing normally. Her bleeding had stopped. Thank goodness.

Claire wrapped her in a big, comforting hug, saying, "Richie is on his way."

Cindy smiled and said, "Oh, good." But then her face crumpled and she started to cry. Claire hugged her friend more tightly and then pulled back to look into her face. Cindy's sobs had turned into laughter that was now verging on hysteria.

"What's going on, Cindy?"

"I'm just overwhelmed," Cindy admitted. "What if you hadn't found me here? Who knows what would have happened to me."

"I know, Cindy, I know," Claire murmured, patting Cindy's back some more.

But then Cindy shook her head and put on her tough face. She wiped her tears and said, "How is it that I missed all the action? Can you tell me that?"

"You're alive, dummy," Claire said. "Could you just be happy that you're alive?"

Their playful exchange was interrupted by a woman's voice that said, "Claire?"

It was Joan. She was walking down the steps, looking cute and unconcerned. It was almost as if she had a new role in a movie and had just walked out onto the set, thinking she could wing her lines.

"Wait, is that Cindy next to you?" she asked.

Cindy said, "Claire, help me up."

"Stay where you are, sweetie. It's better if you sit still until the paramedics arrive. Unlike me, they have medical equipment and will be able to check you out properly."

Joan said, "Cindy, what happened to you?"

"A man up there tried to shoot me. I ducked, but then I also tripped and fell down these steps. It was silly, really. Claire says I'm going to live."

Joan groaned and said, "Oh, that freaking Peter. He's a maniac." She sat down next to Cindy and took her hand.

She turned her head up to look at Claire and said, "I wanted to tell you that those gunshots jogged a memory. Sam Alton. I remember him now."

With those words, she instantly had Claire and Cindy's avid attention.

"I guess you could say he was my boyfriend. We didn't use our real names with each other. I called him Butchie. He called me Princess. We kept each other company from time to time, but it wasn't love between us. Our relationship came out of pure and simple need, on both of our parts." She cleared her throat and sighed, saying, "Still. He was very kind and he didn't deserve to die. I'm so very sorry that he's dead. I never saw who shot him, but I know that Peter has to have been involved. I wish I had seen Butchie's killer. I wish I knew how it happened."

Sirens wailed, amped up, and stopped as an ambulance drove up to the service gate at the bottom of the steps.

Joan and Claire both stood up.

There were the sounds of panel doors slamming and voices shouting. Claire ran down to the driveway and helped the team by opening the gate for them so they could carry a stretcher through.

"Hurry," she yelled. "We need you up here."

CHAPTER 29

INSPECTOR RICHARD CONKLIN WAS conducting a bedside interview at St. Francis Memorial Hospital for the second time this week. But this time, it was more than that. This interview was an official interrogation.

Peter Carter had gone through surgery, had cleared the recovery room, and was now settled in his private room. Hours earlier, his surgeon had pronounced him in stable condition.

Conklin had arrested Carter for his attempt on Joan Murphy's life. If the force was with Conklin, the dangerous fool in the hospital bed was going to admit to being part of a conspiracy to murder Joan Murphy—twice—as well as the plan to murder Joan's friend and proven lover, Sam Alton.

Right now, Peter Carter was in a talkative mood. His hand was cuffed to his bed rail. His eyes were closed, and the sheets were pulled up under his arms. His leg was in a cast and in traction. Prior to this interview, Conklin learned that this man was a person who couldn't shoot straight without his glasses. To Conklin, Peter Carter looked like an ordinary and even pleasant man.

"Feeling okay to talk?" Conklin asked.

"Only if you promise not to judge me," the man said.

"I'm not like that," said Conklin. "I just want to clear up a few things. Before we start, though, I want to make sure you understand your rights."

"Okay. I told you already. I understand them."

"Fine. And I'm going to keep recording our conversation on my phone." He showed the phone to Carter, then set it down on the tray table.

Carter said he understood his rights and Conklin believed him. He also believed that Carter was desperate to be understood and forgiven so that he could return to something like life as he had known it.

But that wasn't going to happen.

Conklin said, "I want to start in the middle, Peter. Look, you should know that Arthur O'Brien is dead. He overdosed in his apartment."

"No way. Are you shitting me?"

"Sorry. I know he was a friend. We have his cell phone and have the phone records. He called you many times while you two planned the hit on Joan at the Warwick. What I don't know is how it all went wrong."

Carter sighed. "Damn it. I told him to always call my prepaid phone. I guess I didn't realize that he'd called me on my cell."

At Carter's words, Conklin silently congratulated himself. He hadn't been positively sure of the connection between these two men until this minute. *Thanks for confirming the conspiracy, bud.*

He said, "People can get rattled. Sometimes they make mistakes when they're doing something they're not used to doing, right?"

Carter agreed. He said, "Artie was an old school friend. I knew I could trust him. He needed the money. He isn't, you know, a professional."

"Sure. We get that. So he was supposed to kill Joan and keep the jewelry, right? But why kill her? Help me to understand."

"I didn't have a choice. Robert doesn't love Joan. He's told me so many times that he loves me, but I know he'll never leave her. I thought if she just happened to die while she was on a date with someone else, he'd be a free man. He'd own the house and we…"

Carter trailed off. Conklin didn't want him to fall asleep. Not now. "Peter. Peter, I'm still here."

CHAPTER 30

CONKLIN REACHED OVER AND shook Peter Carter's arm, keeping him awake before he slipped into a post-operative slumber.

His eyes opened. "Oh. It's you. What was I saying?"

"You were saying that you got Arthur to kill Joan?"

"Well, yeah. Better him than me. I wanted to have a clean conscience. A clean enough conscience, anyway. I mean, if I didn't actually shoot her…"

He winced from pain, looked at the water glass on the tray table. Conklin handed it to Carter and watched while he drank, sputtered, then handed the glass back to Conklin.

Conklin asked, "And what about Samuel Alton? Was killing him in the original plan?"

Carter nodded.

"That's yes?"

"Yes. It wasn't anything personal. He was just collateral damage. It had to be done."

"I see. I understand all that. You had to kill the witness, right?"

Carter nodded, winced, and then closed his eyes.

Conklin said, "Peter. Is that a yes?"

"Yes. For God's sake, are you thick? I think it's time for me to take a nap. Where's Robert?"

Conklin didn't want to answer that one. Because Robert Murphy was a material witness, Conklin's team had him in lockup. Sac and Linden were questioning him, but charges had not yet been brought to the table.

Meanwhile, Conklin pressed on with his interrogation. "Peter, Robert will be in to see you later. I'm sure of it. But for now, we have to finish here. Understand?"

"Go ahead, then," Carter said. "I'm in a lot of pain, man. Let's get this over with."

"Good," said Conklin. "Two more minutes. That's all."

Peter asked, "What was the question?"

"The key card," Conklin said. "We have the key card to Joan's hotel room. It was in Artie's possession. How on earth did Artie get that?"

"Right," said Carter. "That was easy. I went to the Warwick. I paid off the guy at the front desk and told him I just wanted to take pictures. I showed him my camera, and I said, 'One picture is worth a thousand buckaroos.' I didn't have to ask twice. The guy made me a key and even put on this big show of welcoming me to the Warwick. Ha!

"Then I handed that key card off to my buddy Artie. An hour later, he calls and tells me that he'd done the job and that it had gone off perfectly. He was in and out in three minutes. It was such a relief. I figured that after that call, it was all over, except for the funeral, of course. But then, Joan comes home with gunshot wounds. She walks. She talks. She seems to be just about as good as new."

"Huh," said Rich. "That must have been a shock for you."

Carter went on. "She completely wrecked it, man. Everything I'd worked so hard to coordinate. Hey, what's your name again?"

"Conklin. Inspector Richard Conklin."

Carter waved his hand as if Conklin's name was unimportant, after all. He was into his story, though. He wanted to complain.

"The whole situation between me and Robert worked for two years—but then all of a sudden, Joan wouldn't allow it anymore. Like, who gave her the right to say whether the relationship between me and my boyfriend is okay or not? Look, if you really want to know who was behind all this, it was Joan herself. She was the one who started it. She should have left us alone. Okay? Are we done now?"

Conklin knew it was now or maybe never again. The answer to this question was critical.

"So, Peter, you're saying that Robert had knowledge of this plan to kill Joan?"

"No, no. I didn't tell him about that. You gotta be kidding me. She caused it, but it was my plan all along. I figured with Joan out of the way, Robert and I could be happy. I never wanted him to know what I'd done to Joan. Correction, tried to do to her. Honest to God, that's the whole truth. Robert had absolutely no part in it."

"Okay," said Conklin. "I believe you."

"What happens next?" Peter asked.

"Get some sleep. And then you'll want to get a good lawyer."

"Call Robert, will you?"

"Sure."

Peter Carter had relaxed back into a dopey, angelic post-operative doze when Conklin said, "Take care."

Then he left the room with the taped confession in his pocket and said good night to the two officers on guard outside the door.

CHAPTER 31

CINDY WAS IN AN excellent mood.

Her editor, Henry Tyler, had been so happy with "A Miraculous Life." It was her first-person account of Joan Murphy's ordeal. In fact, Henry had liked the article so much that he'd ceremoniously presented her with a little statuette from the fifties that he kept in his office called the Smith Corona. The bone-china figurine depicted a high-stepping young woman in a business suit who wore a typewriter as a hat.

"This, Cindy, this is how I think of you."

She'd laughed and thrown her arms around Henry. She told him that getting the Smith Corona was better than getting an Oscar. And it was. She surrounded the statuette with a forest of candlesticks on the sideboard.

In a couple of hours, she and Rich were having a special dinner in their small, ground-floor apartment to welcome home Lindsay and Joe, who had just returned from their vacation yesterday.

They decided to make the theme of the party "Thanksgiving dinner," because the meal was so good that they didn't want to wait until November to enjoy it. In preparation for their version of turkey day, Cindy had asked Claire to bring cranberry sauce, a vegetable side, and stuffing. Rich had stepped up to make his Thanksgiving specialty of the house since childhood: a yam casserole with marshmallows on top.

Brady had said, "Do not worry about wine. I will take care of the alcohol course, trust me." And Yuki had added, "I can bring garlands with popcorn and cranberries. Believe it or not, I think I saw some of them out at the market this week. Even though it isn't November, we have to make it look festive."

The meal was going to be excellent.

Cindy had roasted the turkey, basting it properly, leaving enough time for the meat to cool before her guests arrived. Richie made his yams and set up the table in the dining room, adding in the extensions they'd never used before.

They had finally gotten the table ready for everyone when the doorbell rang.

Claire and Edmund arrived first, carrying covered dishes. After Rich hung up their coats, they went into the kitchen to help Cindy and warm up their hot side. Claire had an exquisite talent with a carving knife, and as she dissected the turkey, she explained each and every one of her cuts. It sent Cindy into fits of laughter.

Yuki and Brady showed up with wine and the promised garlands, and Brady hoisted Yuki up so that she could tack the garlands to the ceiling and string them across the tops of bookcases. He spun her around a couple of times, and she scissored her legs as if she were a ballerina. Everyone enjoyed the spectacle.

When the doorbell rang again, Cindy opened the door.

Lindsay, Joe, and Julie came through the doorway. Lindsay held up three boxes and said, "I hope triple-chocolate cake is okay. We have a couple of pies for everyone, too. It's all store-bought though. I'm still in vacation mode."

"Cake and pie," Cindy gushed, and she took the treats from her friend. "That's fantastic."

A shout went up when the Molinari family entered the living room. "Yay! The gang's all here."

Everyone hugged Lindsay, Joe, and Julie. Even though it had only been a week, it somehow felt like more time had passed.

Brady opened wine bottles and poured glasses for the adults, while Cindy got a cup of milk for Julie. She asked the toddler if she was she glad to be home and smiled when Julie nodded emphatically.

Rich assembled eight assorted chairs in the living room and passed around the nuts and a cheese platter. While everyone munched on their snacks, they caught up and told stories and jokes.

After appetizers, everyone moved into the dining room. Once they were all settled around the table, with Julie sitting next to Joe on a kitchen stool, Edmund thanked God for their good health and wonderful friendships.

After the amens, Brady suggested they all go around the table and say what they're thankful for, as if it were actually Thanksgiving. Everyone thought it was a great idea. He went first and said, "I'm thankful to be married to Yuki and for knowin' all a y'all. I swear to God."

Joe popped into the kitchen and came back with the turkey. He set it on the table. "It's trite but true," he said, "that I am glad for this big turkey."

Edmund said, "Cindy, I am thankful you got Claire to make her chestnut stuffing because we haven't had it in about five years."

Claire laughed and said, "That's not true." Then she followed up her protestations by saying, "I'm thankful for you, too, Edmund, and for 'all a y'all,'" which got a long round of laughter from the group.

When the laughing finally subsided, Claire added, "And I'm really happy that my folks sent me to medical school. Look where it got me. *Bon appétit,* everyone."

It was a short reach across the table for all to clink glasses, which they did.

Lindsay said, "I'm thankful to Cindy for taking care of Martha while I was away and for putting together this wonderful Thanksgiving dinner. It was such a good idea to celebrate with a turkey. But I'm also wondering what I've missed. Did anything happen? At all?"

Conklin said, "Nah. Nothing."

"Not much," said Cindy. But then she leaned in closer

to Lindsay and added, "We were just on the juiciest case ever."

"Are you kidding me?" said Lindsay.

"Well," said Cindy, "It was in the top ten, anyway."

And Claire said, "It was definitely a murder case for the ages."

EPILOGUE

CLAIRE WAS THE FIRST to open Joan's handwritten invitation for holiday drinks with her new friends, saying it was a "surprise" venue that was for "girls only."

Claire called Cindy, Lindsay, and Yuki, and they were all in.

A driver picked them each up from their offices and drove them out to the Pier 39 Marina at Fisherman's Wharf. The car was a Bentley, and Cindy immediately located the champagne in an ice bucket in the backseat of the car, which made the ride merry and bright.

After a short while, the driver delivered the Women's Murder Club to a slip of land, where Joan and Marjorie were waiting for them. Joan was bundled up in charcoal cashmere and had her mother's large diamond pendant around her neck.

The night was cool, but it wasn't cold, and the sky was clear, providing a beautiful backdrop for the marina. There were at least three hundred double-fingered boat slips docked along the pier, and the women took in incredible views of Alcatraz and the Golden Gate Bridge.

Joan embraced each of her guests, including Lindsay, whom

she'd never met. "I've heard so much about you," she said, giving her shoulders an extra squeeze.

"I've heard a bit about you, too," Lindsay said.

They laughed and hugged again.

A gorgeous motor yacht pulled up in front of them. It was a seventy-two-foot cabin cruiser with a long, open bridge and old-fashioned brass lights hung along the teakwood trim. The captain's name was Gina Marie, and she looked impeccable in her white uniform and red lipstick. She gave each of them a wide smile as she welcomed them aboard.

Lindsay and Cindy cast off the lines, and Gina Marie started up the engine. Then the guests went down to the lounge, where Marjorie served champagne and hors d'oeuvres. She sat next to Joan when everyone was served and joined the festivities. But the question still lingered: what was the occasion?

Once the yacht was skimming the bay at a comfortable ten knots, Joan stood up with her glass in her hand.

Claire thought Joan looked lighter and happier than she'd seen her three months before. She'd healed well. Her hair was longer and blonder. The scarf around her neck flew like a pendant over her shoulder. Her many diamonds sparkled like stars.

"I have an important announcement to make," she said.

Everyone looked up at Joan.

"I've asked Robert to move out of the house. And I've filed for divorce, which I think I'll be able to get without any problems."

Claire said, "Wow."

Cindy echoed the "wow," adding, "Way to go, Joan."

Joan laughed and then lifted her glass. "So I want to make a toast to all of you. Here's to friendship."

It was difficult to maintain their balance on the moving yacht, but everyone stood up to hug each other.

For the rest of the ride, no one answered a phone. Dinner was delicious and memorable. Joan entertained the women with stories from her fabulous life. She'd rubbed shoulders with many celebrities over the years, and even clued the ladies in to a secret romance that she had with a very elusive actor.

There was clapping and laughter and champagne toasts to round out a great celebratory girls' night.

The first, it felt, of many to come.

MANHUNT

A MICHAEL BENNETT STORY

JAMES PATTERSON

WITH **JAMES O. BORN**

CHAPTER 1

MY ENTIRE BROOD, plus Mary Catherine and my grandfather, gathered in the living room. We'd been told to expect a call from Brian between eight and eight fifteen. That gave us enough time to eat, clean up, and at least start the mountain of homework that nine kids get from one of the better Catholic schools in New York City.

We had the phone set on speaker and placed it in the middle of the group, which was getting a little antsy waiting for the call.

At exactly ten minutes after eight, the phone rang and some dull-voiced New York Department of Corrections bureaucrat told us that the call would last approximately ten minutes and that it would be monitored. Great.

My oldest son, Brian, had made a mistake. A big mistake—selling drugs. Now he was paying for that mistake, and so were we.

Tonight was Thanksgiving eve. Tomorrow we would embark on our annual tradition of viewing the Macy's Thanksgiving Day Parade, and it would hurt not having Brian with us.

My late wife and I had begun this tradition even before we started adopting kids. She'd get off her shift at the hospital and

I'd meet her near Rockefeller Center. When the kids were little, she loved the parade more than they did. It was one of many traditions I kept alive to honor her memory.

She even made the parade after chemo had wrecked her body, with a scarf wrapped around her head. The beauty still managed an excited smile at the sight of Bart Simpson or Snoopy floating by.

As soon as Brian came on the line, there was a ripple in our crowd. The last time I'd seen him, he was still recovering from a knife attack that was meant to send me a message.

Tonight, he sounded good. His voice was clear and still had that element of the kid to it. No parent can ever think of their child as a convicted felon, even if he's sitting in a prison. Currently, Brian was temporarily housed at Bear Hill Correctional, in the town of Malone, in northern New York. It was considered safe. For now. Mary Catherine and I talked over each other while we asked him about the dorm and classes.

Brian said, "Well, I can't start classes because I haven't been officially designated at a specific prison. That will happen soon."

All three of the boys spoke as a group. As usual, they took a few minutes to catch Brian up on sports. Football always seemed to be the same—the Jets look bad, the Patriots look good.

Then an interruption in the programming.

Chrissy, my youngest, started to cry. *Wail* is probably more accurate.

Mary Catherine immediately dropped to one knee and slipped an arm around the little girl's shoulder.

Chrissy moaned, "I miss Brian." She turned to the phone like there was a video feed and repeated, "I miss you, Brian. I want you to come home."

There was a pause on the phone, then Brian's voice came through a little shakier. I could tell he was holding back tears by the way he spoke, haltingly. "I can't come home right now, Chrissy, but you can do something for me."

"Okay."

"Go to the parade tomorrow and have fun. I mean, so much fun you can't stand it. Then I want you to write me a letter about it and send it to me. Can you do that?"

Chrissy sniffled. "Yes. Yes, I can."

I felt a tear run down my cheek. I have some great kids. I don't care what kind of mistakes they might've made.

We were ready for our adventure.

CHAPTER 2

IT WAS A bright, cloudless day and Mary Catherine had bundled the kids up like we lived at the North Pole. It was cold, with a decent breeze, but not what most New Yorkers would consider brutal. My grandfather, Seamus, would call it "crisp." It was too crisp for the old priest. He was snuggled comfortably in his quarters at Holy Name.

I wore an insulated Giants windbreaker and jeans. I admit, I looked at the kids occasionally and wished Mary Catherine had dressed me as well, but it wasn't that bad.

I herded the whole group to our usual spot, across from Rockefeller Center at 49th Street and Sixth Avenue. It was a good spot, where we could see all the floats and make our escape afterward with relatively little hassle.

I was afraid this might be the year that some of the older kids decided they'd rather sleep in than get up before dawn to make our way to Midtown. Maybe it was due to Chrissy's tearful conversation with Brian, but everyone was up and appeared excited despite the early hour.

Now we had staked out our spot for the parade, and were

waiting for the floats. It was perfect outside and I gave in to the overwhelming urge to lean over and kiss Mary Catherine.

Chrissy and Shawna crouched in close to us as Jane flirted with a couple of boys from Nebraska—after I'd spoken to them, of course. They were nice young men, in their first year at UN Kearney.

We could tell by the reaction of the crowd that the parade was coming our way. We sat through the first couple of marching bands and earthbound floats before we saw one of the stars of the parade: Snoopy, in his red scarf, ready for the Red Baron.

Of course, Eddie had the facts on the real Red Baron. He said, "You know, he was an ace in World War I for Germany. His name was Manfred von Richthofen. He had over eighty kills in dogfights."

The kids tended to tune out some of Eddie's trivia, but Mary Catherine and I showed interest in what he said. It was important to keep a brain like that fully engaged.

Like any NYPD officer, on or off duty, I keep my eyes open and always know where the nearest uniformed patrol officer is. Today I noticed a tall, young African American officer trying to politely corral people in our area, who ignored him and crept onto the street for a better photo.

I smiled, knowing how hard it is to get people to follow any kind of rules unless there is an immediate threat of arrest.

Then I heard it.

At first, I thought it was a garbage truck banging a dumpster as it emptied it. Then an engine revved down 49th Street, and I turned to look.

I barely had any time to react. A white Ford step-van truck barreled down the street directly toward us. It was gaining speed, though it must have had to slow down to get by the dump truck parked at the intersection of 49th and Sixth as a blockade.

Shawna was ten feet to my right, focused on Snoopy. She was directly in the path of the truck.

It was like I'd been shocked with electricity. I jumped from my spot and scooped up Shawna a split second before the truck rolled past us. I heard Mary Catherine shriek as I tumbled, with Shawna, on the far side of the truck.

The truck slammed into spectators just in front of us. One of the boys from Nebraska bounced off the hood with a sickening thud. He lay in a twisted heap on the rough asphalt. His University of Nebraska jacket was sprayed with a darker shade of red as blood poured from his mouth and ears.

The truck rolled onto the parade route until it collided with a sponsor vehicle splattered with a Kellogg's logo. The impact sent a young woman in a purple pageant dress flying from the car and under the wheels of a float.

Screams started to rise around me, but I couldn't take my eyes off the truck.

The driver made an agile exit from the crumpled driver's door and stood right next to the truck. Over his face, he wore a red scarf with white starburst designs.

He shouted, *"Hawqala!"*

CHAPTER 3

I STOOD IN shock like just about everyone else near me. This was not something we were used to seeing on US soil.

Eddie and Jane, crouching on the sidewalk next to me, both stood and started to move away from me.

I grabbed Eddie's wrist.

He looked back at me and said, "We've got to help them."

Jane had paused right next to him as I said, "We don't know what's going to happen."

As I said it, the driver of the truck reached in his front jacket pocket and pulled something out. I couldn't identify it exactly, but I knew it was a detonator.

I shouted as loud as I could, "Everyone down!" My family knew to lie flat on the sidewalk and cover their faces with their hands. A few people in the crowd listened to me as well. Most were still in shock or sobbing.

The driver hit the button on the detonator and immediately there was a blinding flash, and what sounded like a thunderclap echoed among all the buildings.

I couldn't turn away as I watched from the pavement. The

blast blew the roof of the truck straight into the air almost thirty feet. I felt it in my guts. A fireball rose from the truck.

The driver was dazed and stumbled away from the truck as the roof landed on the asphalt not far from him.

Now there was absolute pandemonium. It felt like every person on 49th Street was screaming. The blast had rocked the whole block.

The parade was coming to an abrupt stop. Parade vehicles bumped one another and the marching band behind the step van scattered. A teenager with a trumpet darted past me, looking for safety.

The driver pushed past spectators on the sidewalk near us and started to run back down 49th Street where he had driven the truck.

The ball of flame was still rising like one of the floats. Then I noticed a couple of the floats were rising in the air as well. The human anchors had followed instinct and run for their lives.

Snoopy was seventy-five feet in the air now.

Several Christmas tree ornaments as big as Volkswagens, with only three ropes apiece, made a colorful design as they passed the middle stories of Rockefeller Center.

I glanced around, but didn't see any uniformed cops close. The one young patrolman I had seen keeping people in place was frantically trying to help a child who had been struck by the truck.

I had no radio to call for backup. I just had my badge and my off-duty pistol hidden in my waistband.

There had been plenty of cops early, but now I saw that some of them had been hurt in the explosion, others were trying to help victims. It was mayhem, and no one was chasing the perp. I was it. I had to do something.

CHAPTER 4

WHEN I STOOD up, my legs still a little shaky, I concentrated on the red scarf I'd seen around the driver's face and neck as he fled the scene. The splash of color gave me something to focus on.

I looked around at my family, making sure everyone was still in one piece. They were on the ground and I said, "Stay put."

I worked my way past panicked parade spectators until I was in the open street and could see the driver half a block ahead. I broke into a sprint, dodging tourists like a running back.

By this point, no one realized the man running from the scene was the driver. The people this far back on the street didn't have a front row seat to the tragedy. No one tried to stop him. Everyone was scrambling for safety, if there was such a place.

I started to gain on the man because he hadn't realized yet that he was being pursued. He had a loping gait as if one of his legs was injured. But he was also alert, checking each side and behind him as he hurried away.

I wasn't a rookie chasing my first purse-snatcher in the Bronx. I didn't feel the urge to yell, "Stop—police!" I was silent and hung back a little bit so he didn't pick up on me.

He took the corner, then slowed. He looked around, as if he was expecting someone to meet him. I paused at the edge of a high-end fashion boutique and watched him for a moment. I still hadn't drawn my pistol, to avoid attracting attention.

Finally, the truck driver decided his ride wasn't here and started down the street again. He looked over his shoulder one time as he approached a packed diner, and surprised me by slipping inside.

I looked in the window as I came to the door of the diner. Every patron and server was glued to the TV in the corner of the room. News of the attack was mesmerizing. The room was silent as the news had just broken—the same TV parade footage was on loop as the newscaster started repeating the information he was receiving. No conversation, no clinking of silverware, nothing.

I immediately stepped to the cashier by the front door, held up my badge, and said in a low voice, "NYPD. Did you see where the man who just came in here went?"

The dark-haired young woman shook her head. She mumbled, "I didn't notice anyone." Then she turned and looked back at the TV.

Even though the attack had happened only a couple blocks away, a few minutes ago, watching it on TV made it feel like it was in another country.

I saw the hallway that led past the kitchen. There was a sign that said RESTROOM, so I presumed a back door was that way as well. So I hustled, squeezing past several tables crowded with extra patrons. Today was a big day for New York eateries.

Just as I started to pick up my pace, I heard something behind me and turned. The man I'd been chasing was lowering himself from an awkward position above the door. What the hell? It looked like it was out of the movies.

When he dropped to the floor and faced me, I realized he had led me into a trap.

CHAPTER 5

THE TRUCK DRIVER and I stared at each other for a moment. He had taken off the scarf, having used it to trick me. Pretty sharp.

He was about thirty, with neat, dark hair and blue eyes.

I reached for my pistol.

He reacted instantly and blocked my arm. That was from training. That's not a natural move. Then he head-butted me. Hard. My brain rattled and vision blurred.

I stumbled back and kept reaching for my pistol. Just as I pulled it from under my Giants windbreaker, the man swatted it out of my hand. I heard it clatter onto the hard, wooden floor—then the man kicked it.

The gun spun as it slid across the floor and under a radiator.

The man nodded to me and sprinted away. He didn't want to fight, he just wanted to escape.

I couldn't let that happen.

I was dazed and unable to reach my pistol, but I had to do something. I just put one foot in front of the other and followed the man.

My head started to clear.

A moment later, I found myself in the kitchen. The cooks and busboys weren't paying any attention to us. They were watching the news, just like everyone else, but on one of their smartphones. The back door wasn't at the end of the hall, like I had expected, but through the kitchen.

The man was almost to the back door when he turned and saw me. He looked annoyed, and he turned his full attention on me and charged forward.

I picked up a bottle of cooking wine and smashed it across his face just before he reached me.

The driver teetered back. Blood poured out of a gash on his cheek. Just as I was about to subdue him so I could call for backup, his foot flew up and connected with my chin.

That was the second time this asshole had made me see stars.

This time he took the opportunity and ran. He was out the door in a flash.

CHAPTER 6

IT TOOK A minute to get my legs under me. One of the cooks made the connection between the events at the parade and the fight in his kitchen. He helped me stumble out onto the street, but I saw no sign of the terrorist. He had fled back into the chaos he'd created and there was no telling where he was headed.

After retrieving my gun, I'd made my first phone call to dispatch, telling them where I was and what had happened. Now I was talking to a heavyset patrol sergeant and two Intel detectives.

Tom Colgan, the senior Intel guy, had been raised in Queens and now lived on Long Island. I'd known him for too long. We had a lot in common. He was from a classic Irish Catholic family and had four kids of his own.

Now he said, "So after this guy kicked your ass, he just disappeared into the crowd."

I nodded. He had summed it up pretty well. Then I remembered when the truck plowed into the crowd and said, "He yelled something before he detonated the bomb in the truck. I didn't recognize it."

Colgan said, "Allahu Akbar?"

"No. I've heard that before. Frankly, I almost expected him to say that. But this was different."

Colgan said, "They're rounding up all the witnesses now. I'm sure more than a few people caught the whole thing on video." He paused for a minute, then said, "Your family is okay, right?"

"They're coming to meet me here in a little while."

Colgan said, "I'm not kidding when I say I'm surprised someone was able to fight you off, then flee."

"What can I say? The guy had skills." I looked over and saw that Colgan had taken several pages of notes, including the description I'd already given him. The NYPD Intel detectives were some of the sharpest people I'd ever met. He had more information on two sheets of paper already than I take down on a whole case sometimes.

The uniformed sergeant, clearly a Brooklyn native with a long Italian name, got on the radio and gave out the limited description I had of the driver. He was clear and thorough. That's exactly what we needed right now. A patrolman was going to drive me down to One Police Plaza to work with a sketch artist.

I could still hear sirens in the distance. Cops were everywhere. The parade was canceled, and everything in a two-block radius was closed off while the bomb squad made sure there were no other nasty surprises. It was complete mayhem.

This was not the Thanksgiving Day I had envisioned.

CHAPTER 7

I WAS TOGETHER with my family by the time darkness fell. Other than when I was at police headquarters, I had been on the phone just about all day with one person or another from the NYPD. There were several still photographs of the bomber holding the detonator where you could see the kids and me in the background. One photo had already appeared on CNN and ABC.

CNN had named the attack "Holiday Terror." The theme music had just a hint of Eastern influence. I wondered if that was intentional.

Even after seeing all the footage and the news that six were dead and twelve seriously injured, all I could think about was how much worse it could've been. I was standing there. I saw the crowds. Just the truck itself plowing into them could have killed twenty people, but the driver hadn't been able to get to full speed, because he'd had to slow down to get around the dump truck that was blocking off the intersection. Thank God.

The bomb itself caused very little damage. Mainly it ripped apart the truck. The blast didn't cause any additional injuries.

Had the explosive been set properly and the blast spread out in every direction, the result would've been very different. Just the idea of it made me shudder. More than one witness interviewed thought it was a miracle the exploding truck didn't kill many more.

Seamus said, "These people are taking it too lightly. It *was* miraculous. God *did* intervene."

Fiona looked at her great-grandfather and said, "Why didn't God stop the truck driver in the first place?" It was a simple question asked by an innocent girl, no trap or guile in it.

My grandfather turned and put his hand on Fiona's cheek. "Because, dear girl, God gave man free will. It's not something he can turn on and off."

Fiona said, "I learned about free will at CCD. Does it basically mean we are responsible for the things we do?"

Seamus said, "Exactly."

I noticed Trent frantically searching something on his phone. Recently he had been making a concerted effort to match his brother Eddie's intellectual output. A tall task by any measure.

Trent said, "C. S. Lewis wrote, 'Free will, though it makes evil possible, is also the only thing that makes possible any love or goodness or joy worth having.'" He turned and gave me a sly smile.

I chuckled and said, "Good job, Trent. Watch out or you might end up studying philosophy."

Trent said, "Why do you say it like that? *You* studied philosophy."

I wanted to say, "Look where that got me." Instead, I just nodded and said, "And enjoyed every minute of it."

Finally, we gathered for our Thanksgiving dinner. When we were all around the long table, with one chair left empty for Brian, as had become our custom, we joined hands and Seamus said grace.

"Thank you, God, for this family being safe after what they witnessed. I can ask no more of you at this moment. The fact that we are all here together makes everything else in life trivial. We thank you for your guidance and understanding as we humans try to figure things out."

The old guy could still make his point in a quick and efficient way.

Later, as I was helping the kids clean off the table, my phone rang. I was prepared to let it go directly to voice mail, but I noticed it was from my lieutenant, Harry Grissom.

I tried to hide the weariness in my voice when I said, "Hey, Harry, how has your day been?" That got the rare laugh from my boss.

"You did a good job out there today."

"You mean except for the part where I let a suspect beat my ass and get away."

"From what I hear, you got a good look at him, you marked him with the cut on his face, and got a few licks of your own in. They all can't be home runs."

"Did you call just to try and cheer me up?"

"You're assigned to work with a joint terrorism task force at the FBI building starting tomorrow."

"Do they know that?"

"Frankly, I don't give a shit if the FBI wants to work with us. But we've gotta give it a chance. By pooling our resources, we have a better chance of catching this jerk-off and unrolling the cell he's connected with. And we gotta do it before they try something else."

CHAPTER 8

I WAS READY to go at six the next morning, but I had been told to arrive at the FBI building at eight o'clock sharp, so I enjoyed having a little extra time with the kids and Mary Catherine. But at eight, that's where I was: standing in front of the Jacob K. Javits Federal Building on the corner of Broadway and Worth Street in lower Manhattan.

The building was the standard, drab government off-white color with an efficient, if not attractive, design. There were low decorative posts all around the property to discourage car bombs.

I had friends here. Agents I'd worked with and analysts who had helped me solve some of my biggest cases. But the Bureau's attitude and ability to work with others was still questionable. Old habits die hard.

A tall, good-looking guy in his mid-thirties took his time coming down to collect me from the front desk. He stuck out a big hand and said, "Dan Santos. You must be Mike Bennett."

We walked slowly to a conference room behind the main FBI door. I was impressed that the entire office seemed to have shown up ready to work.

As we walked, Santos said, "I thought about joining the NYPD after I graduated from Hofstra."

"What changed your mind?"

"I wanted to make a real difference in the world."

I said, "I hear you. Guess I don't mind just collecting a fat city paycheck without doing anything." I could tell this was going to be a long special assignment.

The conference room was the new headquarters for the investigation into yesterday's bombing. I recognized a few of the agents and a couple of the NYPD Intel people who were also working the case.

Santos walked me over to a woman sitting at a table in the corner. I could tell she was making a complete assessment of me with her pale-blue eyes. Apparently, I didn't impress or disturb her, because she didn't say a word and looked back at a report she was reading.

Santos said, "NYPD Detective Michael Bennett, meet our liaison from the Russian Embassy, Darya Kuznetsova."

The woman extended her hand and said with almost no accent, "A pleasure to make your acquaintance."

Her blond hair muted her hard-edged look. She was athletic, with broad shoulders, and attractive in every sense of the word. But something about her told me I'd never want to tangle with her.

Not knowing what else to do, I sat at the long table next to her. I tried to make small talk, without much success. Finally, I came right to the point and said, "What's your job with the Russian Embassy?"

She turned that pretty face to me and said, "For now, I am the Russian liaison to this investigation."

"I realize that. What is your title at the embassy?"

"I am just an assistant to the ambassador. They thought it would be a good idea for me to work with you because of Russia's own issues with terrorists, and I might see or hear something that American police officers might overlook due to differing cultures."

I said, "Am I missing something? Why would Russian culture be important in this investigation?"

That's when Dan Santos said, "I think all your questions will be answered during our briefing. Believe me, we're going to need all the help we can get."

CHAPTER 9

SANTOS STOOD UP in front of the gathered agents and NYPD people to get everyone's attention. There were maybe twenty-five people in the room now. The tall agent looked confident as he straightened his blue tie and faced the crowd. Of course, few people got to run a case like this unless they were confident. It was a key element to getting people to do what you needed them to do.

Santos gave a recap of what had happened, but he didn't say anything I had not already heard or personally witnessed.

We had several videos taken from bystanders' phones that covered almost every angle of the attack. He played all the videos a few times, ending them all just as the truck came to an abrupt halt and the driver stepped out and yelled, *"Hawqala!"*

Santos said, "Based on our analysis and the attacker's accent, we believe he is a Russian speaker from Kazakhstan. To help us with language and context, we have Darya Kuznetsova, who will be working the investigation with us."

Suddenly the attacker's neat hair and blue eyes made more

sense. Perhaps even his training. This was a wrinkle I had not been expecting.

Santos continued. "The Russians have excellent contacts with the Kazakhstan Security Forces and have a shared interest in working with us to curb terrorism."

We watched another video and some of the aftermath, and then Santos broke us down into smaller groups and explained what everyone would be doing. One group was only following up with interviews of witnesses. Another was working with informants to see if anything was being talked about on the street. A third group, which included analysts, was scouring computer databanks to see if it could find information that might shed some light on the attack.

When Santos said, "Any questions?" I could see the annoyance in his eyes when I raised my hand. He said, "Go ahead, Bennett."

"What, exactly, does *hawqala* mean?"

"Literally it means, 'There is no power nor strength save by Allah.'"

"I've never heard it before. Is it common?"

"Not in attacks like this. We're looking into it." He looked around the room. "Anything else?"

Once again, I raised my hand.

Santos just looked at me.

"Is there some significance to *hawqala*? Could it mean he's after something else or representing a certain group?"

"As I said, we're looking into it." Then he quickly moved on and introduced Steve Barborini from the Bureau of Alcohol, Tobacco, Firearms, and Explosives.

The tall, lean ATF man stood and looked around the room. He didn't use notes when he spoke. That meant he knew what he was talking about and he was confident about his subject matter. I liked that.

The ATF agent said, "Obviously we're still processing the van, the explosive, and parts of the scene. It looks like the device was fairly simple. It contained a five-gallon paint jug with an explosive made up mostly of commercial Tannerite, which is a brand name for the most popular binary explosive on the market. We're not absolutely sure how many pounds were crammed into the paint jug, but we're guessing it was at least twenty."

One of the FBI agents raised her hand. "Where could they buy something like that? How is it legal?"

"Tannerite can be bought anywhere. Even on Amazon. There hasn't been any big move to curb it. It's legal because it's sold in two different packages. Unless the packages are mixed, they are not explosive. That's why it's called a *binary* explosive."

That seemed to satisfy the FBI agent as she made a few notes and nodded her head.

Barborini went on. "There were nuts and bolts taped around the paint jug. The idea is that the explosion should have dispersed the nuts and bolts like shrapnel in a wide circle around the explosion. What we believe happened was that the metal paint jug that was used did not have a secure lid. The detonator was a simple blasting cap on an electronic igniter. When the blasting cap went off and started the chain reaction in the Tannerite, it blew the top off the paint can and the power of the explosion went straight up. That's why the roof of the truck blew off so neatly. An explosion will travel the path of least resistance. That's what saved so many lives."

CHAPTER 10

AFTER ALMOST AN hour of briefing, I wondered if all we were going to do on this case was have meetings. This went against my instincts—to get out on the street and start talking to people. In my experience as a cop, that's what always broke open major cases. People talk. It doesn't matter where they're from or what their reasons are for committing a crime. People always talk.

I couldn't find out what they were saying if I was sitting in a conference room in Federal Plaza.

Dan Santos went through the last few things on his list, explaining how the scarf over the attacker's face had thwarted any efforts to use facial recognition to match the attacker with photographs in the intelligence databases.

Santos turned to me and said, "Turns out that Detective Bennett here is the only one who's seen the attacker's face." He held up the police artist's sketch of the man I'd described. "This is based on Detective Bennett's description. There's nothing unusual about him except possibly a cut on his left cheek."

Then I had to speak up. "There's no *possibly* about it. The man has a decent gash on his left cheek from a broken bottle across his face." I could still feel the heft of the bottle, suddenly going weightless as it broke against his face.

Santos continued. "We're covering the leads on the step-van truck—which was a rental—immigration, current gripes against the US government, and even city employees. The last group is because the dump truck at the intersection was too far to one side, allowing the attacker to slip past.

"I know we have a lot of different agencies working together, but there will be an FBI agent in each group. They will document everything you do, brief me, and handle evidence."

He closed his notebook and straightened up to glance around the room. "Are there any questions?" He shot a dirty look at me in an effort to keep me quiet.

As everyone broke into their small groups with different assignments, Dan Santos walked over to me and Darya and said, "I'm on your team. We'll be handling a lot of different things. But no matter what we do, neither of you are to run down any leads without me. Is that clearly understood?"

I was preparing a smartass answer when Darya said, "I sorry. My English not so good. Let's hope I make no mistake." She turned to me, winked, and shot me a little smile.

I was liking this Darya more and more.

CHAPTER 11

I FELT LIKE I'd found a kindred spirit in Darya Kuznetsova after she stood up to the FBI agent, Dan Santos. It wasn't just what she did, but how she did it—it was playful yet said, *Don't mess with me.*

That's why I was comfortable sitting down next to her away from everyone else in the corner of the conference room. She seemed pleased that I had chosen to speak with her. She gave me just a hint of a lovely smile, but her sharp eyes didn't miss anything.

She said, "Do you always carry two pistols? I thought the NYPD usually carried only one gun, their duty weapon on the right hip."

"I decided a backup .380 on my ankle was a good idea considering how tough this suspect was. How did you pick up on it?"

"You dragged your left leg ever so slightly and I noticed your ankle holster. Your duty weapon on your hip is obvious."

"You don't approve of guns?"

"On the contrary, it's smart. The Kazakhs tend to be of a

rougher sort than most Russians. It would be similar to some-one being raised on the frontier in the Old West." She grasped my right hand and held it up to examine it. "Just like I could tell you were not raised on the frontier."

I gave her a smile, though she had subtly just called me a wimp. "New York City is its own kind of frontier."

Darya considered my comment for a moment and said, "Were you ever pressured to join a group and commit crimes?"

I thought about mentioning the Holy Name basketball team when I was a kid. We'd been a tough bunch, and on a dare I'd stolen a bag of M&M's from a grocery store on the corner. But that probably wasn't what she meant, so I didn't mention it. Be-sides, I had gone back the next day to give old man Rogers, who ran the place, money for the candy.

I changed the subject and said, "I know we talked about this, but how did you get this assignment?"

"Part of it was that I happened to be here in New York and my English is better than most Russians.'"

"Your English is better than most New Yorkers.'" It was satis-fying that the comment earned a smile.

"I was raised in Maryland. My father was in the diplomatic corps in Washington, DC. Then I attended MIT on a student visa."

"What did you study?"

"Engineering. I still get to use it occasionally. What about you? Did you go to college?"

"Right here in New York. Manhattan College."

"What did you study?"

"Philosophy." That one earned a little bit of a smirk.

"Do you ever get to use your degree?"

"That depends. If my studies did, in fact, open my mind to help me better understand the human condition, then yes, I do. If I was merely sucked into the factory of higher education designed solely to make money, I still use it every day."

"What do you think we will be doing on this investigation? Will the FBI try to hinder us?"

"I guarantee the FBI will try to hinder us. Some of the NYPD Intel detectives say that the FBI stands for *Forever Being Indecisive*. But sometimes they're useful."

"Agent Santos did not seem interested in some of my suggestions."

"Such as?"

"Reaching out to Russian immigrants who have an excellent communications network. I'm also looking into the word *hawqala,* to see if it has been used in the past. It seems like an unusual change of pace for someone delivering a message from a jihadist organization. Perhaps this will be a link we need to find and destroy a significant terror group."

We sat in silence for a few moments and then I said, "Do you have some personal beef with terrorists, or are you just focused on this asshole?"

"Russia has seen many more attacks than the US. Some are more public than others. It's a scourge that we would like to see neutralized. If it takes a little effort on our part to teach our friends in the United States how to best deal with extremist groups, then I am all for it."

"Let's hope we don't disappoint you."

She smiled and said, "Don't worry about it. Everyone disappoints me."

All I could say was, "Hard-line. I like it."

CHAPTER 12

LESS THAN AN hour after our first briefing, I found myself playing chauffeur to my Russian liaison, Darya Kuznetsova. She apparently had less use for bureaucracy than me. When Dan Santos said he had to go talk to his bosses and directed us to either sit tight or grab something to eat, Darya said, "I'm going to talk to some Russian speakers who might help us. Do you care to be part of such a conspiracy?"

Not only did she have the right idea, she worded the question perfectly. Next thing I knew, we were driving through Brooklyn on our way to Midwood. There were a lot of Russian immigrants from Midwood all the way to Brighton Beach, but I wasn't sure what information they could offer us.

As we were driving on the Ocean Parkway through Flatbush on our way to Midwood, Darya said, "These are ethnic Russians who lived in Kazakhstan. I don't want to explain why an NYPD detective is with me. Don't show your badge. I'll try to speak in English, but if we speak Russian, just smile and nod."

"Did you just tell me to be quiet and look pretty?" That got the laugh I intended.

"I hope that brain of yours is as sharp when we have to act quickly. I don't have a great deal of faith in your FBI."

"With an attitude like that you could be an *American* cop. We hate the FBI, too."

"I'm not a cop."

I didn't know exactly *what* Darya was, but I didn't get a chance to follow up, because we had arrived at our destination.

The first people we talked to were an elderly couple who lived on the first floor of a five-story walk-up. The man said virtually nothing but glared at me like I had stolen something from his bedroom. His giant, bald head reminded me of a pale watermelon.

The little knickknacks around the apartment could've been from any grandmother in the world. I liked a figurine of a burly man in a fur hat driving a wagon with an ox pulling it. It shouted "Russia."

The woman was better dressed than the man and evidently took care of herself. She agreed to speak English with Darya, and while she had a thick accent, I could still understand her.

Darya told me in a low voice as we walked through the apartment that the man still had ties to Kazakhstan and Russia. That was one of the reasons she didn't want to bring the FBI along with us. They just wouldn't understand.

She was also afraid the FBI would use heavy-handed tactics and threaten these people with everything from arrest to deportation—and ruin any chance of getting useful information.

The woman said, "Living in Kazakhstan can be hard in the

best of times. We went with a program to work as teachers at a school for Russian children. The climate is better than Moscow, but as we got older, it was still tough on our bodies. We had a chance to follow our oldest son here and have been quite happy for the past nine years."

Darya said, "Do you talk to others in the Kazakh community?"

"Of course. Every day."

I followed the conversation, but the woman's accent was sometimes tough to understand. I liked the way Darya showed her respect as if she were a daughter visiting a grandmother. The old man just stared on in silence.

Finally, Darya got to the meat of our questions. "Have you heard anyone talk about the attack yesterday?"

"Some. Mostly people just repeating things from the news."

I had considered this question and thought this would be a critical juncture in any interview. Do we reveal the fact that we think the driver was from Kazakhstan? It might make people pay attention.

Then Darya said, "We think the driver was a Kazakh."

The old woman was shocked. "How can this be? The Kazakhs have no real hatred for the United States. Is this some ploy to ship us all out? Do they want us all to move back to our homelands? We live here, but we've never trusted the government."

I said, "Neither do we. Governments try to trick people. But this isn't one of those times."

Then the old man mumbled something. I thought it was English.

I looked at him and said, "Did you say something, sir?"

The old man said it again and I heard it clearly: "Bullshit."

Apparently, he spoke the essential English words.

CHAPTER 13

AFTER WE TALKED to several other Russian families with ties to Kazakhstan, I decided to track down a couple of my informants as well.

Darya said, "I don't understand. If your informants are not Russian, what would they know about this?"

"These are the type of people that hear everything. Small things. Big things. We may get a tip about someone looking for a ride out of the city that could break open the case. The more ears we have listening the better chance we have to hear something."

"But none are Russian?"

"These people aren't Russian, but they're criminals, and criminals often trade in information."

Darya said, "If they're criminals why aren't they in jail?"

I had to shrug at that simple question. "Different reasons. Some are smart. Some are lucky. Some have good lawyers. You can't tell me all the criminals in Moscow are locked up."

"It depends on who is protecting them."

I laughed. "Here in America, we don't care who protects

who. We just found it's easier to let most criminals stay free. Keeps me in a job."

I could tell my Russian guest didn't agree with my flippant logic. I was curious to see how she reacted to some of my informants.

I added, "I also have some Russian mob people who occasionally help me. But these guys are easier to reach for now."

The first place I stopped was a gambling house in Flatbush. It was close and not too dangerous. A good test for Darya.

The small storefront on Foster Avenue looked like a simple diner. Busy, but simple. Few people realized that when you ordered one of only five things on the menu, you also got access to a variety of gambling opportunities from football to soccer in Asia.

I heard someone call out, "Hey, Mike." I smiled and waved at one of the gamblers I knew from somewhere. No one was alarmed to see me. They knew I was a homicide detective and this place was as safe as any in the city.

I ducked into a corridor past a heavy curtain. Darya followed right behind me. When we entered the rear room, a blond man with tattoos smearing his upper arms and neck jumped up in alarm until he recognized me.

He said, "Jesus, Mike, a little notice would be nice. You scared the crap out of me." Then he took a moment and didn't hide the fact that his eyes were wandering over Darya like she was a piece of meat for sale in the grocery store. He flashed a charming smile and said, "And who is this?"

Before I could say anything, Darya gave him a dazzling smile. Better than any I had earned. Maybe she was a softy for lowlife attention and cheap compliments.

My informant held out his hand and said, "Edward Lindell, at your service." Then he winked at her.

Darya grasped his hand and put her left hand over both of them like it was a warm greeting. Then she twisted quickly, put him in an arm bar, and drove Lindell's head into a table that held thousands of betting slips.

To make the point that she didn't care for the attention, Darya ran Lindell's head down the length of the table, using his face to push everything onto the floor.

Then she released her grip and watched him sprawl onto the dirty green linoleum floor that used to be part of the kitchen.

I suppressed a smile as I watched Ed Lindell get up on his hands and knees and shake his head to clear the stars.

"I think that was her way of saying she doesn't have time for your shit."

From the floor, Lindell said, "All she had to say was, 'Cut the shit.'"

"Frankly, I like her way better. But we're wasting time. We aren't here to watch you get the shit kicked out of you by a pretty woman. We need you to put out feelers about anything unusual related to someone trying to get out of the city or trying to buy a gun or explosives."

Lindell slowly rose to his feet and said, "This have to do with the bombing at the parade?"

"How did you know that?"

"Because I went to Penn State and I'm no idiot. That's all anyone is interested in right now. What will it get me?"

The universal question by informants. I thought about it and said, "Depends on what you give us. But it'll save you more lumps from this lady and you'll be in my good graces for a very, very long time."

Lindell said, "That and some toilet paper means I could take a shit."

Still without looking or acknowledging him, Darya raised a closed fist and caught Lindell across the left side of his face, knocking him against the wall and back onto the floor. She walked out without saying a word.

I nodded to Lindell on the floor and hustled out after Darya.

As we walked a block toward the car, she said, "You're not upset that I assaulted that man?"

"He's had worse. *I've* given him worse."

Darya said, "You don't want to know why I did it?"

"I assume you did it to hide the fact that you stole the 9 millimeter pistol he had sitting on the table." I didn't wait for an answer. I just held out my hand.

She slipped the gun out of her purse and laid it in my palm. "This is America. I'll be able to find a gun if I need it."

All signs pointed to her being a pretty good partner. I'd be able to work with her.

CHAPTER 14

THE NEXT MORNING everyone was in the task force meeting rooms early. Even some of the FBI agents seemed a little annoyed at all the planning and meetings we had gone through the day before. As far as I could tell, Darya and I were part of a handful that had actually gone out and done something. Not that we were telling anyone.

And of course, we started off the day with a stupid meeting. At least I thought it was stupid, until things got rolling.

Dan Santos went over some of the information they had learned the day before, including some of the forensic information from examining the destroyed truck.

Santos said, "There wasn't a lot to grab from the truck—mainly chemical residue that will be used to track down the exact manufacturer of the explosive. The ATF did manage to lift a fingerprint off the inside of the steering wheel, so we put a rush on it to every agency and database in the country. No hits came back. But our esteemed colleague from the Russian Embassy"—he turned and opened his hand toward Darya, as if he were a ringmaster announcing an act—"has found the print in a Russian military database."

Santos nodded to Darya, who stood up. She took a moment to gather her thoughts, as if she was trying to make the announcement more dramatic after the dull crime-scene analysis.

Darya said, "The fingerprint belongs to a thirty-one-year-old male named Temir Marat. His father was raised in Kazakhstan and his mother is an ethnic Russian. He spent his early years in Kazakhstan, then bounced back and forth between there and Russia."

I noticed everyone taking furious notes, but I still hadn't heard anything that would tell me where this asshole was.

Darya continued. "Marat served a stint in the Russian army, and that's how we got his fingerprint on file. He has no history of extremism, but the FBI says that's very common. There's little else known about him."

Someone from the back room called out, "Do we have a photograph of him?"

Darya shook her head. "It's printing now. It's five years old. It's from an application to the Moscow police. There is an older photo from when he entered the army, but he is much younger and he has a buzz cut."

I wrote one line in my little notebook. *Applied to police. Why?*

An Asian woman who worked for the FBI said, "I don't think a history of extremist views is necessary anymore. The way some of these groups recruit leads many without previous violent histories to join. In fact, it's a good move to recruit people not on any terrorist watch lists. This guy sounds like the perfect choice. Smart, unafraid of death, and able to blend in with the general population in the US. He could've been recruited from a website."

An Army major in uniform said, "I can see recruiting people inside the US like that, but this was someone living in Russia or Kazakhstan. There were some serious expenses. This is a step above some of the spur-of-the-moment attacks ISIS has inspired."

Dan Santos said, "It's hard to tell exactly what happened until we catch this guy. Our intelligence indicates that shifting to using trucks and cars and simple attacks like this has a major effect on public opinion. Anytime a group uses the fear of something common to exploit terror, they're eating away at our way of life. Berlin and Paris are perfect examples. There'll be kids there in ten years that jump at the sight of a truck. It's important that we move before this guy comes up with anything else to do."

Darya said, "Russia has seen some of this. Several attacks using trucks that plow into crowds."

When she sat down next to me I said, "I haven't seen those attacks in Russia on the news." This was a private conversation, not intended for the others.

"We don't have a need for everything to be public. Perhaps your government should try that approach occasionally."

I said, "Let's not get into a conversation about whose government is more effective."

"You're right, of course."

I said, "This wasn't some kid trying to get famous. I agree with our colleague in the Army. This attack was organized and funded. It was too big to try and keep quiet in a free country. The US government generally makes information about attacks public. Even if keeping things secret works for Russia, it's not the way we do things."

Darya smiled and said, "I know Americans have a fixation with fame and publicity. You also have many more TV networks than Russia. But sometimes it's better to handle things quietly and not cause a panic. I fear this is a lesson the US will have a chance to learn in the coming years."

I hoped that wasn't the case.

CHAPTER 15

DAN SANTOS SURPRISED me. As soon as our early morning briefing was done, he grabbed Darya and me and said, "I lined up some interviews we can do today."

I withheld any smartass comment, because I wanted to encourage this kind of behavior.

Darya looked bored, but stood up and gathered her things.

Santos said, "Pretty exciting, huh? Your first interviews on a major terror investigation."

I mumbled, "Yeah. Our first interviews. Exciting." I could barely meet Darya's eyes.

She had a wide grin, but Santos was too wrapped up in his own world to notice.

The first stop we made was in lower Manhattan near the NYU campus, a small deli on University Place. It was still early and the place was nearly empty.

I caught up to Dan, who was walking pretty fast from the car, and said, "Are you hungry? What would this deli have to offer us for the case?"

"It's not the deli, but who's working there." He pulled a photograph of a young man with a dark complexion and short-cropped, black hair. "His name is Abdul Adair, he's from the United Arab Emirates. He's studying biology at NYU and works here part-time."

"What led you to him?"

"What do you mean? He's a Muslim, first of all. He attends virtually all of the Muslim student union meetings, and we have intel that he has acted suspiciously and taken a lot of photographs of New York."

That response actually gave me more questions than answers, but I wanted to see how this would go. Santos had just described a college student who likes to sightsee.

We stepped in the doors and no one paid any attention to us, the sign of a good neighborhood. A couple of little kids chased the deli cat and a young mother lazily followed them while chatting on her cell phone. The smell of the chicken cutlet hero the cook was wrapping up for a customer reminded me I had forgotten to eat breakfast. My stomach growled.

Santos stepped to the counter and asked about Abdul. A minute later, we were sitting at a small table in the corner, next to a refrigerator stocked with smoothies that cost seven bucks each.

The student from the UAE was twenty-one and small. He couldn't have been over five foot five and 130 pounds, which made him look even younger. The kid was already trembling.

Santos spent a few minutes clarifying Abdul's information. The whole process only seemed to make the young man more nervous. I scooted my chair back slightly because I didn't want to be in the splash zone if he vomited.

Then Santos asked a series of questions. "Have you ever had contact with an organization that espouses jihad? Don't lie. I'll know if you're lying."

The young man vigorously shook his head.

"Do you or any of your friends know anyone involved in a group like that?"

This time Abdul thought about it, then shook his head. He said, "I spend most of my time either studying or working here."

Santos said, "What about the Muslim student union at NYU?"

"What about it? I go there to see my friends. Meet women."

"And what do you plan to use your degree in biology for?"

"This coming summer I have an internship at an institute in San Francisco doing cancer research. That might be what I'm interested in long-term." The young man seemed to be getting some confidence.

The FBI agent made notes, but didn't invite Darya or me to say anything at all.

Now Santos moved on to our case. He pulled up our photograph of Temir Marat and said, "Know him?"

Abdul shook his head.

"Where were you on Thanksgiving morning?"

"Having breakfast with the family of one of my professors who lives in the Village."

"We'll need his name and address. Now."

Santos pushed over a notebook for Abdul to write in. He made more notes and asked more questions, which Abdul answered quickly and clearly. Then the FBI man thanked him, but warned him not to leave the city. That was it. It felt more like a schoolyard bullying session than an interview. When Santos stood up and handed Abdul a card, I did the same thing. The only difference is, I smiled and winked at him when I gave him the card. He gave me a nervous smile and nod in return.

Then all three of us marched out of the deli.

Before we even got to the car, I had to say, "What the hell was that?"

"What was what?"

"Treating that kid like that! We have no reason to believe that he's done anything wrong. Why are we wasting time scaring kids to death?"

Santos stopped on the sidewalk and looked at me like I was a little kid who just asked a stupid question in class. "Do I have to remind you, Detective, that this is a *federal* case? It's not some cheap New York City misdemeanor or dead dope addict." Santos looked at Darya to see if she was interested in getting involved in the argument. Then he said, "The FBI has to look at the big picture and see if we can link different terror networks. It may not seem like it's helping much now, but it could pay off big later. Let me know when you solve a major terror case."

That stung a little bit. As I slipped into the Crown Victoria, I felt like I'd been told off pretty effectively.

CHAPTER 16

AFTER THE INTERVIEW with Abdul, I realized my time might be better utilized. I saw my opportunity when Santos was called to a boss's office to give an update on the investigation.

I tried to quietly slip out of the task force office, ready to tell anyone who asked that I was just going to lunch. It would take a while to drive out to Brighton Beach, the Brooklyn neighborhood with a high population of Russian immigrants. But I doubted anyone would miss me, especially Agent Dan Santos.

As I hustled down the corridor away from the office, I heard someone behind me. I turned to see Darya Kuznetsova with a smile on her face.

She said, "Going somewhere?"

"Yeah, I'm going to do my job." Then, for no real reason, I said, "I'm going to visit some Russian mobsters. Do you want to come?"

She didn't say a word but just kept following me.

"Why didn't we talk to these Russians yesterday when we talked to your other informants?"

"Because Russian mobsters are in a different class. They

could help us, or they could try to find Marat themselves for a reward."

Darya said, "Do you think every Russian living in the US is a mobster?"

"That's ridiculous. Not everyone can be a mobster. Some Russians work in support roles." I waited until she turned and stared at me, then laughed and said, "I'm just kidding. But if you think no Russians are involved in organized crime, you're just as wrong. I know a couple of them. I know they won't be happy about the attack. So why don't we use that?"

That seemed to satisfy Darya and she stayed quiet, but alert, all the way through Brighton Beach. I pulled off Neptune Avenue a few blocks from our destination.

I parked away from the apartment we were headed to. No sense in alerting everyone by driving an NYPD Impala, whether it was marked or not, into one of the tightest, most isolated communities in New York.

Darya said, "What are you hoping to find out?"

"I just want to see if anyone knows anything about Marat. These guys won't have any loyalty to a terrorist. Terror attacks hurt their bottom line. They'll listen for information if we tell them what to listen for."

We walked up to the second-floor apartment, which offered a glimpse of the Atlantic if you angled your gaze just right.

I told Darya, "This guy we're going to see goes by different names. I'll wait until we see him to tell you what his name is now."

A wiry man with a disturbingly dark tan and a cigarette dangling from his mouth answered the door and just stared at us for a moment. He was about forty but looked older. He said, "What a surprise. I have no idea why you are visiting me now. I've been a very good boy lately." He ushered us inside. It was a surprisingly comfortable apartment, even if it did stink of cigarette smoke and beer. He plopped down in an oversize recliner while Darya and I eased onto a leather couch.

I said, "It's nice to see you too, Mr...."

"Vineyard. Lewis Vineyard. Good name, eh?"

"Yeah, I guess."

The Russian said in accented English, "I like it. I figure I work on my English, no one will ever suspect who or what I am."

I shrugged and said, "Except for the fact that you live in Brighton Beach, work at a Russian mob-run bar, and sell drugs and guns to Russian mobsters, I doubt anyone would ever suspect you of being a Russian criminal. I'm sure everyone will assume you're Swiss."

He gave me a smile and said, "That's my hope." Then he turned his attention to Darya. "And who's this lovely creature you brought to my home? If you're looking for a place for her to live, I agree. She can even have my bedroom."

Darya didn't say a word and I immediately realized she didn't want this guy knowing she was Russian as well. It was also useful for people to not realize she spoke their language.

He held up his arms to show off his tan and said, "You'd love it, baby. I sit on the beach every single day. You would, too, if you were raised in a place like Moscow." He gazed into her face and said, "With soft, white skin like that, you could be a Russian beauty yourself."

I said, "This is my colleague. And we're here about something serious."

"I'm listening." Then he threw in, "And what's in it for me?"

"We're working with the feds on this, so there could be some decent reward money."

He clapped his rough hands together and rubbed them. "Sounds good to me." He stubbed out the cigarette in an overflowing ashtray.

I said, "It's about the attack on the parade Thursday. I'm looking for any information about a Russian-speaking suspect. If there's anyone unusual in the area. If there've been strange requests for guns or explosives. Anything you can think of."

Lewis Vineyard said, "I deal mostly with people I know already. But I'll keep my ears open. No one wants to see shit like that happen. There were little kids killed."

"And we're going to catch that son of a bitch."

CHAPTER 17

WE STOPPED AT a few other places in Brighton Beach, but none seemed as promising as Lewis Vineyard. He knew everyone and dealt with everyone. I was confident he'd come up with something.

Darya said, "I can see why these people leave Russia. They left food lines, and found decent weather and good housing. It's hard to compete with America head-to-head. Even your marketing is better than ours."

"What do you mean?"

"You have *land of the free* or *the streets paved with gold*. We have *plenty of land to farm if you don't mind freezing in Siberia*."

I laughed at that.

She gave me a smile and said, "It would be interesting to work with you on a daily basis."

"Let's catch this guy first, then see where it goes."

"And when we catch him, what happens to him next?"

"The FBI will bleed him for information. On everything."

"That's what we thought."

Before I could ask her what that meant—that "we"—my

phone rang. I looked down and saw it was my grandfather. I never like to ignore calls from Seamus because it could be something serious, the fear always associated with an elderly relative's calls.

"Seamus, everything all right?"

His chuckle told me he was fine. "It's not like I'm going to keel over at any minute. I may still be in my prime. It's a new millennium. Age is just a number."

"The fact that you've seen the last few millennia makes me worry about your health."

"For a change, I'm calling to help you with your job."

"How are you going to do that?"

"As a man of the cloth, I have friends in every denomination. One of them happens to be a Muslim cleric. He's the imam of a mosque in Queens."

"I appreciate that, Seamus, but we're not really taking the shotgun approach that all Muslims know about terror attacks."

"But this imam spent some time in Kazakhstan. If I overheard you correctly on the phone last night, Kazakhstan has something to do with your investigation."

All I could say was, "Give me the info."

Twenty minutes later, we were in Jamaica Estates, pulling up to a mosque off the Grand Central Parkway near 188th Street.

As soon as we were out of the car, a small man who looked about sixty-five approached us. He was wearing a suit with a collarless white shirt and a small, white cap.

The man gave us a warm smile as he said, "You can't be

Seamus's grandson, Michael, can you? I am Adama Nasir."
He had a slight accent that was hard to place. His wire-
rimmed glasses gave him the look of a scholar.

I took his hand and said, "I am Seamus's grandson. He's
much older than he pretends to be." I introduced Darya as my
associate.

We stayed outside and strolled through a playground for the
school attached to the mosque. Nasir explained that he was
born in Qatar and had traveled throughout the world as a visiting scholar of the Koran. I noted that he had spent two years in
Kazakhstan.

Nasir said, "Your grandfather mentioned what you were doing. I think it's important for Muslims to spread the truth that,
just like Christians, the vast majority of Muslims just want to
worship in peace. Most Muslims are outraged at attacks like the
one on the parade."

I said, "I can appreciate the sentiment, but right now I'm
only interested in catching who's responsible. It doesn't matter
to me what religion he is or even what his motivation was. We
need to catch him before he does anything else."

"That's why I asked your grandfather if I could speak with
you, because he mentioned that there was a possibility the suspect was from Kazakhstan. There is a bar in Rockaway Park
that's a meeting place for ethnic Russians with connections to
Kazakhstan. It's really quite a festive place. I have visited it myself because of my stay in Kazakhstan. Of course, I couldn't
drink alcohol, but the company was invigorating. If anyone

knows about someone from Kazakhstan looking to hide in the greater New York area, it's that crowd."

This was a good lead. Probably more than the FBI had. I thanked him and turned with Darya to head for our car.

Nasir said, "I hope you find who you're looking for. It's a tricky business, these attacks. I've seen it all over the Middle East. Some are based on religious conviction. Some people are forced to do the attacks and some attacks are not what they seem."

I said, "Not what they seem in what way?"

"I used to see it in occupied Palestine. They've been known to kill other Palestinians in attacks so that Israel is blamed. I've even heard rumors that some of the old Israeli governments allowed attacks in Jerusalem so that they would have a reason to respond. There is a certain return on this philosophy."

He was right, but I didn't see the US government allowing an attack like this. I also couldn't see them putting so many resources into catching someone if they had allowed the attack to occur.

All we could do was follow up on the leads we had.

CHAPTER 18

THE STREETS FELT more alive than ever on the drive to Rockaway Park. It was incredible. Even with the cold weather, people were out in the streets, as if telling the terrorists, "New Yorkers don't hide."

The bar was on Rockaway Beach Boulevard, not far from the Jacob Riis Park. As soon as we stepped in the door, I heard conversation in Russian.

Darya was right behind me as I surveyed the long room with booths on the left and stools against the bar on the right. Bright sunlight crashed through the wide bay windows, saving the place from the usual depressing air of a bar in the middle of the day.

It was also surprisingly crowded, with people shouting good-naturedly from one booth to another while the bartenders called out orders in Russian.

I wasn't sure what to do, so without identifying myself, I told the bartender I was looking for someone. I showed him the picture of Marat and told him he was a Russian, speaking Kazakh.

The burly bartender scratched his red beard and shook his

head and said in English, "No, no, I never seen this man. Sorry. What you want to drink?"

I bought two beers and settled in at the bar with Darya. There were several other women in the place, but the way they were sitting in booths by themselves or with one man led me to believe they might be prostitutes. I hoped no one would make a mistake and approach Darya. For their sake.

I watched our bartender speaking in a low voice in Russian to one of his colleagues, not far from us.

Darya leaned in close and said, "The bartender just said the two men at the end of the bar are looking for the same man we are."

Having Darya undercover was brilliant. They didn't seem to care if we overheard them speaking Russian.

I looked over to the far end of the bar where there were two men standing, dressed in cheap suits with ties, about my age, but heavy and out of shape. One of the men was burly, with a pockmarked face, and the other had cold, gray eyes, and as soon as they met mine I realized someone at the bar had just told them who I was asking about.

I assumed he made me for a cop, because he made no move to come over to talk. That was fine by me. His interest didn't concern me.

I formulated a plan, and appreciated the fact that Darya didn't ask what it was.

After a few minutes, the two men in suits stepped out the back door of the bar and into the narrow parking lot. We wasted no time going out the main door and into the same lot.

I saw them get into a new Lincoln. Comfortable, but not flashy. Once we got into my Impala, I ran the tag quickly and it came back to a moving company owned by Russians. Shocking.

When it didn't look like they were going anywhere, I said to Darya, "Sometimes we have to make our own karma."

All she said was, "I agree."

As we slipped out of the car, I said, "Whatever happens in Rockaway Park stays in Rockaway Park. Is that a problem?"

"Not unless you expect me to dig a hole if you kill them. I hate to dig."

"I'll keep that in mind."

Both the men were still sitting in the car, looking out at the traffic trickling by on Rockaway Beach Boulevard.

I was careful, trying to approach the car from behind and in the blind spot. As we got closer, I realized they were taking a smoke break with both the windows open.

Neither seemed to be monitoring the mirrors. For a couple of mobsters, they weren't terribly observant.

They couldn't have set it up better for me.

CHAPTER 19

I LIKED HOW both men stayed calm and didn't jump when I appeared in the driver's-side window. I crouched low so my face filled the window, and rested my arms across the door with my Glock service weapon in my right hand, casually hanging into the car.

I said, "Hello, fellas, how's your day going?"

The driver, the burly man with a pockmarked face, mumbled, "No English. Go 'way."

"You think you're the first one to pull that kind of shit on me? There is a universal cure for those who don't want to speak English." Without hesitation, I pulled the door handle, reached into the Lincoln, and grabbed the man with two fingers behind his jaw. The pressure made him hop out of the car with no help from me other than the two fingers on his sensitive nerves that ran there.

I spun him around and slammed him into the car.

I was prepared to order the other man out, but he jumped out on his own to help his friend. Just as he reached the rear of the Lincoln, Darya sprang out from behind the car parked next to them. I had no idea what she did, but the guy was on the asphalt in a heartbeat.

I said to her, "You okay?"

She said, "Good."

She was careful to keep her words to a minimum, because even though her accent is barely discernible, she didn't want these Russians to pick up that she knew their language.

I focused on the man I had in an arm bar against the car. I patted him down quickly and pulled out a Ruger 9mm from his waistband. Holding him with one hand, I holstered my Glock and stuck his Ruger in my pants.

I said, "If you don't speak English, you're under arrest for carrying a concealed weapon. If you do speak English, I'll talk to you for a minute."

He said in a remarkably clear voice, "We speak English."

"Good. See how easy that was?" I eased up slightly on my arm bar, then stepped back and let the man face me. I said, "Now, why were you asking about Temir Marat?"

"Who?"

I grabbed his arm again to show him I could get rough if I had to. That's when he surprised me. He was fast for a big guy. He twisted his body and then landed a knee right on my thigh. It hurt. I mean, in an it-made-me-want-to-pee kind of hurt.

I staggered back and he immediately threw two punches at my head. He had some style and looked like he'd boxed at some point in his life. That's probably how he landed a job like this.

I had done a little boxing myself and immediately had my

guard up, fending off his punches. As I stepped back, I saw that Darya, still alert and on top of her man, was watching what was happening.

I let the guy in front of me take a wild swing. I ducked the right fist as it just grazed the top of my head. Then I twisted hard and landed a left, low on his back, right in his kidneys. Ouch—I knew from experience that that location was *painful*.

I spun to his other side and kneed him in the left thigh, making sure things were equal. Then I grabbed him by the groin with my left hand and by the throat with my right hand, and bull-rushed him backward into a parked pickup truck.

He let out an *umphf* as the air rushed out of him. Then I put him on the ground close to his partner.

The partner tried to sit up and Darya blasted him with a forearm right across the back of his head. I could hear his nose crush against the asphalt; blood started to leak out and pool into puddles near his face.

I said to the guy I had on the ground, "This is serious shit. For all I know, you were involved in the attack on the parade. That's why you're about to have the worst day of your life."

The man sputtered, "Wait, wait. It's not what you think."

"Then tell me what it is."

"I don't want to get in more trouble."

"You can't get in more trouble. You're carrying a gun illegally and you assaulted a police officer."

"I don't want to get in more trouble by talking."

I sat there for a moment and thought about it. Darya looked

up at me expectantly. Finally, I said, "Tell me what you want to tell me. Anything you say while I have you on the ground like this is free. Total immunity."

"If I tell you the truth, you let us go?"

"That depends on how much of the truth you tell me."

The man thought about it for a moment, then said, "I don't know your man, Marat. I have the same photo you showed the bartender. Someone contracted us to take him out."

"A mob hit on a terrorist? Why?"

"*Why* is not one of the questions we ask in my line of business."

"Where did you get the photo of him?"

"It was in an envelope with some cash and instructions to find him and kill him." After another moment he said, "That's the truth, the whole truth."

I released my grip and let him sit up. He brushed off a couple of pebbles that were lodged in his face. One of them perfectly filled the biggest pockmark on his left cheek.

I looked at him and said, "Surprisingly, I do believe you."

I got a little more information out of the other, but stuck to my promise to release them. Besides, I had gotten the information through an illegal interrogation. There was nothing I could do to them.

After I stood up, I took his Ruger out of my waistband, took it apart, and tossed two pieces in a sewer drain. He started to object, then kept his mouth shut. I would toss the rest of the pistol, including the magazine, down a few different drains on our way back to Manhattan. I appreciated his groan as the gun disappeared.

I stepped over to the other man standing next to Darya and started to pat him down. Just as I did, the man said, "She took it already."

I gave Darya a look and she reached in her purse, then pulled out a Smith & Wesson revolver. She shrugged as she slipped it into the palm of my hand.

She gave me a smile and said, "A girl has got to try."

CHAPTER 20

AFTER WE TALKED to the Russian mobsters, I drove us back to the task force headquarters. Darya said she had calls to make based on some of the information we'd found. We agreed to meet up later.

She was very quiet on the ride back, and I found myself wondering what her role in all this was. Dan Santos trusted her, and even though he was a fed I didn't think he'd put someone in the middle of the investigation who couldn't be trusted. But still, something nagged at me. The moment I got to my desk, my cell rang. I didn't recognize the caller, a man's voice with a thick Russian accent. He said his name and I still couldn't place it. Then I realized who it was: the silent husband of the woman we had spoken to in Midwood yesterday. The only English word he had said was, "Bullshit."

Now he spoke in halting English. I guess Darya's idea of not letting people know you spoke their language wasn't a unique trick.

I said, "What can I do for you?"

"When you and the pretty Russian woman came here—we told truth."

He spoke slowly and carefully so I could understand him. Aside from the accent, his English was not bad at all.

I said, "But some of your truth has changed since we were there?" I was trying to think how he had reached me, then I remembered that Darya had written my number as well as her own on a sheet of paper.

"Nothing has changed, except I met someone who might know the man you're looking for. He gave me some information that I thought you might use."

On every big case, there are thousands of leads. God help me, but I was a sucker for someone giving me new information, even if the odds of it being accurate or useful were small.

The old man said, "A man I ran into said he knows the family of the man who did this terrible crime."

"In Russia or Kazakhstan?"

"In New Jersey."

That caught me by surprise and made me pull a notepad from the FBI desk I was sitting at. I couldn't help but look around the room to make sure no one was eavesdropping on my conversation. Technically, all official leads were supposed to be put into a computer program for review before anyone followed up on them.

I said, "It's interesting he has family in New Jersey. That's nothing I had heard."

The old man said, "There are lots of Russians trying to live the right way. Many of us fled terrible conditions and appreciate all the advantages we have here in United States. Most Russians are perfectly respectable. It might not seem like it in your line of work, where everyone is a potential suspect. But this isn't Russia. You can't think that way."

"I don't generally think that way about any group. Nevertheless, I am a cop and I have to follow up on leads. Can you narrow down where his family might live in New Jersey?"

"A little community called Weequahic, in Newark. The name you're looking for is Konstantin Nislev."

"Do you want to give me some details about the person who gave you this information?"

"No. No, I don't." Then the phone went dead.

If nothing else, it gave me another excuse to get out of the Federal Building for a few hours. With Manhattan's usual Saturday traffic, I knew I could be in the car for a while.

A little work in Google and in the New Jersey public records database gave me an address for a Konstantin Nislev, right where the old man said he'd be.

Traffic wasn't as bad as I feared, and I was cruising past neat row houses in the Newark community of Weequahic. I found a parking spot just across from where I was going. I sat there for a minute, checking out the situation.

It was a well-kept row house, and an old oak tree rose up from the front yard and sent branches toward the house like a giant monster. Other than that, the yard was immaculate. Just a few short strips of grass and a lot of decorative stones. It looked like a comfortable home.

I stepped out of the car and tried to look casual as I walked up toward the front door. But I didn't feel casual. If this lead was accurate, it was a big deal. A *giant* deal. So big I might have a hard time explaining to the FBI how I managed to get the lead, not file it in the proper system, not tell anyone where I was going, and then question the suspect's family.

It was probably nothing.

I rang the bell and heard soft chimes on the inside of the house. A moment later, a man who looked about sixty, with thinning hair, wearing heavy-framed glasses, answered the front door.

He smiled and had a noticeable accent when he said, "May I help you?"

I held up my badge and said, "Konstantin Nislev?"

The man said, "I wondered how long it would take the authorities to find us."

CHAPTER 21

I SAT ON a couch with an uncomfortable wooden frame on the back. I took the tea that Konstantin's wife, Vera, offered as we all chatted in a small living room almost overwhelmed with photographs.

Temir Marat's aunt and uncle had heard through the Russian grapevine that he was a suspect in the attack on Thanksgiving. The older couple didn't deny the relation, or that they were worried about their nephew.

I gave them a few minutes to settle down and we chatted about other things before I got to the serious questions on my mind.

I said, "You have a lot of photos of Seton Hall."

Konstantin said, "I have been the facilities manager there for five years. I was an engineer in Russia, and it fit in perfectly with the needs of the university when I started to look for a job here."

"How long have you been in the US?"

"We moved here about six years ago. I had lived in the US before for extended periods, while I worked on different projects for a construction company based in Switzerland. My children and the rest of the family came over four years ago."

"And your nephew, Temir?"

Vera answered that one. "We were hoping he would come with his cousins four years ago, but he had a wife who was pregnant, and already had one young child at home."

"Where was he living?"

"Moscow." I just nodded and let the story continue.

"Temir had a decent job doing something for either the city or the Russian government. He had a nice apartment and a little bit of money. He speaks English so I thought he might want to come. But he decided to stay."

"When's the last time you talked to him?"

"He always sends me mail on special occasions," Vera said. "He loves his aunt Verochka."

"And you had no idea he was here in the US?"

"None at all."

"Do you have any photographs of your nephew?"

Vera stood up quickly and went to a series of framed photographs sitting on a bookshelf. She walked back with a particularly large one that showed a group of more than twenty-five people.

Vera pointed to a young man, no more than fourteen or fifteen, in the corner of the photo. "That is Temir. This was at a family gathering in Moscow about fifteen years ago. His father had died and we thought it was important for him to have male role models. Konstantin's brothers all spent time with him."

"Do you have any idea when he might've become radicalized and interested in attacking the US?"

Konstantin said, "I'm not sure I understand. Radicalized in what way?"

"Had his belief in Islam twisted to where he felt he needed to participate in a jihad?"

Konstantin said, "That's ridiculous. I don't understand any of that. We're not Muslim. We are Russian Orthodox. The whole family is Russian Orthodox. We are all, to my knowledge, devout and law abiding. Are you sure you have the right suspect?"

Suddenly I had some doubts. They had identified their nephew through the photograph I had. The ATF had taken the fingerprint from the truck used in the bombing. I had fought the man in the photograph hand-to-hand. He was the right suspect, but did we have the correct motive?

I'd have a lot of explaining to do when I got back to Manhattan.

CHAPTER 22

AFTER I'D INTERVIEWED Temir Marat's family in New Jersey, I took my time driving back to the Federal Building. I lingered in the lobby and called home to make sure everything was all right. Then, God help me, I sneaked back into the task force office. I felt sheepish, like a dog who had peed on the carpet.

Now I had to figure out how to explain my trip to New Jersey and all the interesting information I'd found out.

Darya was working on some notes at a table on the side. When I sat down next to her, I noticed the report was written in Cyrillic.

Darya glanced up and said, "When I'm in Moscow, I write in English. It's quite convenient. Like my own secret code. Because no one tries to learn anyone else's languages anymore."

I said, "Thanks, grandma, for the lecture. Besides, you've been with me during most of the investigation. There's nothing you could write that I haven't already heard firsthand. Probably from someone with a thick Russian accent."

"Where have you been?"

"Jersey."

Darya gave me a smile and said, "Seeing a girlfriend?"

"Ha, that's funny. Until I think about my Irish fiancée. Then it's scary. If I went to see a girlfriend in New Jersey, it would probably be my last trip to New Jersey ever."

Darya said, "While you have been out sightseeing, your friend the FBI agent and I have come up with an interesting wrinkle."

"What's that?"

"We've found the phrase Marat said before detonating the bomb, *hawqala,* the one that means 'There is no power nor strength save by Allah.'"

I said, "What do you mean you 'found' it?"

Just then Dan Santos strutted up to us and said, "It's a phrase that has been used by people being blackmailed into committing an attack." He looked between Darya and me, then just kept talking. "A Georgian soldier said it before he detonated an explosive vest at a police station, killing eleven, including himself. Turns out his mother was being held by a group that forced him into the attack. Apparently Georgians love their mothers."

"What happened to his mother?"

Darya answered. "They released her. They want people to believe them when they say they'll release someone for carrying out an attack."

Then Santos said, "Last year a former Russian security agent said *hawqala* before he charged a speaker at a meeting of businessmen in Chechnya. He managed to kill the mayor and a deputy with a hand grenade. The mayor was opposed to Russian influence in Chechnya. That attacker survived four bullets by security. He said he'd been told to do it. He regretted it. He also said the reason he shouted *hawqala* was because he heard it would show he wasn't a monster. It's a weird situation. The military and some law enforcement types know the phrase. This is the first time it's been used outside the former Soviet Union. It might be the wave of the future."

That all started to make sense with what I had just learned in New Jersey. Now I had to find a way to tell them I'd been working on my own.

I looked at Darya and realized I wasn't built for keeping secrets. I just started to talk. "I've developed some information I want to discuss with the two of you."

Neither of them offered any encouragement so I kept going.

"I got a tip that Temir Marat had family that lived in Newark."

Darya said, "Right here in the US."

I nodded.

Santos said, "Did you put the lead into the system?"

"Not yet." I paused, but I could have been just as easily yelling, *I ignored you and went out on my own.* Instead, I said, "I wanted to make sure it wasn't a prank."

Santos calmly said, "I'm listening."

"So to ensure the information was good, I took a ride across the river."

Santos glared at me and raised his voice. "What?"

It was about as emotional as I had seen an FBI agent.

Santos said, "Was there something not clear about your place in this task force and how the investigation was going to be conducted?"

I shook my head. "All I can say is that it was not a prank. Marat's aunt and uncle moved here years ago and are still in touch with their nephew."

Now Santos slipped into the chair next to me and said, "Tell me everything they said."

"Oh, so I can't break the rules unless I find out something important?"

"No, but this case is bigger than politics."

I ran down the information I had gathered from Konstantin and Vera Nislev.

Both Darya and Santos took notes with interest.

Finally, when I had come clean and told them everything, Dan Santos looked at me and said, "This is good stuff. Now collect your shit and hit the road."

I stared at him for a moment. "What are you talking about?"

"It's a privilege to work on a case like this, on a task force like this. We all have certain procedures and everyone was briefed. Yet you are the only one who decided to go out on his own."

Darya started to come to my defense and I was afraid she was going to mention our earlier interviews. I held up a hand to stop her. I knew when a decision had been made. It didn't matter why it was made.

Without saying a word or acting like a spoiled brat, I picked up my notebook and a few other things I needed and strolled out of the task force with my head held high.

CHAPTER 23

THAT EVENING, I sat on the couch after dinner and doodled on a pad, making a few notes and my own version of a chart that showed the connection between everyone in the case.

The only call to the NYPD I had made since I left the FBI was to my lieutenant, Harry Grissom. I told him exactly what had happened, what I had found out, and that I had been told to leave. His response was pure Harry.

Grissom said, "On the bright side, at least you weren't kicked off the task force for stealing something."

I gave him half a chuckle.

He said, "Seriously, Mike, this isn't going to change anything between us or on the squad. Maybe some bosses will be pissed off, but they're so used to the FBI bullshit that I doubt anyone will care. I'll talk to Santos, then call you back when things have leveled out."

That made me feel better. Seeing the kids and having one last dinner of Thanksgiving leftovers set my head on straight. I also decided that just because I wasn't officially on the task force investigating the attack on the parade, that didn't mean I couldn't do anything about it. I was still a cop.

Now I was a pissed-off cop. And I wanted to find out what the hell was going on. Things were not as they appeared, and my unrelenting need to understand events kept pushing me.

Jane plopped down on the couch next to me and said, "What'cha workin' on?"

"Nothing, really. Just putting a few thoughts down on paper."

She laid her head on my shoulder and pointed at the page where I'd been doodling and said, "I especially like your thoughts about this boat and the giant shark behind it. Did you watch *Jaws* again last night?"

I let out a laugh. "No, but I'll let you in on a little secret."

She turned that beautiful face toward me and looked at me like I was about to explain the meaning of life.

I said, "The only things I can draw are boats, sharks, and swords. Anything else looks like a chimpanzee grabbed the pencil."

Jane said, "That's incredible. I'm in the same boat."

"You can only draw a few things?"

"No. Mine is with reading. I can really zip through novels I like by great writers like Michael Connelly and Tess Gerritsen. But when I read the history books I'm assigned at school, I just can't get into them. Now that I know it's just a family issue, I won't worry about it as much."

Even though I liked her sly smile, I said, "Sorry, that's not gonna cut it. It's an interesting argument and I admire the effort that went into it, but you'll read every history book assigned or I'll try to draw your portrait and post it at school."

Jane said, "I like that kind of out-of-the-box thinking. You're turning out to be a pretty good parent."

That was the kind of praise I needed about now.

I was still smiling at the remark a few minutes later when my phone rang and I heard Harry Grissom's voice. As usual, he got right to the point.

"Mike, it was too hard to listen to that jerk-off Santos. He was jabbering on about you not following regulations. But all I could say was, 'So what else is new?'"

A smile crept across my face, though I'd been dreading this call.

Grissom said, "I've never seen them quite like this before."

I said half-jokingly, "So you don't want me to show up at the FBI office tomorrow?"

"I don't even want you to show up at an NYPD office tomorrow. You've earned a day or two off. Enjoy yourself."

If I was a good parent, Harry Grissom was a great lieutenant.

CHAPTER 24

I SPENT SUNDAY with the family and on Monday was up early to make sure everyone got off to school without a hitch. It was fun. We played a couple of quick games over breakfast and on the short ride to Holy Name. We even arrived more than five minutes early. I was afraid it might give Sister Sheila a heart attack.

She surprised me with a simple smile and wave.

I ran some errands, cleaned up the apartment, and in general sulked about not being at the task force. Then, in the afternoon, I stopped in to say hello to my grandfather. He was busy at his desk when I walked through the front door of the administrative offices for the church.

I said, "What are you working on, old man?" I expected a smart-aleck reply.

Instead, Seamus said, "I've got to get this grant into the city before the close of business today."

"Since when do you worry about grants?"

"Since I want a way to bring kids in the neighborhood, who aren't Catholic and don't attend the school, to an afterschool program that would include a meal and tutoring."

"That sounds like a worthy project."

"At my age I only work on worthy projects." He set down his pen and looked up at me. "Is this how you're going to spend a precious day off? Harassing an elderly clergyman? Do you think you could find something better to do with your time?"

A broad smile spread across my face. "It's odd to have the shoe on the other foot for a change. You know how usually I'm trying to work and you're bugging me about something. How does it feel?"

Seamus said, "You tell me. How does it feel to block my efforts to bring underprivileged kids in for a snack and extra tutoring every day?"

"Okay, you win this round, old man. But I'll be back." Just then, my phone rang. I said to Seamus, "You were saved by the bell."

I backed out of the office as I answered the phone. I didn't recognize the number. "This is Michael Bennett." I shaded my eyes from the afternoon sun.

"And this is Lewis Vineyard."

It took me a second to realize that was my Russian mob informant's new name. At least one he was trying out. "I'm a little surprised to hear from you."

Lewis said, "We need to meet. Today."

I thought about explaining that I was off duty, but I could tell by the tone of his voice he needed to see me. We picked a diner we both knew on the West Side.

I said, "What do you got? Did you find Temir Marat?"

"No. But I know where he'll be tonight."

CHAPTER 25

LEWIS VINEYARD HAD hooked me. I wanted to meet with him right away, but he said he couldn't. He had other commitments. And it would look suspicious if he slipped away right now. He met me four hours later, at a diner near West End Avenue. I knew that meant he was serious. He didn't want to risk any of his Russian friends in Brooklyn seeing us together. I was in the booth waiting for him thirty minutes early. I never did that. It took me a moment to notice Lewis coming down the street toward the front door. I craned my neck to look out the window at my overly tan informant wearing a nice button-down shirt and jeans. He almost looked respectable. He was dark, but not leathery; he hadn't started spending all his time in the sun until the last few years.

As soon as he plopped into the booth across from me I said, "It's not cool to tease me with important information, then not meet me immediately."

He held up his hands to calm me down and said, "No way around it. I called you as soon as I had the information, but things got hopping around the bar and I couldn't just leave. And there was no way I could have you show up there."

"I believe that the information you have is good, otherwise you wouldn't come all the way up here to see me."

Lewis said, "It's nice to see how the other half lives. Just walking down the street, I'd say you guys live pretty good up here. I prefer Brighton Beach. But that's just me."

I couldn't wait any longer. "If you're done with your monologues about New York City, can you tell me where Marat will be tonight?"

"It's not quite that easy. This is worth a lot."

I said, "What about the time there was a hit on you and I stopped the hitter in Brooklyn Heights? What was that worth?" I just stared at him and waited for an answer.

"You have a point. You've never screwed me, and you help me out. So I'm going to give you this information—if you tell me you'll make the FBI pay. This is so big the NYPD won't have the cash."

"I doubt that."

His smile told me he had some good info. Finally, I nodded and said, "If it's good information, I'll do everything I can to get you paid. That's the best I can promise."

Lewis Vineyard said, "That's good enough for me." Now he took a moment to gather his thoughts and glanced around the diner to make sure no one was close enough to hear us speak.

Lewis said, "Your man, Marat, will be at the Harbor House, down by Battery Park, at eight p.m. tonight. He may be meeting someone there. A couple members of the Russian mob are going to intercept him."

"How do you know that information so precisely?"

Lewis perked up and said, "I sold them the guns. Two SIG P220s. It's a shame they'll probably toss them in the river after the hit. They're some nice guns just to use one time."

I looked down at my watch and realized I didn't have much time. I didn't have time to verify the information or even scope out the restaurant. But that's how things with informants usually worked.

CHAPTER 26

I RACED SOUTH on West End Avenue until I could slip onto the Joe DiMaggio Highway. It was too late to call in the troops and plan anything worthwhile. Besides, this could still all be bullshit. I'd know soon enough.

I had to catch myself when I realized I was driving like a lunatic. My driving was the reason people always cursed at New Yorkers. I cut off a UPS truck and tried to wave my apology to a heavyset driver who was not happy.

I'd zipped past all the Trump buildings, some with plywood hiding his name. The vents for the Lincoln and Holland tunnels barely registered on my right.

I tried calling Darya, just so someone knew what was happening. No answer. I didn't leave a message.

Now I started to consider the questions that were popping into my head. Why would someone pay the mob to kill a terrorist? Who gained from his death? Were the local Russians worried about backlash? Did they really love America that much, or was it their bottom line? All the same questions any homicide detective would ask.

I didn't know the answer to any of them.

I didn't call Harry Grissom. There was no need to put him in the trick bag if I screwed this up. I had to let things unfold.

And I wanted Temir Marat alive. I had questions to ask him before he was in FBI custody and no one got to talk to him again.

It was true, our last meeting had not gone the way I planned. He was tough and he had skills like no one I had seen in a long time. But I was determined. I had my Glock. And I had a backup revolver on my ankle.

I was as ready as I would ever be.

I exited the highway just before the tunnel that would loop me around to the East Side, parking illegally before I started running through the maze of parks and benches before the water. I scouted the area thoroughly, hoping to see Marat out in public. What the hell, it seemed to happen all the time—fugitives caught by someone who was keeping their eyes open. There had been a baseball hat in my car, left there after the last police league softball game of the season. I'd pulled it on as low as I could, since Marat would no doubt recognize me.

I didn't see him, so as I approached the Pier A Harbor House, I slowed down to take it all in, peering into some of the windows that didn't face the water. I finally stepped inside.

The heat inside the restaurant made me realize how strong the chill in the air was, which I hadn't registered as I ran there. I scouted for other exits and windows while standing in the corner of the bar, noting that a long bar led to the dining room.

There was no one here I recognized. Lewis Vineyard had told me that one of the hitters who bought the guns from him was a well-built man about my height in his early forties, with a distinguishing characteristic of a purple birthmark on his cheek below his left eye. Lewis said the man worked with a tall female who had long black hair. There was no one that fit either of those descriptions that I could see.

I stepped farther into the restaurant, then saw someone I recognized. And frankly, it caught me by surprise. I might even say it shocked me. Sitting alone at a table by a window overlooking the river was Darya Kuznetsova.

What the hell?

I was about to get her attention when it hit me. This couldn't be a coincidence. What was she doing here? Was she luring Marat to be killed by the Russian mob? Why? Why not do it with her own government people?

That line of questioning led me to wonder—why had she provided a photo of Marat if she just intended to kill him?

Then I understood. At least that part of it. She didn't have a clue where Marat was hiding. The more people looking for him, the better.

She's the one who spread the word in the Russian community. That's how his aunt and uncle knew he was a suspect, why Konstantin said, "I wondered how long it would take the authorities to find us."

Shit. I was a fool.

CHAPTER 27

ONCE I MADE up my mind, I didn't dawdle. I stepped up, crossed the room, and sat down directly across from Darya Kuznetsova. I removed my hat like a gentleman, and smiled as if I were her date.

The look on her face and the way her eyes darted around the room told me she didn't want me there and expected someone else.

Darya took a moment and sipped her water. Then she said, "Hello, Michael, what a surprise."

I said, "Do you mind if I join you? Are you waiting for someone?"

She gave me a flat stare and said, "Why do you ask?"

"Just curious. All cops are curious. I noticed you're quite curious. Are you a cop in Russia? Or a spy? C'mon, you can trust me."

"I've learned I can trust no one."

I shrugged and said, "Too bad. Life's a lot easier with friends."

Darya said, "It's longer if you don't trust friends." She paused. "You're very sharp. I'm used to dealing with FBI bureaucrats. You're not like them at all."

"Flattery won't help you now."

Darya said, "I want this terrorist stopped as much as you do."

"Dead or alive?"

"That's how Russia views all terrorist hunts."

"There's a lot more to this than just hunting for a fugitive." I waited while she seemed to ponder my question and consider whether she could trust me.

Finally, Darya said, "Are there factions within the NYPD?"

"Yes. All agencies have factions."

"So do we. I suspected it was the same everywhere. Some in my government have different ideas about the war on terror. Unfortunately, they've acted on them. You might call them cowboys or rogues."

"What kind of different ideas do these factions have?"

She brought those intense, blue eyes to rest on me. "We all have the same goal: stop terrorism. Some people in the Russian government feel like the US has not participated the way it should."

I couldn't hide my shock. "Are you saying this is a Russian government–sanctioned attack?"

Darya stayed calm and steady. She didn't rush what she had to say. That was the mark of a pro.

She said, "No, just the opposite. Now this is all hypothetical, of course. But suppose a rogue element, which was now neutralized, had forced a Russian agent to carry out an attack like this."

"Temir Marat worked for the Russian government?"

She lifted her hands and said, "I was just giving you a theory.

I'm doing this because I know you're actually trying to help things."

I said, "I want to capture Temir Marat and question him. What do you want?"

Darya gave no answer.

Before I could press her on it, I glanced up. There, near the front door, at the end of the bar, stood Temir Marat.

CHAPTER 28

IT FELT UNREAL to have been searching for someone so hard and then see him in person not far away. I guess part of me thought Lewis Vineyard was full of shit.

I stared at Marat. A bandage on his cheek covered the cut I'd given him with the bottle. He wore a NY Rangers baseball cap pulled low. He was gazing around the room, looking for someone. I suspected I knew who.

I eased out of my chair, getting ready to make a casual stroll across the dining room to get next to him.

Then I saw the couple coming into the bar behind Marat. A tall, burly man with short hair, and a woman nearly six feet tall with black hair. The man's birthmark told me exactly who he was. The birthmark looked like a smeared tattoo of a purple house.

All I could think was that the FBI was going to owe Lewis Vineyard a truckload of cash.

If I wanted Marat alive, I would have to act quickly.

Then the mob hitters made their move. It was smooth and professional—if I didn't know what I was looking for, I might've missed it.

The man stepped up right next to Temir Marat, folded his hands across his waist, and casually slipped his right hand under his dark linen coat.

It was subtle, but not too subtle. Marat immediately picked up on the man right next to him. He moved like a cat.

I could clearly see the Russian mobster as he pulled his blue steel SIG Sauer P220 semiautomatic pistol. It was an ugly thing, out of place in a nice restaurant like this.

But Marat was smooth as he turned and used both hands to block the gun before it could come up. He locked the man in close, with the pistol pointing almost straight at the floor.

The killer struggled with the gun under the power of Marat's grip. I could tell he was also struggling with the shock. He'd thought this would be easy.

Marat head-butted him, then ripped the gun right out of his hands. Now the woman got involved, reaching into her Louis Vuitton purse to pull out an identical pistol.

Marat reacted immediately, jerking the dazed man right in front of him as the woman pulled the trigger, shooting her partner twice in the chest.

Marat shoved the motionless man toward the woman. The dead weight knocked her off balance.

This all happened before I could even reach the bar. Everyone was looking around, startled by the two gunshots. The echo had made it difficult to pinpoint. This guy really did have skills.

I was a few feet away from the bar when the female hitter regained her balance and had Marat in the corner. The man with the two bullet holes in his chest was dead on the white tile floor. His blood was swirling into dark red pools and running along the grout lines.

Marat didn't have his pistol up yet. He was at the mercy of the female hitter.

I kept coming full speed and threw my entire body into the hitter. It was just a gut reaction.

We both hit the tile hard, but I landed on top of her.

She was out cold, the pistol loose on the floor.

Marat gave me a faint smile, raised the pistol to his forehead, and saluted me before disappearing out the door.

Darya appeared at my side as I was kneeling to make sure the woman was breathing properly.

I said, "Watch her." Then I was on my feet and out the door.

As soon as I hit the open area beyond the restaurant, I had my head on a swivel. There weren't many people out. Then I caught just a glimpse of someone running. It was the way his head bobbed up and down, and the blue and red of the Rangers cap.

He was running south, along the water. I drew my Glock and started to run the same direction. I fell into a measured pace, not knowing what I might have to deal with once I caught this unusual suspect. At least he wouldn't surprise me with his abilities this time.

The park was flat and relatively empty as it got closer to the street. I would see him if he moved away from the water.

Just as I paused by a cement column that depicted the construction of the World Trade Center, I heard a gunshot. The bullet pinged above my head on the column.

Great. Now this was a gunfight.

CHAPTER 29

I CROUCHED ON the other side of the column and brought my pistol up. There were several low concrete shapes in the park designed to be artistic and give people a place to sit and rest.

I crouched low and ran to the first of the cement structures. It wasn't until I dropped behind it that I realized Marat was just beyond, crouching behind a closed food kiosk.

I leaned from behind the cover and popped off two quick rounds, hoping to scare him out of his position. Instead, I was met with two quick rounds back at me.

I knew the gunfire had to attract attention and if I could just hold him in place, help would be on its way soon. But I still wanted to take this guy alive. A patrol officer rolling up on a gunfight wasn't going to take that kind of care. I wouldn't blame any officer that fired a weapon in this situation.

I popped around the edge and fired twice more. Just to let him know I was here and I wasn't giving up. That's when he used his skills once again. Most people, when they are being shot at, will find cover and stay there. Marat started to move as soon as

I fired the two shots. He came low and fast from his cover along the edge of the cement block I was behind.

Next thing I knew, he was right in front of me. I turned and raised my pistol, but he had already twisted and slapped it hard. Then his foot came off the ground in a blur and struck me in the side of the head. I was dazed as I pitched over.

But he didn't want to fight. He just wanted me to stop shooting. He turned and sprinted away toward a series of decorative concrete walls designed to block the wind and give people something to look at. It looked like a tiny maze.

Once again, after I cleared my head, I was running after him as quickly as I could.

I slowed as I came to the walls. I had my pistol up and scanned the whole area, hoping to get a glimpse of Marat. I entered the little maze carefully.

As I came to the last wall, expecting to see Marat in the wide-open space between here and the Clipper City Tall Ship anchored in the water, I spotted some movement out of the corner of my right eye. Just a blur.

Unfortunately, the movement was Marat's fist as it connected with the side of my head. I had to look like a cartoon character with my face twisting under Marat's fist, my eyes spinning, as I tried to protect myself. I thought I was losing consciousness as I dropped my gun and heard it clatter against the rough cement. Then I steadied myself as I bounced off one of the six-foot-high concrete walls.

Marat was on me in an instant.

He threw his whole body into mine, knocking me flat on the ground. Then he picked up my pistol and flung it hard toward the river.

Marat said, "Just stay here. I still have a pistol." He held up the SIG Sauer like I needed some kind of visual cue.

Now he was jogging away again. He thought he had disarmed me. That was his mistake.

CHAPTER 30

I HATE TO admit that I sat on the hard cement for a few seconds just to gather my wits. This guy could've killed me several times over. Why hadn't he?

Now I had an advantage. He thought I was unarmed. I reached down and drew the Smith & Wesson model 36 revolver. I wasn't crazy about going up against a man armed with a .45-caliber semiautomatic while I just had a five-shot .38, but there was no way I could let this guy disappear.

I knew he'd been headed south, so I got to my feet and started to jog unsteadily toward the masts of the Clipper City Tall Ship I could see in the distance.

It was cold and dark, so there were few people in the park or near the ship. I spotted his Rangers cap about halfway between me and the ship. He was walking fast, trying not to draw attention to himself. I knew he was trying to get out of the area. That's what I'd do.

As I closed the distance, I suddenly felt like the .38 in my hand was a BB gun. Where the hell was my backup?

I scanned for cover to get behind before I shouted for him to stop. A drop of blood from a cut on my forehead slipped into my eye. I felt like I'd been run over by a Volkswagen.

The best cover I could find was a heavy, freestanding billboard that advertised tours out of the mouth of the Hudson. I stood behind it, raised my revolver, and sighted from the groove near the gun's hammer to the front sight, with Temir Marat's body taking up my entire sight picture.

I shouted, "Police—don't move!"

He froze.

I spoke loudly and enunciated carefully. "Put the gun on the seawall!" He was right next to the low wall with the open water beyond it. If he tried anything, he had to pull the gun, turn this direction, and then find me in a split second. I liked my position.

Marat just stood there, facing the water. I could still see his hands hanging at his side. There was no telling what a man like this was thinking or how far he'd go.

I shouted again, "Put your pistol on the seawall!" I waited a moment and added, "Do it now."

He never moved his hands as he stepped up onto the seawall and spun to face me. This is not what I wanted to happen. I didn't want him to have a chance to survey the area and see where I was standing. But I didn't feel I could pull the trigger when I saw both of his hands clearly, and didn't see the gun at all.

He glanced over his right shoulder as if he were thinking about jumping in the river. It wouldn't be the first time a suspect tried it. Most people overestimated their swimming ability.

I shouted, "Don't do it, Temir!"

That caught his attention. He just stared at me.

"That's right, I know your name. I know everything about you. I even visited your aunt and uncle in Weequahic. Aunt Vera and Uncle Konstantin."

He was listening. It was a nice change from him punching me.

I stepped out from behind the sign and started to walk slowly toward him. My pistol was still up as I said, "You didn't attack the parade because of a jihad. You're not even Muslim. You're Russian Orthodox like the rest of your family."

Now I was only about ten feet from the seawall. After what this guy had done to me in two different fights, I wasn't about to get any closer.

I was careful how I phrased my next statement. "I think I know who you're working for. We can protect you. All you have to do is surrender."

His right hand twitched and eased toward his jacket's front pocket.

I said, "Don't do it."

The hand froze about halfway to the pocket.

"Surrender and we can work this out."

Then Marat spoke. His voice was even and he clearly had an accent, but his English was good. "If I surrender, you can ignore the people I killed?"

I just stared at him for a moment. I had no answer.

Marat said, "Neither can I." His voice had a catch in it. "I had to do it. They have my wife and daughter."

"Is that why you said *hawqala?*"

"I didn't know if anyone would pick up on it."

I kept the pistol trained on him. I was still expecting some-one to come help me shortly.

Marat said, "They told me I had to do this one job. Drive the truck into the parade, then detonate the explosive they had built into the truck. That was my first clue they'd abandoned me. When I hit the detonator, it was supposed to give me thirty seconds to escape. Then there was no one waiting to drive me away like they were supposed to. They've been trying to kill me ever since. Now it looks like they tricked you into doing their dirty work."

All I could say was, "Who? Who is trying to kill you? Who do you work for?"

He looked like he wanted to tell me. Like he knew it was over. He started to speak, then hesitated.

His right hand moved. That's when I heard two gunshots.

CHAPTER 31

AS SOON AS I heard the shots, I couldn't keep from turning to see where they came from. Behind me, partially hidden by a wooden bench, Darya Kuznetsova kneeled with the other Russian mob hitter's pistol in her hand.

I spun back to Marat. He seemed to be frozen. Somehow, in that split second, his right hand had reached the gun in his jacket pocket. Now he held it loosely with the barrel pointed to the ground.

He looked at me and tried to speak. That's when I noticed the two red stains expanding on the front of his jacket. Both were close to his heart.

The pistol dropped onto the seawall. Marat stood for a second longer, then toppled over into the river.

I raced to the seawall and leaned over to look at the dark water. The tide was going out and there was a serious current. But there was no sign of Temir Marat. The swirling black water would hide anything more than a few inches below the surface.

Darya joined me at the seawall. She carefully placed the pistol next to the one that had dropped out of Marat's hand.

I looked at her and simply said, "Why?"

"I thought he was going to shoot you. You have no idea what men like that are capable of."

"I'm starting to get an idea."

"He would've shot you."

I said, "That's bullshit. He's one of yours. You're just trying to cover his tracks."

Darya shook her head and said, "He's not one of mine. I had nothing to do with anything this man was involved in." She was convincing. Then she said, "And I really thought your life was in danger."

Two patrol cars pulled up to the edge of the park and the four patrol officers started jogging toward us with their weapons drawn.

I immediately set down my revolver, pulled my badge from my back pocket and held it in my right hand. To be on the safe side, both of my hands were above my head before they got too close.

Darya took my lead and raised her hands as well.

A female patrol officer who was leading the pack charging toward us recognized me. "Do you need a hand, Detective Bennett?"

Immediately, I felt relief wash through me.

It was over. Maybe not the way I wanted it to end, but the manhunt for Temir Marat was finished.

CHAPTER 32

TWO HOURS LATER, I was sitting on the same seawall where Temir Marat stood when he was shot. My feet dangled over the seawall as I watched the search for Marat's body.

A crime scene was set up where Marat had been shot. The three pistols, mine and the two mobsters' SIG Sauers, were still sitting in the same place on the seawall.

Several harbor boats, two NYPD boats, and the Coast Guard rescue ship were shining lights and casting nets into the murky water.

Someone sat down next to me, and I was surprised when I turned my head to see that it was Dan Santos.

He just sat there watching the water with me for about half a minute. Neither of us said a word.

Finally, I said, "How did your interview with Darya go?"

Santos said, "About how you'd expect. She claims she followed you from the restaurant to help you catch Marat. She picked up a pistol from the floor of the restaurant that came from one of the people trying to kill our suspect. When she found you facing Marat, she thought he was about to shoot you so she fired first."

"But did she say anything about Marat's motive or who he worked for?"

"C'mon, Bennett, give the FBI some credit. As soon as we figured out how *hawqala* had been used in other bombings, and consulted some counterparts at the CIA, we had a pretty good idea what was going on."

"Did you suspect what Darya was up to while she was working with us? I mean, she never intended for us to get our hands on Marat."

Santos smiled and said, "Did you ever see me do, or say, anything classified in front of her?"

I said, "Maybe you're not the dumbass prick I thought you were."

Santos laughed and said, "Once again you're underestimating the FBI. I'm not a dumbass, but I am a prick. Sometimes you have to be in this line of work. Especially when you deal with the NYPD every day."

The only answer I had to that was, "Touché."

CHAPTER 33

I'LL ADMIT TO being a little uncomfortable when Darya asked me to grab a cup of coffee after we were released from the shooting scene. But curiosity got the better of me and I agreed to slip into a coffee shop right at the edge of the financial district.

We sat in silence as I made a show of stirring my coffee until she finally said, "I have no idea why it is important to me that you know I had nothing to do with the attack."

I just nodded. My grandfather had taught me that running your mouth without thought is always a bad idea. When I was a kid I believed he followed all of his own advice.

Darya said, "There is nothing about this incident that I agreed with. I shouldn't even have to say that I'm against terrorism. I'm against any government trying to trick other governments. And I was against the way my government chose to handle the whole situation. And if you repeat anything I say here, I'll simply deny it. I just felt like you had earned an explanation."

"And you didn't want me to think you were a cold-blooded killer."

She shrugged and said, "Frankly, I prefer you think I'm a killer than a liar."

I stared at her, trying to get a feel for her sincerity. She really was striking with those deep-blue eyes and high cheekbones. No matter how I focused, I couldn't get a clear read on her.

Darya said, "I'm pretty certain Dan Santos will never deal with me again, but I would love to hear who hired the two Russian mobsters and tipped them off that I had arranged a meeting with Temir through a mutual acquaintance. If you were able to talk to the woman who survived, is that something you might be able to find out for me?"

I just smiled. There was no way I was going to commit to helping her on anything until I knew more about what had happened during the investigation. I was in a weird no-man's land between the FBI and an official envoy from Russia.

I drank about half my coffee as we sat there and watched the few people on the streets at this time of the night.

Finally, I asked the one question that had been on my mind. "Will the US see any other fake attacks?"

"Not from Russia. Who knows what others have in mind. It's too easy to bend public opinion. Why should a government make a good-faith effort to do the right thing about terrorism or any other hot-button issue, when one incident like the attack on the parade will galvanize the population?"

"What about you? Are you going to stay in New York?"

"For a while. I like it here. I'm starting to understand American police politics and I am certain there will be more incidents where we all have to cooperate."

"I'm afraid of the same thing."

Darya surprised me when she reached across the small table and grasped both of my hands. "I am your friend, Michael. In time, I hope you learn to trust me. I think we could each help the other in a number of ways."

I couldn't deny the logic, but wasn't sure I grasped her entire meaning.

She released my hands and stood up. I immediately stood as well. She stepped toward me, rose up on her tiptoes, and kissed me on the cheek. Then she whispered in my ear, "We'll meet again."

Then she was gone.

CHAPTER 34

THREE NIGHTS AFTER Temir Marat was killed, I sat in the only safe place I knew in the entire world. In my living room with Mary Catherine, nine of my kids, and my grandfather.

Mary Catherine was snuggled in next to me on the couch, with Chrissy and Shawna tucked in on the other side of me. The older kids all sat on the carpet as we watched the Jets on Thursday Night Football. It was a game against the Dolphins in Miami and every camera shot between commercials showed people walking along the beach in shorts. It just didn't feel right to a New Yorker.

Before the game, I had watched the news, where everyone was reporting the attack on the parade as just another terror incident. They went on to say the terrorist was shot by "authorities." Reporters made it a point to say the suspect acted alone.

That seemed to put an end to the terror attack that had rocked the city. Even Ricky said, "So you solved another one, huh, Dad?"

"*Solve* isn't the word I'd use. We *cleared* the case. That'll have to do."

Eddie said, "It's got people on their guard now."

I smiled. "For now, but people forget. Always. It's got to be one of the fundamental laws of the universe."

Mary Catherine said, "You really think the attack will be forgotten?"

"Not totally, but no one will think twice about next year's parade. That's how these things always go. People talk about never forgetting, but they forget remarkably fast. The Freedom Tower is a good reminder, but you have to be in lower Manhattan to see it."

Shawna looked up at me. "We'll still go to the parade next year, won't we?"

Jane chimed in. "We have to, otherwise the terrorists win."

I didn't know if she was serious or joking.

Shawna still stared up at me. "Can we go?"

I smiled. "Of course we'll go. That's our thing. Your mom loved it. In a way, we're honoring her memory. St. Patrick's and Macy's are two parades we won't ever miss."

There were smiles and cheers all around. Mary Catherine hugged me, then kissed me on the lips.

ABOUT THE AUTHORS

JAMES PATTERSON has written more bestsellers and created more enduring fictional characters than any other novelist writing today. He lives in Florida with his family.

MAXINE PAETRO has collaborated with James Patterson on the bestselling Women's Murder Club and Private series. She lives with her husband in New York State.

JAMES O. BORN is an award-winning crime and science fiction novelist as well as a career law enforcement agent. A native Floridian, he still lives in the Sunshine State.

JAMES PATTERSON
RECOMMENDS

JAMES
PATTERSON

THE PEOPLE
vs.
ALEX CROSS

THE
WORLD'S
#1
BEST-
SELLING
WRITER

THE
CHARGES:
EXPLOSIVE

THE
EVIDENCE:
SHOCKING

THE
ACCUSED:
ALEX
CROSS

THE PEOPLE VS. ALEX CROSS

Alex Cross has always upheld the law, but now for the first time I've put him on the *wrong* side of it. Charged with gunning down followers of his nemesis Gary Soneji, Cross has been branded as a trigger-happy cop. You and I know it was self-defense, but the jury won't exactly see it that way.

When the trial of the century erupts with the prosecution's damaging case, national headlines scream for conviction and even those closest to Alex start to doubt his innocence. He may lose everything: his family, his career, and his freedom. Things couldn't possibly get worse—until they do.

As Alex begins the crucial preparation for his defense, his former partner John Sampson pulls him into a case linked to the mysterious disappearances of several young girls. The investigation leads to the darkest corners of the Internet, where murder is just another form of entertainment.

Alex will do whatever it takes to stop a dangerous criminal . . . even as his life hangs in the balance.

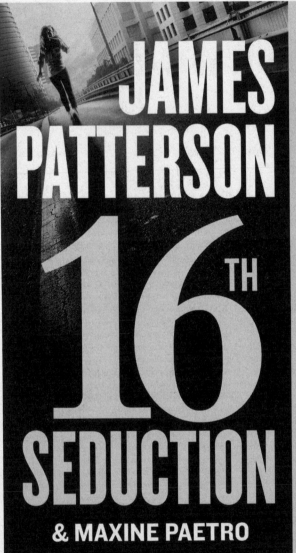

JAMES
PATTERSON

16TH
SEDUCTION

& MAXINE PAETRO

16TH SEDUCTION

Fierce. Determined. Smart. Unstoppable. That's Detective Lindsay Boxer in a nutshell. As the leader of the Women's Murder Club solving crimes in San Francisco, she's been tested time and time again. Now I've put even more pressure on her—as everyone she's ever relied on turns their back on her.

After her husband Joe's double life shattered their family, Lindsay is finally ready to welcome him back with open arms. And when their beloved hometown faces a threat unlike any the country has ever seen, Lindsay and Joe find a common cause and spring into action.

But what at first seems like an open-and-shut case quickly explodes. Undermined by a suspect with a brilliant mind, Lindsay's investigation is scrutinized and her motives are called into question. In a desperate fight for her career—and her life—Lindsey must connect the dots of a deadly conspiracy before *she's* put on trial and a criminal walks free with blood on his hands.

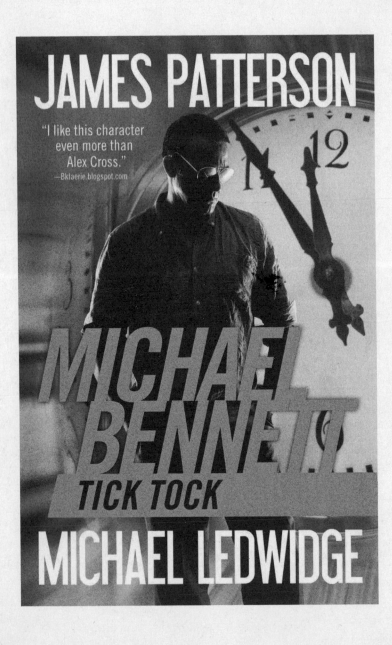

TICK TOCK

Sometimes a setting is so rich, vibrant, and alive that it's very much a character in a book. That's how I think of New York City. In TICK TOCK, she's under attack again, and this time the crime tearing through the Big Apple is so horrifying—so perfectly planned by a deadly mastermind—that Detective Michael Bennett is pulled away from a seaside vacation with his children so he can investigate. Things heat up as Michael comes across one of my favorite twists yet, and you'll see why the city that never sleeps is the city that never stops needing Detective Michael Bennett.